About the Author

Born in London, Robert was raised in New Zealand, where his family emigrated to when he was eleven.

Robert initially used his creativity for mechanically related projects in his forty-year career as an engineer. But as time went by, Robert was eventually persuaded by his friends and family to start turning some of the many plots that he had developed over the years into meaningful dialogue that was fleshed out into full-length novels, including *The Ghost Bus*.

robertgordonauthor.com

The Ghost Bus

Robert Gordon

The Ghost Bus

Vanguard Press

VANGUARD PAPERBACK

© Copyright 2024
Robert Gordon

The right of Robert Gordon to be identified as author of
this work has been asserted by him in accordance with the
Copyright, Designs and Patents Act 1988.

All Rights Reserved

No reproduction, copy or transmission of this publication
may be made without written permission.
No paragraph of this publication may be reproduced,
copied or transmitted save with the written permission of the publisher, or in accordance
with the provisions
of the Copyright Act 1956 (as amended).

Any person who commits any unauthorised act in relation to
this publication may be liable to criminal
prosecution and civil claims for damages.

A CIP catalogue record for this title is
available from the British Library.

ISBN 978 1 83794 116 2

This is a work of fiction. Names, characters, businesses, places, events and incidents are
either the product of the author's imagination or used in a fictitious manner. Any
resemblance to actual persons, living or dead, or actual events is purely coincidental.

Vanguard Press is an imprint of
Pegasus Elliot Mackenzie Publishers Ltd.
www.pegasuspublishers.com

First Published in 2024

Vanguard Press
Sheraton House Castle Park
Cambridge England

Printed & Bound in Great Britain

Chapter 1
(February 1945)

The man's shaking hands slowly unfolded the worn piece of paper that he had carefully removed from its equally worn envelope. With the paper now placed flat on a small table, the man repeated the task that he had followed religiously each morning since first receiving it.

As he looked down at the familiar words, he was not concerned that some of the writing was now faded and hard to read; the paper it was written on had succumbed not only to wear and tear but to the ravishes of time as well.

The man knew every word of every sentence that comprised the document. This faded letter was the last piece of correspondence he had received from its author—the person he loved more than anyone else in the world.

With the turn of a latch and a gentle push, the small upstairs window opened just enough to allow the prevailing breeze to carry the aroma of salty sea air into the room. It also permitted the distant sound of waves crashing against solid, unforgiving rocks to be heard, which, ironically, was a sound that always comforted and soothed him.

The sound and smell of the cold winter sea symbolised the void that lay between himself and the writer of the note, for it was the sea that had taken the author away, and it was the sea that would return the person that he cared for beyond measure.

As the man looked at what remained of the worn letter, he knew that he and the author would one day be reunited. But there was one thing he did not know. Would today be that day of unimaginable jubilation? Or would it be just another day of tormented loneliness?

Chapter 2
(August 2019)

Luke Spitz was an investigative journalist, and a very good one at that. He had learned at an early age that he had an amazing way with words. Luke's mother, Joy, would proudly show her friends the letters her young son had written expressing his love for her in a style that was far beyond what would be expected from someone his age.

In high school, Luke headed up production of his school's yearbook, amongst other projects. That was no mean feat considering that he hadn't sacrificed his studies or social life in order to achieve what was undisputedly a top quality product.

After several years writing articles for local papers, Luke made the move to investigative journalism and soon realised that it was his true calling in life. While the last few topics Luke had been assigned to write about might not have been the juicy, gripping subjects he hoped for, he always gave each task his total commitment. So having focussed on giving one hundred percent of himself to the task at hand, Luke had no concerns about his performance on recent assignments.

Knowing this, Luke had no reason to suspect anything negative from his employer, yet he was aware of feeling a little nervous as he knocked on the door that separated Skip Newton's office from the main work area.

"Come on in, Luke, and take a seat."

"Is everything OK, Skip?" The first words out of Luke's mouth betrayed his concern. Being summoned to the chief editor's office could only mean one of two things—either Luke had done something really good, or he had done something really bad.

Skip Newton was not just Luke's boss. While their work relationship was purely professional, in a strange sort of way there was an unspoken bond between the two men that felt much like friendship. Luke had always just assumed their closeness arose from their shared Jewish American ancestry.

Skip's real name was Solomon, and after falling in love with a visiting Australian girl, he had followed her to Melbourne in 1975, married her, and launched a very successful career in journalism. When his marriage split up fifteen years later, in 1990, Skip had returned to America to take over and eventually purchase his newspaper, *The Independent Eye*, or just *The Eye*.

Fifteen years is not long relative to an entire lifetime, but it was long enough for Solomon Newton to acquire an accent that blended Australian and north eastern American tones. He had also picked up the habit of using Australian slang, which had earned him the nickname Skippy from his American friends. It was soon shortened to Skip and became the name he would forever be known by.

Luke had been employed for the last three years as a journalist at *The Eye*, which was a small investigative newspaper based in Silverleaf, Virginia. Knowing Skip well, Luke could tell from just the look on Skip's face that something was not right; hopefully, it was nothing that he had done.

"I am going to be up front, open and honest with you, Luke. You're not stupid, so what I'm going to tell you should come as no surprise." Skip hesitated and turned to pour himself a glass of water from a crystal decanter that sat on an oak cabinet at the back of his office.

"Can I offer you some water, Luke?"

"No, I'm good. Thanks, Skip."

The pause had given Skip time to compose his words carefully. "All is not good with *The Eye*. It's no secret that sales have been steadily declining for the last few years. There are several reasons for that, none of which are in our control. We can't compete with online content; people want to pick up their phones and read things instantly. Of course, there is our online subscription, but social attitudes are so different from when I started *The Eye*. People today have access to so much information. Many people will only read what they want to read, and they'll only pay to read what they want to see in print. I guess I'm a dinosaur because I'm not politically affiliated with anybody and will publish a story about anyone from either side of the house whilst carefully tiptoeing through the minefield of political litigation. I'm all about truthful, unbiased reporting. That's what made *The Eye* what it is.

"Our online content is just not holding its own in this world where people select what they want to believe out of the thousands of online articles written by thousands of online journalists. Luke, it's like being in a candy store; you open a jar and take the candy you like but leave the ones you don't. I haven't even touched on how the cost of printing is going up and up, and experience has shown us that only a small cost in unit price reduces circulation quite disproportionately.

"*The Eye* has been my life. So, yes, we're going down, but I'm not going down without a fight. I'm looking at ways to adapt and keep costs down, but I'm also realistic and know that there will come a point when you shut up shop and walk away, if for nothing more than your own sanity. I hope what I'm planning will at least steady circulation and *The Eye* can stay alive, but to be honest, at the moment, I can't see lasting another twelve months. You're the first one I've talked to, but I'm going to tell everyone, just so there will be no surprises."

Luke was well aware of *The Eye*'s declining circulation but had been unaware that things were as bad as what he'd just been told. A mixture of shock, disappointment and sadness was apparent on his face.

"Oh, I am so sorry, Skip. I never realised things were that bad."

"I really like you, Luke, so here is some advice. Change careers. There's no future here. Leave *The Eye* before I have to tell you there's no job. I'll give you a glowing reference. I hear this girl you've been seeing lately is a real keeper. Perhaps you two can start a business together and get the rewards that you deserve."

"Rachael sure is a keeper, and I'm hoping it will last. If she likes me at least half as much as I like her, then we have a future together. But we both have our own careers, and I am not deserting my mine because things are tough. I am also not deserting you or *The Eye*. If you're not going down without a fight, then neither am I. So, what can I do to help?"

Skip whistled lightly and shook his head. Then he grinned as he replied, "Well, Luke, all I can say is that you're either extremely loyal or really stupid. But whatever the reason, I am grateful for your help."

"Maybe I'm both loyal and stupid. But I have never been as determined as I am to stick with you and *The Eye*."

Skip smiled before speaking. "If you want to help, then go out and get me that one in a million story, the one that nobody else has. Not the space-filling rubbish that we use to bulk up the paper, but rather the sort of story that will give us national coverage and make *The Eye* a household name."

"That's a tall order, Skip. I can't promise that exclusive a story, but I can assure you that I'll do my best to look for it."

"You're a good man, Luke. I'm proud to have you on the team. But anytime you want to bail out, you have my full support with no hard feelings."

Skip's voice had an undercurrent of sadness, although not in what he said. Rather, his tone told Luke that he fully expected him to abandon *The Eye* in the not too distant future.

Chapter 3
(October 1941)

The woman walked briskly and boldly forward after exiting the train. Her forceful manner portrayed a false sense of confidence as she hurried along in the cool autumn air. It was not a route she felt comfortable taking, especially at eight thirty in the evening and in this particular part of town. Life, however, had determined that it was a walk she had to make five days a week. After all, what other options did she have?

From a distance, she appeared to be smartly dressed in quality clothes. A closer inspection, however, would reveal they were not expensive items of attire. In fact, quite to the contrary, a very modestly priced dark-red pleated dress and matching fitted jacket had been lovingly altered by her mother to make them appear more fashionable, whilst a white blouse and a once expensive hat bought second-hand from a jumble sale promoted the false image of wealth. On her feet, the shiny red shoes she wore appeared new, but they had considerable mileage on them, making them unsupportive and uncomfortable. The woman's thick coat, also sourced from a jumble sale, completed the look. The coat was also necessary to ward off the chilly wind on this particular evening.

Since the unexpected death of her husband two years earlier, the woman in the dark-red dress had faced considerable financial hardship and had reluctantly made the decision to move back in with her parents. Reality now dictated that she work long hours to support her two young children. Her job was exhausting, and in a different world, it would not have been her first choice. However, finding herself with limited options, she approached each day with a seemingly endless amount of energy and enthusiasm, something that was slowly taking its toll on both her mental and physical health.

Her parents' house, although modest, was warm and comfortable. It was located in what could only be described as a low-income area, although not the worst area of the city. But it would never be a neighbourhood that people would aspire to live in.

The twenty-minute walk from the train station to her parents' house always had an element of uneasiness. But this night, it felt a little worse. The rhythmic clunk of her low heels against the pavement gave a clue to the speed she was walking, which was somewhat faster than usual. She had a heightened sense of urgency to get to the safety of her parents' house. Maybe it was just her imagination, but the feeling that she had of being followed was nevertheless spurring her on. Turning around to check did not seem like a good idea, so instead, she continued her brisk pace, trying not to appear alarmed or subconsciously take on the role of victim. She reminded herself that every step was one step closer to the safety of home.

Suddenly, the sound of a second pair of shoes on the pavement confirmed her worst fears. There was someone behind her. With her heart now pounding quickly in her chest, she finally turned her head to peek over her left shoulder and noted a briskly walking man about twelve feet behind and to her left. What she didn't see was the second man who approached on her right.

The woman struggled bravely as a hand brought a thick, damp cloth over her face, and she tried to scream, but her cries were muffled by the cloth. Reality began to blur into a sea of drowsiness as the chloroform completed its task. The woman's now limp body was soon roughly bundled into the dark Ford sedan that had pulled up alongside them.

The evil from which her family had spent their life savings trying to escape had now spread its dark tentacles over 4,600 miles to claim another of its carefully selected victims.

Chapter 4
(August 2019)

The evening had gone extraordinarily well, as well as any fourth date could go. Luke had caught up with Rachael numerous times for coffee over the last few weeks, but this was their fourth real date. Farrington's restaurant had provided the perfect location and had certainly lived up to its reputation; with its antique furniture and the ambiance of its cosy, dimly lit interior, it was a great place to relax and impress a special someone.

Lazarus Lashenco was the larger-than-life owner of Farrington's. Now in the twilight of his hospitality career, Lazarus had a succession of award-winning eating establishments to his credit, and there was not much about creating a special experience that he did not know. Lashenco was a man who had built each of his successful ventures on three principles: great food, great atmosphere and, most important of all, great service. The third one meant that Lazarus very selectively hand-picked his staff, and everyone who worked for him had to have that special something, particularly his waitstaff.

Connor, Luke and Rachael's waitperson for the evening, typified all that his employer valued, with a friendly and almost flirtatious manner for both male and female clientele. He made you feel like a long lost friend just returning home, but without being overbearing or making you feel uncomfortable. Luke's budget did not allow for the kind of tip he would have liked to leave, but as the true professional he was, Connor acknowledged all gratuities with the same enthusiasm, regardless of their size.

Parking right outside Rachael's apartment, Luke shut off the car before rotating to face his beautiful passenger.

"Thanks for your company. Talking to you tonight made me feel good."

Rachael smiled before returning the compliment. "It's me who should be thanking you. I've been totally spoilt this evening, eating at Farrington's. Wow. But I guess you've been there a number of times before."

"No, I haven't been there before. What makes you think that I would have?"

"I just thought you would've taken all of your previous girlfriends there." Rachael's mischievous smile revealed that she was just playing with him and did not expect a reply. "Well, then, I am honoured I was the first person you've taken there. I had always wondered what having a meal at Farrington's would be like. Next time, though, I'm paying, OK?"

Luke's nod of acknowledgement was followed by a brief period of awkward silence. Like any young man in the early stages of a relationship knows, there is, between the extremities of not being keen enough and appearing to be overly enthusiastic, a middle ground, a place that is comfortable and safe for both parties.

Am I in that place? Is this the right time to kiss her? Will there ever be a better time? The thoughts raced through Luke's mind and were momentarily overwhelming. But then Rachael's sudden smile was just the prompting Luke needed.

He caught Rachael off guard when his lips met hers. But Luke's bold move received a positive response as she made no move to break off the contact.

When the kiss ended, she asked lightly, "Do you want to come in for coffee?"

Luke's' heart missed a beat and then galloped in an adrenalin fuelled rush. *Does she mean come in for a coffee, or does she mean would I like to stay the night?*

Chapter 5

The location was not familiar; it was a wooded area with a tree canopy that extended far out to cover the distant hills. The night air was cool and without the slightest breeze so that the mist rising from the ground halfway up the pine trees remained silent and stationary. Luke was standing at a clearing in the woods where the road had been widened to make a now long abandoned bus stop. In the distance, a rhythmic mechanical sound grew increasingly louder; the noise was eerie and its pulsing beat sent a shiver down Luke's back. The unfamiliar tones were a hybrid of a human heartbeat, a chugging steam engine and an old, slow turning, stationary oil engine. As the sound gained volume, it induced more fear and dread.

"The bus is nearly here," one of the two other men also waiting at the bus stop noted.

"We have to get the seats fixed quickly before it leaves to collect more people," the second man added. The urgency in his voice was evident, and his look of uneasiness added an element of mystery as he fidgeted in place.

Luke looked down at the toolbox in his left hand. He somehow knew, despite his growing alarm, that the man was right—they had a job to do fixing the seats of the bus.

Like many dreams, the scenario Luke now found himself in was utterly bizarre, yet in the context of a person's brain unloading during that mysterious phenomenon we call dreams, anything and everything can make perfect sense. This occasion was to be no different.

A bus finally made its way out of the mist and rumbled towards them. It was old, with a rounded shape that identified it as being from the 1930s or '40s. The passing of time had taken a toll, and the vehicle's once shiny exterior was now worn and pitted with rust, making it a mere shadow of its former glory. The front of the bus was distinctive: large triangular chrome surrounds stood proudly on each of the two front guards, and within each of these imposing fixtures, there were three lights.

As the bus moved slowly forward towards where they were waiting, Luke could feel the moist heat from the steam that hissed out of its radiator like an angry dragon spitting flames from its nostrils. The bus continued forward and eventually came to a stop adjacent to the three men. Luke was already consumed with fear, yet his heart rate managed to speed up even further when he noted to his horror that there was no driver. The angry beast was alive and driving itself.

The single door located halfway down the right-hand side suddenly popped open to expose a completely empty passenger compartment. The opening of the door allowed a cold, spine-chilling breeze to flow out from the bus's interior. It was a chill that consumed everything in its path. Fear had now engulfed Luke down to his very core. Shaking uncontrollably, he did not want to board the vehicle, but he was prompted by one of his two colleagues, who stressed the urgency of the job he had been assigned.

Slowly, Luke placed first one foot, then the other on the steps as he prepared to board. But first he insisted that one colleague remain right behind him and the other stand in the doorway to prevent it from closing. Assured by his fellow workers that they would remain right where he wanted them, Luke proceeded to hurriedly fix the broken wooden trim on the offending left-side seat.

"Where is this bus heading?" Luke enquired nervously as he started his repairs.

"It's going to go collect the souls of the dead."

The answer from one of the work colleagues further horrified Luke and prompted him to turn suddenly, just in time to see that his two colleagues were no longer there and worse, the door had just finished closing, trapping him inside. Luke felt the bus lurch forward.

Gripped by sheer terror, he shouted as loudly as he physically could, "Let me out! Let me out! Let me—"

The two hands that now gripped his right arm were shaking Luke with enough force to wake him from his nightmare. He sat up straight and quickly moved his shaking hand to turn on the bedside light.

"Are you OK?" the anxious voice that came from beside him asked.

It took Luke a few moments to realise that it was a very worried looking Rachael who was enquiring as to his well-being. Luke found that he was literally out of breath as his heart pounded uncontrollably in his chest, and his mumbled words did not sound convincing.

"Yeah, I'm OK. It was just a nightmare, but it was so real and terrifying. I'm so sorry I woke you."

"Do you often get nightmares like that?" Rachael's concern was apparent.

Of course not; what a stupid question. Luckily, Luke's thoughts would never have been transposed into words, and as guilt crept in, he began to see the situation from her perspective.

But then again, how would she know? This was the first night we've spent together.

Up to this point, things had gone so well for both of them—the meal, the wine, the laughs, the realisation that he had been invited to stay the night, which in turn, had led to the full-body massage and the wonderful lovemaking. Luke knew he had made a good impression, at least up to this moment. This girl was special, and he didn't want to get anything wrong. But he'd just made a complete fool of himself. Would she ever want to see him again, let alone spend the night together?

Chapter 6
(June 1940)

The large wheels of the 1938 Cadillac V-16 crunched the white gravel as its two-and-a-half tons of luxury turned through the opened gates and moved along the driveway that led to a magnificent estate. The occupants seated in the back of the Cadillac town sedan were used to the best things in life, and being chauffer driven in one of the finest cars ever built was but a glimpse of the wealth and luxury that Rupert K Smidt surrounded himself with. Mr Smidt was a true captain of industry, a self-made multimillionaire who owned a multitude of heavy industry businesses, most of which had lucrative contracts with the government in both civil and military capacities. Rupert K Smidt was also a man with Washington connections that went right to the top of both politics and the military.

This was the first time that Mr Smidt and his wife, Ellinore, had visited this location. They, along with their equally successful business acquaintances, Walter and Gloria Bloomfield, were to be weekend guests at this fine, gothic inspired mansion on a magnificent Maryland clifftop site.

The Smidts had nearly everything money could buy. However, they had long ago realised there are some things in life that money can't acquire, and genuine friendships were one of those things. Despite being surrounded by yes men, all ready to tell him whatever he wanted to hear, along with countless others keen to make a positive impression, genuineness or, rather, the lack thereof was always an issue that frustrated Rupert.

With no close family and a constantly growing mistrust of the intentions of the people they found themselves surrounded by, the Smidts were both incredibly lonely, despite their business and private successes and the image of completeness they presented to the world.

Rupert was also well aware that a pitfall of their lofty position was that once you aspire to and reach such heights, letting down your guard and exposing human weaknesses becomes a truly unthinkable action. Life proves to be very shallow when you can only be yourself when you are by yourself. There was, however, a glimmer of hope in that if you could surround yourself with like-minded people, a situation where everyone in attendance was aware that they were equals and could be unafraid to expose their secrets; then a man could truly relax and freely be himself, knowing that any secrets or weaknesses uncovered would remain safely within the group.

Finding such an opportunity was a rare occurrence, but their host for the weekend was an exceptional man. He and his wife were both charming beyond measure, and it was a charm that felt comfortable and genuine. As they spoke to you, their words did not appear superficial. The things this couple said always penetrated your defences and spoke to your soul, and their company inevitably left you craving more of their attention.

Just like the common masses, powerful people also need to relax and unwind, and there was a heightened sense of anticipation as the Smidts' Cadillac pulled up outside the large door of their entertainer's home. Their chauffer, Nixon, soon had the door open.

Unlike the Bloomfields, the Smidts had not yet met their hosts for the weekend, but they had heard a lot of good things about them. Those who had met the owners of this fine house all relayed similar stories of a couple who made you feel so welcome and comfortable that they became the long-lost family you never knew you had. It was a house where you could relax, let your guard down and expose the real you. With no expectations or pretences, a visit to this location and time spent with its owners did not mean giving up on life's luxuries; it just meant that far away from prying eyes, it was a chance for the wealthy and influential to do something that money couldn't necessarily buy—indulge in rest and relaxation.

With impeccable timing, at the very moment that the Bloomfields' car came to a stop, an imposing figure appeared at the top of the staircase leading into the house. Even before introductions were made, there was something about their host that commanded a sense of awe in his presence. It wasn't until he descended the stairs that his single most noticeable feature became apparent, however. He had deep blue eyes, the sort that stared right into the depths of your soul and that would cause nervousness, even fear, had it not been for his deeply comforting smile. His first four words alone, "Welcome to my house," told the Smidts in their delivery that they were going to have a weekend they would not forget.

Chapter 7
(September 2019)

Protecting her modesty by wrapping herself in the silk robe that had until that moment been draped over the chair adjacent to her bed, Rachael made her way from the bedroom to the source of the noise that had roused her from her deep slumber.

Waking up in her bed alone a few minutes earlier, her initial thoughts had been that Luke had made a run for it sometime between when she went back to sleep following their midnight disturbance and when she awoke just then. It would have been quite conceivable that Luke was extremely embarrassed and decided to leave rather than face her in the morning. But as her body and mind slotted back into reality, she realised to her relief that the clunking of crockery and the smell of freshly brewed coffee could only mean that Luke had not left but, rather, was making breakfast. By the time she walked in to greet her guest, Rachael had decided it was probably in both their best interests to not make mention of the night's events.

"Morning, handsome. What are you up to then?"

"Hi, Rachael. You were fast asleep, so I thought I would see what I could put together as a little surprise. Trouble is, I wasn't sure where everything was, so it's taken a lot longer than I expected. But if you'd given me just another two minutes, I would've brought you breakfast in bed."

Luke pointed to a tray on which stood a boiled egg in a cup, a plate of toast with spreads and a vase containing a few flowers he had hastily picked from the garden. "I was just waiting for the coffee to brew so I could bring it as well."

"Well, aren't you just a man full of surprises."

The words had no sooner left Rachael's lips than she had the horrible thought that Luke may take her comment as a reference to his nightmare, prompting her to quickly clarify her remark.

"You surprised me with Farrington's, then that awesome massage that just made me feel so relaxed, then our intimate time, and now breakfast. Wow! You really are amazing!"

It was lunch time on Tuesday before the opportunity presented itself to Luke to catch up with Rachael again. The two days between had been a mixture of pleasure as he thought about Saturday night and anxiety as he pondered how to approach the subject of his nightmare. He knew that he had to say something, perhaps a few words of reassurance that it was a first and a one-off event, and as such, she should not worry about being in bed with him.

Once Luke started the conversation, the right words came surprisingly easily. Rachael's response was both comforting and reassuring as she drew the conversation from the past to the upcoming weekend.

"Are you free Saturday?"

"Yes, at this stage I am. Can I ask what you have in mind?"

"Well, you took me to Farrington's, and now it's my turn to take you somewhere nice. The Grand has a special Great Gatsby evening, if you're interested?"

"That sounds good. What exactly does that involve?"

"I just saw it in the paper today. It runs from six thirty till midnight and starts with a brief introduction from a Professor William Roberts about F Scott Fitzgerald and the original book. Then there's a showing of the 1949 film, which is about an hour and a half. After that, there is an hour break, where they serve dessert and wine, and then they are playing the 2013 movie, which runs from nine thirty till midnight. One last thing; this is entirely my treat."

"Great, that sounds very interesting. I've only seen the film that had Robert Redford in it. I think it was made in the early seventies, and it would've been at least ten years ago that I saw it. So I can't actually remember much of the storyline. How about I come over at four and bring you back to my place, where I can cook us a nice meal and we can leave from there."

The thought of another evening with the most beautiful woman in the world made for a very long week. Killing the time by immersing himself in his work, the countdown changed from days to hours and, eventually, to minutes before his car pulled up outside Rachael's apartment at four, right on the dot.

They shared a bottle of cabernet sauvignon with the meal, which made the decision to catch a taxi to The Grand just common sense, especially given the wine that was included in the ticket price. If Luke had been honest with himself, the extra glass of wine could necessitate his staying over at Rachael's when the taxi dropped them off, which would hopefully include a repeat of the last Saturday, except, of course, the nightmare.

Her invitation for coffee really did include coffee. As Luke and Rachael sat facing each other sipping the caffeine loaded beverage, they discussed the subtle messages underlying the contents of the two films. Luke then found his imagination drawn to his mind's perception of the opulent lifestyles lived by the mega-rich of the time.

"The lavish parties of the twenties must've been amazing. Such decadence and extravagance, and the thirties, as well, I guess. Before the war slowed things down a bit in the forties," he mused.

"But wasn't the nineteen-thirties when the Depression hit?"

"For most, yes. But there were those who still had wealth and used the money that they had to their advantage as they acquired assets from mortgage sales and businesses that had no choice but to go into liquidation. To be honest, Rachael, nothing, not even wars, plagues or famines have ever really changed the lives of those people who have the real financial power and political influence. And it's no different today. Some of the research that I've carried out in the course of my job has given me just a peek into the world of the unimaginably wealthy, the people who hold the real power. It's the sort of men and women who dictate policy to politicians and would make the characters in *The Great Gatsby* look like peasants. That, however, is a story for another time."

"That sounds very interesting, and you have to tell me more about it one day. But for now," she cooed, "would you like to stay the night?"

A shiver of excitement fuelled by a rush of sexual energy flowed up Luke's spine.

"I thought you would never ask."

Chapter 8

There must have been well over 500 people, men and women of every colour, shape and size, but despite their physical differences, they all had the same objective: get to the bus depot and board a bus home. Work at the factory had finished, and this was not a safe place after dark. The crowds briskly, but in an orderly fashion, made their way through the gates of the depot to their awaiting transportation. Luke followed them through, aware of the urgent need to board the appropriate vehicle. Looking for clues that would indicate the various bus routes, Luke struggled to find the correct but that would be going in his direction. Everybody else seemed to know exactly what they were doing, and the buses were soon filling and leaving the depot. Luke's attempts to ask for advice only compounded his confusion. But then he suddenly nodded and quickly proceeded to a nearby ticket window.

Explaining where he wanted to go only led to increasing frustration with every attempt. Luke knew where he lived, but relaying that to the man behind the counter proved to be an almost impossible task. After what seemed like an eternity, the man finally asked for the money for the cost of the ticket, and Luke reached into his pocket. It was full of coins, but no matter how hard he tried to provide the fare, he was thwarted by the coins falling back into his pockets. The little he managed to get onto the counter proved inadequate after another frustratingly long time. The man behind the counter eventually informed Luke that he didn't need a ticket after all, but he had better get going because there was only one bus left.

Luke turned around. The vast crowds had disappeared, all whisked away by a fleet of now departed buses. Every one of the vehicles had left—except for one. The man pointed towards the remaining bus. It was a vehicle that Luke instantly recognised. There were the 1930s' style front fenders that incorporated the matching triple-headlight modules, the single entry door halfway down the right-hand side, and the frighteningly familiar sound emitting from its engine as it burst into life, once again causing steam to sputter from its radiator. Each rhythmic pulse from the mechanical beast sent a surge of mind numbing terror though Luke's whole body. The same bus that threw fear into Luke's mind the first time he saw it was once again there, waiting for him and him alone.

"No! Not that bus. Don't let it take me!" he pleaded.

His own voice calling out combined with Rachael shaking his arm to rescue Luke from his sweat-inducing second nightmare.

Jumping straight out of bed, Luke flicked on the main light switch in Rachael's bedroom. The now illuminated room confirmed that he was not in a deserted bus depot, and there was no terrifying bus waiting to take him to goodness knows where. Reality, however, still didn't immediately bring down his elevated heartbeat or return his rapid breathing back to normal conditions.

"Luke, are you OK? You were calling out about a bus again. Do you want to talk about it?"

Luke struggled to get his words out and initially just nodded as Rachael walked up to him and wrapped her arms around him in a sympathetic hug. The warmth from her naked body was comforting as Luke held her closely in return.

"I am so sorry. What must you think of me?" he muttered.

"It's OK, Luke. It was only a dream." Rachael gently patted Luke's back as he snuggled his head into her neck.

Although Rachael's embrace was the best thing that could be happening, Luke realised the nightmare was far too scary to just dismiss it like a bad joke. He felt like a scared child being comforted by his mother rather than a grown man trying to impress the woman he hoped to have a serious relationship with. After a few moments, he reluctantly broke out of the embrace, letting his hands slide down Rachael's arms till they held hands.

"I really would like to talk about this nightmare, if you don't mind."

"Of course. But let's get back into bed and we can cuddle whilst you tell me."

Luke laid on his back and put his right arm around Rachael as she positioned herself up close against him.

"I can't say for sure that I've never had nightmares before. I do remember waking up frightened on one or two occasions when I was a young boy, but that was a long time ago. I've never had them as an adult. Last week, the dream I had was just so scary—as stupid as it was, it felt so real. I didn't want to talk about it because I was scared you might think I'm a nut case and not want to see me again. So I told myself it was just a one off event that would disappear into the past and we'd just both forget about it and move on. Now, I'm really worried that you'll think I have nightmares all the time. But I swear to God, the only two I've had since I grew up were on the two nights we've spent together." He paused for a moment as he realised how that had sounded. "Oh, shit. I didn't mean you're responsible. No, definitely not. It's just a coincidence. I know it's not you; you're the best thing that's happened in my life."

"Can you tell me exactly what happened in both dreams? Perhaps there's some coincidence I'll spot."

Luke spent the next fifteen minutes relating the two nightmares in as much detail as he could remember. Most dreams seem to quickly fade into obscurity, apart from a few details, but it was different with these nightmares, and Rachael was surprised by the amount of detail that was imprinted in Luke's memory.

"Well, here's how I see it," she said. "Last week, you had a nightmare. They do happen. Maybe it was your mind or body reacting to something you drank or ate, or maybe it was just the whole thing about us spending the night together. It was obviously very real, and therefore, it was still alive in the back of your mind, which meant it easily came back, particularly since you hadn't talked about it and tried stuffing it down. But now that we've talked about them and brought them out into the open, it'll be different. When I was a young girl, I remember my dad telling me that evil only lives in the darkness, and if we want to deal with something bad that we've done, seen, heard or thought, then we have to bring it into the light and talk it through with God or people we trust. So I'm sure this will be the end of this episode. Do you agree?"

"You're absolutely right. Thank you."

"Well, now we can go back to sleep… or since we're awake, we could have a repeat of earlier. That's if you're up to it, of course."

Chapter 9
(June 1940)

Rupert K Smidt felt unusually relaxed as he sipped the whisky their host had poured. Walter Bloomfield was also feeling that his everyday worries were a thousand miles away as the soft leather chair cradled his tired body. The three wives had retired to the drawing room after their five-course meal, leaving the staff to clear the dining room and the men to retire to the library for a post-dinner indulgence of fine Cuban cigars and aged Scotch whisky.

"This had better be my last," Rupert stated as their host offered to refill his empty glass.

"Well, in that case, I have a little surprise. I always believe in keeping the best for last, so just give me a couple of minutes, and I'll be back."

Their host soon returned holding a small round tray on which stood three crystal glasses and a bottle filled with amber liquid. Only those with the finest appreciation would know how special the contents were.

"That wouldn't be what I think it is, would it?" Rupert asked, wide-eyed.

"Well, if you're thinking it might be a bottle of McDrumond's 1934, then you are correct. There are only a handful of bottles still in existence of this arguably finest Scotch whisky produced in the last twenty-five years. Gentlemen, I can't think of a better time to open it."

"I am definitely honoured. But it's far too rare to open now; you should save it for a special occasion," Walter protested.

"Well, gentlemen, I have saved it for a special occasion. I would be honoured to share it with you both."

In the excitement of the moment, neither Rupert nor Walter had noticed that two of the three glasses had already contained a single drop of a clear, odourless and tasteless liquid. It was those two glasses that were passed to the guests after the whisky had been poured. Their host made certain that the third glass and its contents were left for him. A few minutes earlier, after returning from the wine cellar with the bottle of McDrumond's, the tall blond host of the evening had stopped at his solid oak liquor cabinet. The heavy counterbalanced door folded down to reveal a selection of spirits and fine crystal glasses in varying shapes and sizes.

The cabinet also contained a sinister secret; hidden behind the contents of the second shelf was a small brown bottle with a dropper built into the cap. It contained an innocent, but potentially deadly, liquid called HCF. German chemists had developed HCF in the early 1930s as part of a government research plan. The digestion of six to eight drops would cause a person's body and organs to go into a state of relaxation and slow to a point from which there was no recovery. The end result would be the person going to sleep and not ever waking. Being virtually impossible to detect, it was perfect for the purpose of simulating a natural death without arousing any suspicion. Apart from its primary purpose, HCF had the secondary result of providing a feeling of total relaxation when administered in small doses; a safe recommended maximum intake was only three drops within a twelve hour period for the average mature male.

The Smidts and Bloomfields had all received welcoming drinks containing a single drop upon their arrival. Now the two men were about to receive their second. As their wives chatted freely about topical issues, the three men shared their views on world events. The two visitors were too at ease to notice how their host skilfully manipulated the conversation, and the subject matter soon turned to the ongoing war in Europe and America's perceived neutrality.

Rupert K Smidt was quite convinced that America would yield to the increasing calls to join the Allies, and when they did, he would be ready to mobilise his workforce and resources for the war effort, something that would not only be patriotic but also potentially very profitable. Bloomfield, in contrast, was not quite as sure. He knew there was no appetite for war among the majority of the population, even as the unfolding events in Europe became more troublesome.

Their host listened carefully whilst placing the odd question to secretly gauge the two men's true feelings about the situation. Slowly, but surely, the host started to direct the conversation towards why, for its own self-interest, America should not become involved in what was a localised conflict. He proposed to his guests the theory that Germany would battle it out with the Allies, headed by England, and the eventual victor, whoever it was, would be weakened to the point of being dependent on the United States, who could then capitalise on the situation and gain extreme influence over world events and unrestrained access to the Earth's resources. It was not the points of the argument but, rather, the way the facts were presented that made for a very convincing theory, and it had Rupert re-evaluating his own views, much to his surprise.

Even with Rupert's apparent change of heart, the host cemented the logic of his argument with the analogy of two men fighting over the affections of a bountiful girl. Once the two suitors had beaten each other to a pulp, a third man, who had been quietly watching on the sidelines, stepped forward and took both their wallets, then left with the girl. The host's story was a catalyst for all three men to burst into hysterical laughter.

After interesting discussions on an array of topics and a second glass of McDrumond's that Rupert initially tried to decline, the host again led a change in the topic of conversation. This redirection eventually led to the subject of time spent at a private boarding school and the personal experiences each man had whilst enrolled in their respective institutions. Extended education at an all-male boarding school was something that the three men had in common, and in their unguarded state, it meant that the conversation flowed freely.

It was two fifteen in the morning when the host and his wife finally made their way to the master suite. It had been a long but rewarding evening, with much learned from and about their unsuspecting guests, information that seemed harmless on the surface but could, at the appropriate time and under the right circumstances, be put to good use.

Now, after all the formalities of the day, there was one thing left to do before retiring for the night. With the door to their suite firmly shut, a press on the side of a piece of artwork caused the picture to release from its frame. With the original masterpiece fully rotated out of the way, the couple gazed at the image that was usually masked by the innocent watercolour, a portrait that was normally hidden for good reason as its presence spoke of evil that could bring a man to his knees with fear. It was a chilling portrait of none other than Adolf Hitler.

Despite the warmth of the June evening, a cold and unexplained chill swept through the room as two outstretched arms gave the Nazi salute whilst two voices quietly spoke the words, "Mein Führer."

Chapter 10
(September 2019)

It was a clear, frosty night and the surreal silence meant that Luke's footsteps were audible on the concrete pavement despite the soft soles of the shoes he was wearing. The surrounding area was faintly illuminated by a dull incandescent glow from the streetlights above. There was just enough light to notice how the scenery of old boarded-up houses lining the road had turned into a collection of abandoned industrial buildings, each one a testament to better economic times. Luke stopped as a noise in the distance suddenly generated feelings of dread that caused a tingling throughout his body. The sound was faint, but it was recognisably the familiar chugging of the bus that always instilled fear right to his very core. As the noise slowly got louder, Luke became gripped by uncontrollable panic and started to run.

The scenery had changed yet again, this time to tall buildings so close to the footpath that their proximity cut off any possible escape route. The more Luke ran, the more his legs hurt, and although he was expending a lot of energy, forward movement felt like trying to run through water. The puffing and chugging sound increased in both volume and intensity as the bus got continually closer; Luke retreated down an alley just wide enough for the bus to follow him. He suddenly realised all exits were now totally blocked as the alley came to a dead end. Turning to face his nemesis, Luke knew there would be no escape from the inevitable.

Like an evil demon, the bus hissed and spat steam at Luke as it slowed its advance. The bold radiator grille's badge containing the large chrome letters OMD was now only inches from his chest, and he could feel the intense heat of the engine as the gap narrowed further.

"*Help*! *Help me*!" Luke's screams roused him from the nightmare that had engulfed him, mind and body. Drenched with sweat, Luke jumped out of bed to quickly flick on the light switch. Although he knew it was a dream, logic had not yet caught up to his sudden awakening and return to consciousness. Luke peered through the side of the curtains, carefully checking that the bus was not parked outside. Assured that the coast was clear, he opened the window and placed his ear to the screen, listening to the cool outside air for any trace of the sound that had become to him the representation of pure evil. To his relief, and as expected, nothing could be heard.

It may have only been a dream, but the intensity had provoked so much terror, it had caused him to do something he hadn't for over twenty years. He had wet himself. Still trembling from fright, he looked at his urine-soaked bed and slowly released the quiet words, "Thank you, God, that Rachael wasn't here. A third nightmare, and now this, would've been the final straw for such a level-headed woman."

The fact that he was alone that night was in one sense a blessing, but it also created a dilemma. How could he spend the night with Rachael ever again knowing that an early morning screaming session was now a distinct possibility. What had been up to now just a couple of easily dismissed events now took on a whole new meaning. This had to be sorted out once and for all, and Luke knew he was about to embark on a quest.

"Hello, Luke, I'm Stephen." The man's handshake and smile exuded calmness and tranquillity. His many years as a psychologist had taught Stephen Boswell that the most important moments in a therapist–patient relationship were the first fifteen seconds. With the introductions and formalities out of the way, it was time to get down to business—the reason that Luke had made the appointment.

"Well, Luke, how can I help you?"

"I know this is going to sound stupid, but I've had several nightmares—three, to be exact—all about the same thing. Now I'm too frightened to spend the night with my girlfriend. She witnessed two of them, and I'm afraid that if I have another, she may decide she doesn't want to see me ever again. And I wouldn't blame her as it's just so ridiculous."

"First, Luke, nothing you tell me will sound stupid or ridiculous. You would not believe what people have told me in the forty years I've been dealing with people's problems. I still struggle to comprehend how complicated the human mind is. Our generated thoughts can take us from the top of the world to the depths of despair and back again in an instant. Our minds can recreate the experience of events that we know will never occur again, and they can also give the weakest of men superhuman feats of strength in times of trauma. The one thing that runs true every time, though, is there's always a root cause. What we have to do is uncover what that is, and then we can look at what we need to do to refocus your mind in a positive direction. So let's start with you telling me about those dreams."

Chapter 11

It was two weeks to the day after his first appointment that Luke once again strode into Stephen Boswell's reception area.

The receptionist looked up and sheepishly relayed, "I am so sorry, but Stephen had an emergency out of the office today, and he's running about thirty minutes late. Please, help yourself to some coffee and cookies and have a seat." She pointed to the coffee machine and glass jar holding a selection of chocolate and shortbread treats, gesturing for Luke not to be shy or hold back.

Luke moved to sit in a luxurious leather chair, but with a coffee and chocolate chip cookie in hand, he struggled to keep his balance. The chair proved to be much softer than its appearance indicated, and he sank deep into the cushions.

His previous session with Stephen had been very constructive, and Luke hadn't had anything even resembling a nightmare or disturbing dreams since that visit. The two men had not been able to ascertain any link between Luke's nightmares and some event, known or unknown, in his life up to that point.

Stephen had covered the obvious scenarios. Had Luke ever been abandoned on a bus? Did someone he love go away on a bus and not come back? Was a family member ever killed by a bus or piece of machinery? As the scenarios were discussed, it became apparent that there was nothing obvious to explain the horror he felt at something so common as a bus. The cause of his nightmares still lay rooted quite deep in his mind.

Rachael had been understanding. They had continued dating, with each occasion inevitably leading to intimate time together, and Luke's reluctance to spend the night with her had made him determined to find answers.

Talking about the three dreams with Stephen had helped. The clinic was a safe place for Luke to discuss his fears, hopes, accomplishments and perceived failures. In fact, he'd been startled at how much he'd already told the therapist, as some things were of a quite personal nature.

Will today's session shed any additional light on this situation? Will Stephen ask a magic question or offer words of wisdom that will unlock a part of my mind long closed off from the outside world? Could there—

Luke's thoughts were abruptly interrupted by the receptionist. "You can go on in now."

Five minutes into their session, Stephen suddenly stopped the conversation's current direction, and after a brief pause, he resumed with a new approach.

"Luke, I must confess that I've taken a bit of a liberty. In fact, quite a big liberty. After our last session, I was thinking about the bus in your dreams and what you told me about it. I contacted an old school friend who is a walking encyclopaedia about trucks and buses, and I described the bus to him. I didn't mention you or the reason why I was asking about it. My friend first said I could have been describing a multitude of buses until I mentioned the letters OMD. Then, he knew exactly what I was talking about and why a Google search might not have produced any results.

"I would normally never do anything like that without first asking my client, but I was very concerned about how those dreams were affecting you, so I broke my own rule. The point I'm getting to is that my friend emailed me a picture of a bus that might be like the one you've dreamt about. I have that picture here. You can see it if you feel comfortable, or we could take it to the fireplace and burn it if that might help. Or you could even look at the picture and see that it's just a bus in a picture and it cannot hurt you. We could also pretend that I never made that call, if you prefer, and I will destroy the picture myself. It's totally up to you and what you're comfortable with."

"I want to see it," Luke replied without hesitation.

"I thought you might."

Stephen handed Luke a large envelope holding a folded piece of paper, and Luke carefully withdrew the sheet, pausing before opening the fold. Luke's heart raced and his skin tingled as he looked at the scanned picture. Every curve of every panel on the bus in the photo caused a flashback to his nightmares.

"Are you OK, Luke?" Stephen was genuinely concerned at the reaction Luke was having to even something so benign as just looking at the image. To Stephen's relief, Luke eventually replied.

"Yes, just a bit shaken. This is it. The shape, the style. It's missing the big OMD badge I clearly saw in the third dream, but the rest is all there, just as I saw it. How could I dream so clearly about something that I'd never seen before and then find out later that it's actually a real thing?"

"The human mind baffles people far more clever than me," Stephen replied softly.

Stephen was about to say something else when Luke suddenly jumped out of the chair and dropped the picture to the floor. Then, a moment later, the look of panic eased, and Luke apologised for the interruption. "I'm sorry, Stephen. I heard the demonic sputtering that bus makes when it's starting, but the sound is gone now."

"Please, Luke, don't apologise. Dreams can have adverse effects that last a long time. The thing to remember is that it is something that was created in our minds, so we can also use our minds to destroy it. As I suggested, you can burn the picture. Or we could… now, please trust me on this, you could draw all over it. I have some coloured pencils. You could turn it into a circus bus, all brightly coloured and driven by clowns, so that it becomes something funny rather than scary. And we can laugh and make fun of it."

"I don't want to destroy the picture; I need to find out more about it and why this thing chose to come into my life. What else did your friend tell you about it?"

"Not much. He said only a few were ever brought into the country, so there's not a lot of information available. But he'd probably have more information than anyone."

"As a journalist, my job is digging up all the information I can find about something. At times, information is obvious, but other times, I have to dig deep holes and turn over rocks to find what I need to know. This is no different. I need to learn as much as I can about OMD buses, and the obvious place to start is your friend. Are you able to give me his number?"

"I'm sure he wouldn't mind. Larry loves to share his knowledge with anybody who takes the time to listen. I never said why I was asking about the bus, so you don't have to say that you're a client."

"That doesn't bother me. I'll tell him the truth. There's a reason those nightmares happened, and I'm going to find out what it is."

Handing Luke a slip of paper, Stephen replied, "OK. Here's his number. When you've found out all you can, come back, and we'll talk it through."

Anxious and not wanting to waste time, Luke made the call from his car in the clinic parking lot. Even in such a brief conversation, Luke could tell that Stephen had not been kidding about Larry Breen being a walking encyclopaedia of all things motor vehicle, particularly trucks and buses. He lived only about forty minutes from Silverleaf, and Luke arranged to meet him at seven the next morning.

Chapter 12

As he walked up the path to the free-standing, single level house, it was obvious Luke was at the right place. Lining the walkway was a collection of ceramic and galvanised planters in the shapes of cars, trucks, buses and heavy moving equipment.

Luke's press of the doorbell summoned the plump, smiling house owner.

"Hi. I'm looking for Larry Breen," Luke said.

"That's me! You must be Luke, the man I spoke with yesterday who knows Stephen. Right?"

"That's me. I'm Luke Spitz," Luke replied as a he reached to shake Larry's hand. "I'm actually a client of Stephen's, and he suggested you might be able to help me."

"I will try my best," Larry acknowledged as he led Luke through the modest home to a table in the dining room. It appeared to be the only piece of furniture in the house not covered by stacks of books or models of trucks and buses.

"You have to excuse the mess, but ever since my dear wife, Betty, died, I haven't got anyone to tell me that I can't purchase some truck model I've seen. Maybe I have let things get a little out of hand, but there are much worse vices I could have. Anyway, enough about me. Stephen said you're looking for information about OMD buses?"

"I believe you are the expert on them, which is good because I've only been able to find practically nothing about them online."

"Let's start by clarifying the fact that I'm not an OMD expert, and I very much doubt that there's any living person who is. There were not many vehicles manufactured under the OMD brand, and all the OMD records kept by the parent company were destroyed during the war. So I'm not surprised you haven't been able to find out much."

"But you do have some information?" Luke asked hopefully.

"Well, I am a truck and bus enthusiast. So I probably know as much about those buses as anybody in the country, and I'm happy to share what information I do have about them with you."

"That's fantastic! Thank you."

"Please, have a seat. Can I get you a coffee?" Larry offered.

"No, I'm good, thanks. Just any information that you have."

"Well then let's start with the name. OMD stands for Ottinger-Mayer-Dieter. There was a misconception that the D stood for Deutschland, but it was definitely Dieter. Albert and Michael Dieter inherited the family bicycle manufacturing business after their father died. The two brothers were very forward thinking, and not wanting to stay stuck in the past, they began fitting small engines to their bikes for an assist with peddling. That, in turn, led them to design and fit sidecars to their bikes. They looked more like motorcycles then, and they were a cheap form of transport. That business was sold as a going concern, and by the mid-twenties, they'd used their capital to start a business building sidecars for motorcycle manufacturers. Times were tough, but labour was cheap, and they made some good business decisions. So it wasn't long before the company was venturing into making and fitting custom car bodies for auto manufacturers. Their company, known as Dieter Brothers, was small, but they produced high quality work. So by the early thirties, both Albert and Michael were looking for new challenges.

"The next part of the story is a bit vague, but for some reason, they became obsessed with trying to build the best motorbuses in the world. They wanted to become the Rolls Royce of quality bus manufacturing, a strange decision considering the economic times. Anyway, they convinced a German financier, Helmut Mayer, that when Germany recovered from its downturn, they would be the only manufacturer of luxury buses in the country. Mayer put up most of the capital, and the Dieters, their staff and equipment all moved into new premises in Ottinger, Germany, close to the Czech border. Naturally, the Dieters didn't have it all their way, and one of the stipulations of their new partnership was changing the company's name, which is how OMD came into being. OMD only produced two models, the K-eighteen and the K-twenty-five. Both were built on rolling chassis acquired from a company in Czechoslovakia that were shipped to their factory before being disassembled so the suspension could be modified for a much more comfortable ride.

"All the bodywork was built from scratch, and most of the work was done in-house. Some components were contracted out, like with the specialist company that carried out the engine and driveline modifications. Rumour has it that the engines were so well balanced, even the driver couldn't tell if the bus was running at idle without looking at the gauges. A lot of the design was groundbreaking, and when it was finished, the bus had features rarely seen on buses, even today. It had seats that reclined and were rubber isolated from the body, air vents underneath each seat that could blow either warm or cold air and the ride that was second to none. The K-eighteen was the trial vehicle for many of their innovations. I believe only three were made, and they were sold at a loss.

"Mayer began to get frustrated about the rising costs and was ready to cut his losses and walk away. But somehow, the Dieters, who had also put everything they had into the business, convinced him that with the development work finally done, they could start producing the slightly bigger K-twenty-five. Nationalism had started to take hold in the re-emerging Germany, and they were convinced that OMD would proudly be one step ahead of the competition as the world awoke to a brand new future where Germany was at the forefront of technology.

"The K-twenty-five was released in mid-1936, but not everything in the world had turned out the way the Dieters had imagined. Nationalism had unfortunately spawned Hitler's rise to power, and the clouds of war and uncertainly hung ominously over Europe. As good as it was, the world was just not ready for the K-twenty-five. I don't know how many were actually produced. Estimates range from sixteen to twenty before the business went under and was absorbed into DKM. The company ended up producing vehicles for the German war effort. Nothing else was ever produced under the OMD brand.

"The reason we don't know much about the K-eighteen or K-twenty-five, including total numbers built, is that all of their records were destroyed when the factory was bombed during the war. However, I do know that four were imported into the States."

Luke paled, revealing his horror. "So there are four of those buses in America?"

"It's probably more a case of there *were* four in the States. As good as they were, that was over eighty years ago. They'd have all been retired and scrapped long ago."

"But if one did survive, where would it be?"

"I really don't think any could have survived. All four were imported by Allen's Luxury Bus Services, which operated out of Youngtown, North Carolina. The company is still around, but now they're called Allen's Transport. They do bus charters out of their new HQ in Wisdom, North Carolina. And that, Luke, is about all I can tell you."

"Have you got any pictures of the bus other than the one you sent to Stephen?"

"Only one other. Just like the first picture, it's of a K-twenty-five in Allen's livery. But in this photo, the K-twenty-five is parked next to an REO. They also operated a couple of those. You can't mistake a K-twenty-five, with its triple lights on each fender and the big OMD badge on the grille."

Larry passed Luke a small picture of the two buses before commenting, "This picture is obviously pre-December of forty-one."

"How do you know?"

"Because after Pearl Harbor, an anti-Japanese and German backlash spread across the nation. As I said before, there was a misconception that the D in OMD stood for Deutschland, so Allen's removed the OMD emblem from the grille. They replaced it with a chrome-plated Allen's logo."

"That's an interesting scenario."

"If you want to find out more about what happened to the four trucks imported here, then maybe you should contact Allen's. Their current records might not go back that far, but it's worth a try. To my knowledge, there are no surviving K-eighteens or K-twenty-fives anywhere in the world, let alone here in the States, but if you do find anything out about what happened to them, please do keep me informed."

"I will certainly be contacting Allen's. And no matter what I find out or don't find out, I'll let you know. Did Stephen ever tell you why I am enquiring?"

"No, he didn't. And I never asked, but to be honest, I'm intrigued. In all my years, nobody has ever asked me about OMDs."

"Well, if you're keen to hear the story, I'd like to tell you why. It's really bizarre, but my need to find out what's going on has outweighed any embarrassment I initially had," Luke began. "You see, I have met the most wonderful woman in the world, and I just want to get this sorted so I don't freak her out and have her leave me."

Stunned by Luke's honesty, Larry encouraged him to continue, eager to hear what was driving his visitor. "Now you really have me intrigued, Luke. I would love to hear! It might help me to help you."

Luke took a deep breath before embarking on a twenty-five minute recap of the events of the last few weeks.

Chapter 13

Luke's seven a.m. meeting with Larry should have given him enough time to still get to work, with just a slightly late start, at worst. But after his conversation with Larry, Luke knew that Allen's Transport would hold part of, if not the entire, answer. He was left with no choice but to contact Allen's, or maybe even make the trip to where the next clue on the trail may lie. A quick check of Allen's address on Google Maps indicated a driving time of four hours and twelve minutes. The decision was all but made as there was no other option. He'd call Allen's first, and if there were any indications that would guarantee the long drive would not be wasted, he'd contact Skip to let him know he was on the trail of a story and wouldn't be in the office today. It was a decision that required no guilt; after all, he would not be lying.

A quick search on his phone for information about Allen's Transport gave him a link to the company's website. Ignoring the first few paragraphs about its modern day services, Luke clicked on a tab labelled 'Company History'. It took Luke to a page that had a selection of photographs, but none were of an OMD. Moving on to the text, Luke saw the opening paragraph proudly informed readers that the company's beginnings went all the way back to 1923, when Ronald and Sherman Allen formed Allen Brothers Motorbus Company. Readers were then informed how, in 1933, as the country was still deep in the economic doldrums from the Great Depression, Allen's defied the norm. After rebranding to Allen's Luxury Bus Service, the company proceeded to provide an upscale and high-end service for wealthy travellers. In 1961, the company rebranded again, this time to Allen's Transport, the name they still operated under, although they'd gone through a couple of livery changes since 1961. Unfortunately, the historical information on the site was only relevant to the general outline of the company and made no mention of bus types other than using words like 'comfortable', 'modern' and 'reliable'.

Clicking back to the home page, Luke found the company's contact information, one for bookings and one for general enquiries. The office hours were listed as eight till five. Luke looked at his watch and saw it was now ten minutes to eight. It was a very long ten minutes. Luke thought how strange the perception of time was. Two hours spent with Rachael seemed to pass in a heartbeat, but this ten minutes staring at his watch felt like forever. Eventually, the minute hand hit twelve.

After a bit of explaining what he needed to find out, the Allen's Transport's very helpful receptionist, Glenda, transferred Luke to Mark Western, the general manager. Sympathetic to Luke's request, Mark invited Luke to make the drive; there were some company archives that he could look through. In addition, Mark informed Luke that he would invite Ernie Taylor to come in. Ernie was their longest serving employee, and although he was now retired, the two men kept in contact. Ernie would be the best source of information, and Mark knew he would be keen to help. Luke's mind was made up. He'd make the long drive, but first, he had to send two texts.

Taking several incoming calls and dealing with various interruptions by staff during the short time the two men were chatting in his office did not seem to faze Mark Western, who was clearly a very busy man. Mark told Luke that as much as he would like to tag along with Luke on his investigation, he couldn't do so in person. But he did know there were some records that could hold helpful clues for Luke. They were kept in the company archives, which went back to Allen's early days, although there had been a big clearing out when the company moved into their new premises.

Ernie Taylor's arrival was a relief to Mark. Perhaps because of knowing how far Luke had driven, Mark had behaved as though he had a moral obligation to keep Luke company until Ernie showed up, regardless of his busy schedule.

"Hello, I'm Ernie," the man greeted Luke.

"Hi. I'm Luke. I hear you can help me with my research."

"I'll certainly try my best."

Mark interrupted briefly. "I'll leave you two to chat. Just let me know if you need anything." Mark quickly left the room and closed the door behind himself.

Ernie spoke. "Thursday, thirty-first January nineteen-fifty-seven."

The seemingly meaningless statement momentarily confused Luke. "Sorry, what's the relevance of that date?"

"That was the day I started working at Allen's, just a naive sixteen-year-old boy keen as anything to learn about mechanics. I remember it as if it was yesterday. Cecil Allen ran his business like a well-oiled machine. He was firm but fair and expected an honest day's work for an honest day's pay. On my first day, I turned up at seven twenty to start work at seven thirty. By eight thirty, I had completed all of the formalities. I'd been shown around the depot, met the people I needed to know and had my coveralls on, ready to start. There was no mucking around in those days," he mused. Then he returned his attention to the visitor. "Mark said you want to talk about the old OMD buses we had."

"Yes, definitely. Any information you have about them would be much appreciated. I'm a journalist and doing a bit of research. I also have personal reasons for being here."

"I was employed at Allen's for fifty years, to the day, from start to finish. My wife wanted me to retire before that, but I was determined to make a real milestone out of my employment, so Wednesday, thirty-first January two thousand and seven it was. When I started at Allen's, we only had two of the OMDs left. The other two had been scrapped after twenty years of solid service. Of the remaining two, one was still operational. The other was parked and was used as a source of spares for the working one. Parts were impossible to get for those. The operational one was in the workshop getting serviced the day I started, so it was actually the first bus I worked on. What an amazing vehicle it was. I guess they would be considered primitive by today's standards, but when they came along, they must've been revolutionary compared to anything else that was available at the time.

"So there I was, straight into it on my first day. I was put with the head mechanic, Joe Brown, and I clearly remember his first words to me: 'Son, grab those two half-inch spanners, and I'll show you why these are the best riding vehicles ever made.' And that's just what he did. The rear axle had two sets of leaf springs on each side, set at different load rates. But the secret to the suspension was the hydraulic dampeners, which did what shock absorbers do on a car today. The fluid compressed a piston that acted against an enclosed spring. There were two units on each corner of the bus that were reversed to each other, so it was the porting of the hydraulic valves that did the dampening. Now, the really clever thing was that each pair of dampeners could be adjusted according to load. The driver would go to each wheel well and independently put a lever in the correct position corresponding to the loaded weight. The whole system was terribly complicated, but the results gave a class A ride that couldn't be beat. I remember Joe taking the bus out after we'd finished. He drove straight over a speed bump, and I'll tell you what, I hardly felt a thing! Joe said he was probably the only man left in the country who could adjust the suspension correctly. I remember once helping him set up valve porting on a test rig he'd made himself. It was only about eighteen months after my first day that the last OMD was decommissioned, and they were both taken away to be scrapped."

"I heard they were rumoured to be very quiet. I guess that means they wouldn't have made a chugging sound, sort of like a heartbeat, when they were running. Is that right?" Luke asked.

"Goodness, no. They were so quiet and smooth that even sitting in the driver's seat, you couldn't tell if it was turned on. There was a green light on the dashboard that illuminated when the motor was running, just in case the driver thought they'd stalled out."

"What about overheating? Did they ever hiss steam out of the radiator?"

"Certainly not that I can remember."

Luke went on. "Can you describe what they were like inside?"

"Sheer luxury, Luke. A bus that size would normally have up to twenty-four seats. But our OMD had twelve individual leather seats that reclined, and each had individual outlets for fresh or heated air. I can't really remember much more. It was a long time ago. I did work on the OMD during the first eighteen months of my time at Allen's, but during that period, I also worked on the other vehicles in the fleet."

"I understand, Ernie. But can you remember if the seats had fold-down trays with cut-outs that acted as cup holders?"

Ernie thought for a few moments and then looked up at Luke with a sense of amazement. "Why, you know, yes, they did! I remember it was a routine thing to adjust the trays so they stayed level."

Luke pressed on. "And down the aisle, was the floor recessed and carpeted, with two L-shaped chrome brackets running down either side?"

"Yes, it was that way. I remember the floor sections were removable for maintenance. Those chrome brackets had a quick-release feature, and you could lift up each floor section. Each piece had about two inches of sound deadening material underneath. How in the name of God did you know that?"

"Actually, I had a dream about getting on an OMD bus. It was all so clear and vivid, I just had to talk to you to verify everything."

Ernie stared at Luke for a few moments in total disbelief. Then he smiled. "Ha! Well done, son. I nearly believed you. I bet you found the fifth one, haven't you? I thought it would've been long gone, but you hear about those rare barn finds every now and then."

Luke gaped at the older man. "What do you mean, the fifth one? I thought there were only four."

"No. I said Allen's operated four, but they'd actually bought five. They ended up selling one. I know all four of ours were scrapped, so you had to have found the other one. Where the heck was it?"

"Look, I honestly haven't found another OMD bus. Until just a minute ago, in fact, I didn't even know there was a fifth one brought into the country. I swear, I'm telling you the truth. I dreamt about one of these buses on three separate occasions. And they weren't just dreams; they were nightmares, bad ones. I woke up screaming and freaked out my girlfriend, so now I've been going to bed and not sleeping, concerned I might have another, and I'm terrified Rachael will leave me. So please believe me when I say I need to find out what is going on. Now that you've told me there's another OMD somewhere out there, I'll have to chase it down and see if it still exists." Tears had started rolling down Luke's cheeks as he choked out the last few words.

Ernie's expression changed. He'd seen a lot in his seventy-eight years, enough to know when someone was lying and when they were telling the truth.

"Well, I'll be darned. Ain't that just the strangest thing! I believe you, son, and I'd really like to help, but I don't know anything more about it."

"But you know it exists."

"Existed, yes," Ernie emphasised. "At one stage. But if it's still around, well, heck, it'd be older than me. It's probably long gone to the scrapyard, just like our four."

"Is there anything at all you can think of that might help me find out what happened to it?" Luke's voice was tinged with desperation.

"All I know is what Joe told me. He said that Allen's bought five OMDs from Germany in nineteen-thirty-seven, but they sold one to a private party somewhere upstate. Joe did say that they handled the service on that one for a while, but then he never saw or heard about it again. That's really all I can tell you. I never heard any names, addresses or any other details."

"Would Allen's have any record of who bought the fifth bus? Mark said something about an archive and that I'd be welcome to look through it."

"Well, son, when Allen's moved here in nineteen-ninety-five, it was a chance to really clear out the other depot, which was the original site they'd bought only a couple of years after the company was formed. You can imagine how much Allen's accumulated in all those years, so they had a lot to clear out. I know they saved some records, but not everything.

"They'd kept most everything, going right back to when they started. Mark wanted to get rid of everything that was no longer relevant, but Marie stopped him. Mark isn't an Allen, of course. Well, not a blood Allen. He married into the family when he took William Allen's daughter Marie as his wife. Mark took over running the place in nineteen-ninety-two, but between you and me, I think Marie makes all the big decisions, or probably actually all the decisions. Mark doesn't do anything unless Marie gives the OK. I guess Marie sees the old records as part of her family's history. She once told me about plans to put up a small outbuilding and make it an Allen's heritage display. I haven't actually seen what they have saved, but Mark did give the OK to access the old records, so I'm thrilled to get to help you look through what they have."

Ernie led his eager guest through to the storeroom where boxes of records had remained untouched since they'd been placed there twenty-four years ago. What initially appeared to be a daunting task was made easier by the fact that some of the documents were grouped by year. Unfortunately, 1937 was one of the years that remained elusive.

As they opened each box and reviewed the contents, Ernie occasionally stopped to reminisce over photos showing Allen's buses in the various colour schemes that were applied for special occasions or contracts.

Finally, a box that held an answer was located. Luke placed the documents on the small table, readying the contents for examination.

"Ernie, look! Here are the bookkeeping journals from nineteen-thirty to nineteen-thirty-nine."

Luke held the journal labelled 1937 in trembling hands. There were no documents or photos inside, just pages and pages listing income and expenditures. The faded ink and ornate writing made interpretation a little tricky.

"Just look for big numbers, Luke," Ernie offered.

"Exactly what I was thinking."

"There, that must be it." Ernie pointed to an entry. "There, that must be it!" The number was so large that it could only have been the purchase of five new buses. However, it was another ten minutes before they found what was the true quest of Luke's search, a cash purchase of one of the OMD buses by a Mr E Linderman. Another two hours passed. Luke became so engrossed in searching the files for further details that he had missed Ernie's hints about getting tired. Another two hours had passed before Ernie finally just came straight to the point.

"I'm sorry, Luke, that the name was all you could find. But hopefully, it can lead to what you're looking for. This has been a wonderful experience, bringing back so many memories. But I'm exhausted and need to get home and rest. I can see if Mark is OK with you staying here alone."

Luke realised that if he remained, he'd have overstayed his welcome with both Ernie and Mark. The day hadn't been wasted; he had a name. In his job, he'd found answers with far fewer clues than that.

"I am sorry, Ernie. You're right; we should go now. I really appreciate all your help with this. And it was a success—I now have a name. Let me just stack these boxes back as we found them and then we can go."

The walk back to his car reminded Luke of not only how long the day had been but also how long it had been since he'd eaten or, more importantly, had a cup of coffee. That was his first priority when he got to the café directly across the street.

The cup of black coffee hit the spot the way only a strong hot brew could, reviving Luke's thoughts and letting him ponder the options for his next actions. There were only light snacks on offer at the café, and Luke remembered the roadside diner he'd passed on the way into town. It had an unforgettable name that was impossible to resist. It seemed like the perfect place for a long overdue nourishing meal.

At the café, a quick Google search for E. Linderman on his phone had produced no initial relevant hits. But Luke saw it as just a minor hiccup. He had a name, and that was a major breakthrough. If anybody could find out about the person who'd bought that fifth bus, it was Luke.

Several minutes later, Luke was seated in the restaurant with his phone to his ear. "Hi, Rachael. I thought I'd give you a quick call now as I am going to get back too late to catch up tonight."

"Oh? Where are you?"

"I'm at Skip's."

"So you're at work?"

"Ha, ha. No, not exactly. The diner where I'm eating happens to coincidentally be named Skip's. When I saw the place from the road, I figured it was a sign from above telling me I should stop here and not the other place two blocks down. I'm in a town called Wisdom, in North Carolina. I've been following up some leads on the bus, and you're not going to believe where the trail has led me. I don't want to get into much detail now, but I'll tell you everything tomorrow. If it works for you, we can catch up at lunch, and I can tell you all about what I've found after I prepare you for what to expect at my family's party tomorrow night."

"OK, you can tell me tomorrow. But how are you, Luke? That's a long way to drive, so it had to have been a long day. Aren't you tired?"

The yawn Luke had tried to stifle at the end of his last sentence had clued in his girlfriend that he was, indeed, both physically and emotionally tired.

"Well, actually, yeah, just a bit. But I've had a good meal and several cups of coffee."

"Why don't you get a motel room and have a good night's sleep so you can drive home safely in the morning," she suggested.

"I'll be fine."

"OK, then. It's your choice."

The tone of Rachael's reply made Luke realise that her idea about the motel wasn't a suggestion; rather, it was a request. He conceded. "No, you're right. There's a motel right behind this diner. I'll see if they have a vacancy."

"Thank you, Luke. I just want to see you kept safe."

As the conversation moved to a more personal nature, it became clear from Rachael's concerns and her gratitude following his decision to stay, that it had been the right choice for him to make, and the conversation had left him on a high. But Luke had to put that aside as he checked in at the motel and made a quick call to Skip, following up on the text he'd sent earlier from Larry's.

Neither the pillow nor the bed was as comfortable as his own, but they seldom are. So it was further proof that attempting to drive back would not have been a good decision when it didn't take long before alertness gave way to the effects of fatigue and mental stress.

The blue glow of the numbers on the bedside alarm clock indicated five after three, a time when arousal from sleep would normally only mean a few quiet minutes before drifting back to sleep, but this time was different. Luke was wide awake as his mind started working on the question of who E Linderman was and whether his family would still have the bus.

Luke logically wanted to build a profile of the person in question, which he did by quietly speaking his thoughts aloud to an invisible audience.

"First, I assume E. Linderman was a man, so I can Google a list of men's names that begin with E. That'll be a start. Second, he must've had a reason to buy the bus. Either he was a transport operator, or he needed it for his own private use. If he was a transport operator, Larry Breen would probably have known about him and the fifth bus. So let's start by assuming he needed it for himself. Third, he had to have been rich to pay that much cash; if he was financially well-off, he probably ran in the circles of other rich and possibly well-known people of the time.

Additionally, the bus was German built, and Linderman sounds like a German name. That could be a solid connection, so I will also initially assume he was German. Maybe he was a businessman, in which case, a search for businesses using the name Linderman might produce a lead."

As the ideas continued to flow into his head, Luke decided he needed to write them all down before he forgot any. That was a wise decision; it wasn't the first time Luke had awakened to an overactive mind full of ideas, but then woke up later in the morning with no clue what those thoughts had been.

A simple plan to record his ideas, however, turned into having to get out of bed and start his laptop to begin the task of following up on some of these ideas. Dead end after dead end made crawling back into the bed an attractive option, but then an article about pre-war German society on the American East Coast gave a first hint of progress. It was a story about the lavish St Patrick's Day party held at the estate of a mover and shaker named Eric Linderman.

"Yes, yes, yes and yes!" He shouted.

Forty-five minutes later, Luke was convinced he'd found his man. Eric Linderman was a rich German-American who threw opulent parties at his mansion on the Maryland coast. Linderman was also known for his views on America keeping out of the war that was raging through Europe at the time. Eric's life came to a tragic end, however. Unable to control his grief when the two countries he loved became sworn enemies, he committed suicide along with his wife shortly after America declared war on Japan and Germany. Luke had been able to determine approximately where Linderman may have lived, accomplished with a little help from Google Earth.

Could that be where the bus was taken and later stored?

The thought of detouring in that direction before heading home briefly occurred to him, but that would mean he'd have no time for his promised visit with Rachael and still be on time for the family party they were to attend later in the evening. By then, it was nearly six a.m. and because there was little chance of getting back to sleep, he decided to get ready to head home.

Chapter 14

Luke's acceptance that talking about his nightmares was a means to an end had made exposing his vulnerabilities to Stephen, Larry and Ernie easier than he'd thought it would be. Another life or another time would have seen his emotional self-protection causing him to hide much of what he had now openly shared.

Nonetheless, Luke was still reluctant to show any signs of weakness to Rachael. He believed that he had to show nothing less than impenetrable strength of character if he was to present himself to her as a viable lifetime partner.

So it was in that state of mind that Luke carefully chose his words as he recounted the prior couple of days to Rachael. Nothing he said was untrue; he just made sure that some things that had occurred were emphasised, whilst others were glossed over.

Reciting the facts of his newfound knowledge helped put a degree of justification on what Luke still considered an embarrassing episode in their relationship. The woman who had captured his heart had to have no doubt in her mind that his nightmares were not a reflection of any physiological or psychological problems. Rather, they had to have a purpose, and what that purpose was comprised the reasons for Luke's journey of discovery. When Rachael herself suggested there appeared to be some reason for the nightmares, Luke breathed a sigh of relief, and his concerns that a repeat performance could destroy their relationship momentarily subsided.

"Rachael, I feel like I've been cleansed."

"In what way?" Rachael queried.

"Well, I mean cleansed of the nightmares and any effects they might have had on our future together."

"I'm sure that once we know what's behind the dreams, all thoughts of the nightmares will be a thing of the past."

As excited as she was about Luke's progress on his quest to track down the bus, Rachael currently had more important things on her mind. Having not yet met any of Luke's family apart from a brief introduction to his mum and sister, she felt vulnerable about meeting his entire family later. She was certain they'd want to find out all they could about her, and she wanted to know what to expect from them.

Rachael's first meeting with Luke's mum and his sister, Nina, had gone well. The hospitality and genuine warmth they'd shown her had calmed her nerves and made her immediately feel that she'd been accepted into Luke's immediate family circle. Rachael knew that if her move into the outer echelons of the Spitz family went as smoothly, there'd be nothing to concern herself about. But she didn't want to take that for granted.

Luke had been only five when his father passed away, and despite his young age, he remembered that day with great clarity, from being called into the principal's office to be taken home by his aunt to his pregnant mother, Esther, being inconsolable.

Rueben Spitz had been a man of traditional values who put his family above all else. No one in the family had any memories at all of him being angry in front of his family. Luke's father had led his life based on a set of self-imposed standards. To Reuben, it was a basic principle that as the head of the family, it was his duty to be a tower of strength who modelled restraint and never let anything bring him down, at least not in front of his family. He believed that when faced with a stressful situation, the best option was to take your anger out into the garden, out of the sight of your children. However, Rueben didn't always find it easy to keep his emotions from showing, and despite his best efforts, his family did often see displeasure on his face.

Being so young when his father passed away, Luke had only a few memories of their time together. Most centred around Luke sitting on his father's knee, watching western movies and eagerly awaiting the horse riding scenes. That was when Rueben would bounce his leg so that Luke would be getting his very own, albeit simulated, horse ride. The best pretend ride was what Luke and his dad called the *Bonanza* ride, named after Reuben's all-time favourite western.

"Dum-did-a-dum, did-a-dum, did-a-dum, Bonanza! Dum-did-a-dum, did-a-dum, did-a dum, dum-did-a-dum-dum-dum." Singing his rendition of the show's well-known theme song, Reuben would bounce Luke higher and higher on his knee, eliciting shrieks of laughter and joy from his son.

"Hold on tight, Luke!" Reuben would admonish, his words confirming that Luke should maintain his tight grip on his father's arm whilst also reminding the boy that should he fall off and hurt himself, both father and son would receive a sharp reprimand from Luke's mum.

Following her husband's funeral, Luke's mother had been forced to take on the roles of both mother and father to Luke and his soon to be born sister. Esther had found an inner strength that she had been unaware she had. A small insurance pay-out allowed Esther to give her children a life that, while not extravagant, was comfortable and met their basic needs. Strong family support helped, too, as relatives rallied around to help the family through their grief.

Rachael wanted to make the best impression that she could for her Spitz family debut. Their original plans to meet the previous night would have given her plenty of time to learn all she could from Luke about what to expect and consequently prepare for. But now, with the clock ticking, she was starting to get nervous.

"I want to start getting ready at three o'clock. That gives you two hours and forty-five minutes to tell me everything I need to know about your family. It's really important that I know what to expect and don't get caught off guard by anything. I want to be with you, Luke, and I really want us to work out. So tell me what I need to know. Let's start with your Uncle Errol since that's whose house the party is at."

Luke could see her uneasiness as she spoke, so he launched into the rundown to try to ease her mind. "As you know, Uncle Errol isn't really my uncle by blood. He's actually my mum's cousin; mum's father and his father were brothers. Also, his sister Ruth isn't my aunt, but I still call her Auntie Ruth. I know it's a bit weird, but there's a big age discrepancy between Mum and her cousins because my grandfather married later in life. So Mum always called them Uncle Errol and Auntie Ruth, and it's just something Nina and I did as well.

"Now, I know this will also sound strange, but there's quite a bit about Uncle Errol that I don't know and probably never will. It's a case of the unspoken family rule that you just don't ask. But I do know that he's a self-made man who started with nothing and made some good business and financial decisions over the years to get where he is now.

"Neither he nor Auntie Ruth ever married, and for as long as I can remember, they've lived in the same house. He seems to have half of it, and she has the other half. I also know that Uncle Errol owns the house, and in return for living there, Auntie Ruth cooks for him and looks after him to a point. And while they sometimes squabble like an old married couple, they do really love each other and are a good case of blood being thicker than water.

"Uncle Errol did have a girlfriend once. Her name was Beryl. She was a short, pretty woman with white hair. I remember meeting her a few times when we were visiting, and apart from the obvious rhyming of their names, I always though Errol and Beryl had a deep meaningful sound. But for whatever reasons, they decided to go their separate ways.

"Auntie Ruth is the true force behind our family keeping in touch. Maybe that's because she never had a family of her own. Today's party is not specifically to celebrate any particular occasion; it's more an opportunity to stop family members from quietly drifting away from each other. However, there are a number of family birthdays this month, so there's going to be a group birthday cake. Auntie Ruth organised today's party with Mum's younger sister, Auntie Val. Obviously, Auntie Val is also cousin to Errol and Ruth, but she also calls them Auntie Ruth and Uncle Errol because of the age difference. Let's see, Mum is fifty-one, so Auntie Val is fifty. Auntie Ruth, however, is seventy-nine, and Uncle Errol is eighty, so yes, there's quite a gap between them. Mum's other sister, Aunt Beulah, is married to a Norwegian man and lives just outside of Oslo, so we never see her. In fact, the last time I did was when I was around nine or ten."

The allotted time was ticking by as Luke did his best to sort his family into neat little groups that allowed for an easier understanding of where everyone fit in. A few additional stories helped cement an overview of the more colourful personalities in their clan.

As he wrapped up the family overview talking about his two closest family members, his mother and sister, Luke shared how his father's passing had torn his mother down to her very core. They'd been totally devoted to each other, but Luke had been too young to fully comprehend what, "Daddy won't be coming home," meant. Because his mum had been pregnant at the time with his sister, Nina never got to meet her father, something that had always seemed so sad to Luke, although Nina assured him it didn't bother her. Luke was secretly quite sure that it actually did.

"Even I don't really remember much about Dad except for sitting on his knee watching western shows and movies. Any horse riding would get him to start bouncing his knee like I was riding, and he'd hand me a plastic toy gun that he kept under his chair, saying, 'That man there is a baddy. Quick, shoot him, Luke!' I'd aim the gun at the TV, and he'd make shooting noises. When I have a family, I want to be to my children the sort of dad he was to me."

The tear that Luke was unable to hide running down his cheek cued Rachael to draw him close for a hug. "Luke, you're going to be the best dad there ever was."

The late afternoon drive was an opportunity for Rachael to return the favour and give her beau a bit more information on her own family. Luke did his best to show enthusiasm about the conversation, but there was only one thing that currently consumed his thoughts, even crowding out thoughts about the bus and the drama playing out about Eric Linderman. Very soon, he and Rachael were going to be seen by his extended family together, in a partnership. For Luke, their entrance as a couple was going to be a bold message to his family. It would be the first time he'd brought a woman to a family event, and she wasn't just any lady, but rather, the most beautiful woman he could be seen with. It would be an unspoken but visually loud statement saying, 'Look at me! I'm not a loner. I'm not unattractive to the opposite sex. And I'm definitely not gay. I was just waiting for the right woman, and now that I have her, she's been worth every minute of my wait. I know, and now you do, too, that I am a very lucky man.'

Rachael was not the first girl Luke had dated or been keen on, but for a variety of reasons, none of the previous women who had captured Luke's attention had ever graced a family event with their presence. Bridget had been Luke's first love. An unfortunate fact of reality is that the naivety of youth can cloud one's judgement, even when friends and family quietly give warnings about the person's integrity. Now, more than a decade of maturity later and aware of how much truth there'd been in the words of those who cared for him, Luke shuddered at the thought of what could have been.

The second girl who had captured his heart was Monika Fenton, a very pretty but insecure girl from Virginia. Monika was kind and loving, but her insecurities led to a life controlled by constant jealousy, which is not a good characteristic for a life of matrimonial harmony. Then there was Annie, an incredibly beautiful woman who had, on their first date, unintentionally got Luke so sexually excited that, by his own admission, he'd made a complete fool of himself. Embarrassed beyond belief, Luke didn't dare ask for a second date, even though it would've given him a chance at redemption.

No synopsis of Luke's love life would be complete without mention of Justine Smith. Justine had a couple of cogs in her head that didn't mesh quite right, which was not initially apparent to Luke. It was only two days before his family's last gathering, eight months ago, that Luke received a text from Justine asking him to stop sending her abusive texts. Floored at the thought that she could suspect he'd send any such messages, Luke insisted she show him the offending texts so the matter could be immediately cleared up once and for all. Justine's refusal to show him her phone and her continued insistence that Luke was the perpetrator, even claiming that he'd used another number to mask his identity, sent Luke into a total state of disbelief. If she could dream up something like that scenario, and seemingly believe it to be true, then what other unpleasant surprises could present themselves in the future? The thought was too scary to even contemplate.

"Am I really the first girl you've brought to a family event?"

Rachael's voice brought Luke's wandering mind back to the present.

"Now, you already know the answer to that. I've been an open book about all my previous relationships, with you and with my family. Unfortunately, for some of them, the concept that a man of twenty-eight could always attend family events without a female companion is too strange to understand. I'm sure that my cousin Billy doesn't believe anything about my previous bad choices of women and is convinced I'm gay. I can't wait to see his face when I turn up with you."

In fact, Rachael had known the answer to her question, but Luke's words reassured her of his sincerity. Although Rachael knew the names and a few details about his ex-girlfriends, Luke had found it best not to go too deep into the reasons why he'd had such rotten luck with women up till now.

"Here we are." Luke's words coincided with the right-hand turn onto a curved, tree-lined driveway. The tone of his car's tyres changed from the relative quietness of the concrete road to the clattering of the gravel being flung up from the driveway surface.

The anticlockwise rotation of the key and subsequent quieting of the motor was Rachael's cue to open the car door.

"Wait, wait, wait."

Initially perplexed by Luke's sudden outburst, Rachael soon realised that he planned to exit the car first so he could open the door for her.

"My, oh my. What a gentleman you are!"

His proud grin said what his lips didn't.

Their entrance as a couple made Luke feel like the centre of attention as they walked up the steps and through the doorway into the house. His body tingled from the multitudes of stares that penetrated like tiny arrows through his clothing to hit his skin. Luke's attention alternated between his beautiful companion and the task of exchanging greetings with those who acknowledged him.

"This is my girlfriend, Rachael." How sweet those words sounded as, time after time, he made introductions.

With Rachael now deep in conversation with his female relatives, Luke made eye contact with the man he knew he should be seeing more of, the party's host, Uncle Errol.

"Luke, we don't have nearly enough family events, and when we do have these occasions, I realise there are some like yourself who I just don't see often enough. It seems to only happen on occasions like this, weddings, or heaven forbid, funerals."

"It's always good to see you, too, Uncle Errol. And I agree, life just gets in the way."

"Where is your lovely companion, Rachael? Can I just say that she definitely looks like a future member of our family. You've done well."

"She is lovely, and yes, I have done well. She got hijacked by Auntie Ruth, who has taken it upon herself to introduce Rachael to everyone here. Auntie Ruth is introducing her as 'Luke's special lady friend, Rachael' instead of just Rachael. I hope that's OK with Rachael. I guess I'll find out later."

Uncle Errol gave a slight laugh. "That is so typical of my sister. She loves to take possession of any new person. At least your father's side of the family is normal." The two men laughed at the inside family joke.

"One thing, though, Luke. Having her otherwise occupied keeps you free to catch up with old acquaintances and family like me. You said when you came in that there's something you wanted to ask me. Now's a good time, if you'd like."

"It wasn't anything important. I've just had a few related bizarre dreams that have, in turn, put me on a trail of discovery. I'll spare you the boring details, but I hit upon a clue in the name of a man from the nineteen-forties who might have some connection, and I wondered if you've ever heard of Eric Linderman."

It was a harmless statement, but as soon as the words had left Luke's mouth, he knew his question had opened up something related to his family that had, up to now, been long since locked away. Luke watched the expression on his uncle's face morph from happiness to total disbelief. Errol's body remained stationary, but his mouth was locked wide open as the colour drained from his face. When Errol eventually regained his composure, it was only just enough to pull Luke into an adjacent room and shut the door behind them.

"Tell me again why you want to know about this man," Uncle Errol demanded. His tone had become very formal, with all traces of joviality now gone.

"I know this may sound silly, but my nightmares all revolved around a bus. And not just any bus, but one made by the German company OMD. A bit of research led me to learn that only four or five were ever imported into this country, and most of them went to a tour bus operation. But one went to Eric Linderman. Maybe this vehicle still exists, and maybe it doesn't, I really don't know. But Eric Linderman is the connection. You obviously knew him."

"No, I didn't know him. But I knew of him. I was only four when he died in nineteen-forty-two."

"Yes, I read that he and his wife committed suicide in the early part of that year. I did some research about him and got the basic facts, but what do you know about him that I might not have found?"

Errol spoke as if reciting an entry from an encyclopaedia. "Eric Linderman was born in Stuttgart, Germany, in eighteen-eighty-six. In eighteen-ninety-seven, when Eric was eleven, his parents came to America, where his father started a very successful import/export business. In nineteen-oh-six, much to the surprise of his parents, Eric's mother gave birth to another son, Peter. That was the same year that Eric's father commissioned the building of the family estate, an architectural masterpiece inspired by German and Eastern European styles.

"In nineteen-eighteen, Eric met and married Edith Holtz, a very young actress. Her family, like Eric's, were quite wealthy. Eric and Edith never had any children, but after Eric's parents died, Eric inherited the family home, and he'd also promised to take care of his younger brother, who was fourteen when they took him in.

"Edith slowly built up their social network, and after they completely renovated the Lindermans' house between nineteen-thirty-three and nineteen-thirty-six, it became the must visit location for any person to be seen. By nineteen-forty, everyone who was anyone on the East Coast knew the Lindermans. History tells us that Eric never tried to hide the fact that he had loyalties to both Germany and America, and for that reason, he always argued for American staying out of the war in Europe. So when war with Germany was declared, Eric was inconsolable to the point that he and his wife took their own lives by jumping off a cliff not far from the house.

"All of Eric's wealth was left to Peter, but that was no consolation for a man who'd idolised his brother and then had to identify their bodies. Peter lived in the house until he died in nineteen-ninety-nine at the grand old age of ninety-three. He'd always had everything he needed, including food, delivered to him daily, right up to the end. With his considerable wealth, he was able to hire security guards to keep unwelcome visitors away. Even after his death, a trust that Peter's lawyers had set up for him continues to pay all the bills for the estate, including security, even though no one has lived there for nearly twenty years.

"Historians and other writers tell us that Eric Linderman was a kind and well-respected man who loved both his country of birth and his adopted country; some even hail him as a hero. I believe Eric Linderman was someone completely different, but it's too late now to prove anything."

To say Errol knew a bit about Mr Linderman was quite clearly an understatement, but all of that was merely a recitation of facts, the sort of facts that Luke could have found with just a little more research. Luke was thoroughly confused about why his uncle knew so much about Eric Linderman, yet appeared immensely uncomfortable at the very mention of Linderman's name.

"Wow! I am quite taken aback by your knowledge about him, Uncle. But everything you just told me I could probably have found on my own with some research. What I want to know now is how do you know so much? You must have done your homework on this man. Can I ask why? And what else are you not telling me?"

Errol's piercing stare caused Luke to realise he shouldn't have put forward those questions. After an uncomfortably long pause during which Luke squirmed secretly under his uncle's withering glare, Errol finally spoke again.

"We have talked enough about this man. You now know all that you need to! No good can come from digging any deeper. I think we should go mingle with the other guests. I'm sure Rachael is wondering where you have got to. Come, let's go back outside, and you go rescue your young lady from your Aunt Ruth."

The firmness of his uncle's tone and the dismissive hand gesture made clear that the conversation was now completely finished. Luke was now certain that Errol knew much, much more, but was unwilling to share what he knew; well, at least at this time.

Chapter 15

Letting out a big sigh, Luke fell back onto the bed. "You've worn me out. I really need to catch my breath."

Rachael didn't reply other than moving to wrap her body around Luke's as she regained her own composure. Once she'd caught her breath, she spoke.

"Well, mister, weren't you the dynamic one? Tell me something. If you could be a Marvel superhero, who would you be?"

"A Marvel superhero? Where did that come from?"

"Go on, humour me. It doesn't have to be an existing character. In fact, you should just make one up."

"Well, I don't know, really. I'd have to think about. How about The Investigator. I'd appear when people couldn't solve some troubling issue, and I'd find the answers they need. Then, I'd disappear before they had time to thank me. I would have a magnifying glass on the front of my golden suit, and a big, red letter I in the glass lens. And of course I'd have a cape, maybe a purple one. When I disappeared, people would say 'Who was that masked man?' just like they did for the Lone Ranger. Now, what about you, Rachael? Who would you be?"

"I don't think I can compete with that! But maybe I'd be Mystery Woman. Nobody knows who she is, but she turns up at exactly the right moment to help people in need. She would also have a suit and cape, but all in white." Rachael paused for a moment before continuing. "If I was naming you, I'd make you Captain Orgasm, and you'd be Mystery Woman's companion who helps her relax after a hard day helping people."

"Ha, ha! That's so funny. Well, if I'm Captain Orgasm, then you'll be my companion, and you'd be called Naughty Girl. So you'd have a big N and G on the front of your outfit."

"OK, then. I'm going to call your bluff. If we're ever invited to a superhero party, I'll make our costumes. Yours will have a cape, a mask, and a big O on the front of the suit. And mine will have the letters N and G. We would both have to wear them, too. Do you agree?"

"OK, I agree."

"Great. But there's one last thing. Whenever someone asks what the letters on our outfits mean, we have to tell them the truth. Do you agree to that, too?"

"OK, Rachael. Now I'm going to call your bluff. Yes, I do agree, but I'll also tell them how it was all your idea."

"In that case, let's hope we never get invited to a superhero party," she chided. "Thank you so much for a marvellous evening, Luke. I really enjoyed meeting all of your family. Everybody was just so nice and friendly. Your Auntie Ruth seemed to think I was her new best friend. She introduced me to everyone as if she'd known me for years! Did she do that with your other girlfriends?"

"You are so not subtle, Rachael. You know that the couple of girlfriends I've had in the past were nothing serious, and to answer your question, you also know you're the first one I've been serious enough about to introduce to my whole family."

"Well, that explains it, then," Rachael declared.

"Explains what?"

"It explains why they were so happy to see me. Maybe they were just relieved you're not gay."

Luke rolled his eyes. "Oh, ladies and gentlemen, she's not just a beautiful woman; she's also a comedian."

"I do have my moments," Rachael crowed.

"I'm sure you do. Anyway, thank you for inviting me back."

"Wait. That sounds like you're leaving. You will stay the night, won't you? Or are you worried about your bad dreams? I can learn to live with them, you know."

"You won't have to. I'm pretty sure they're firmly in the past, and I haven't had any more. But I do need to go. Before I do, though, I really want to tell you about some of the other things that happened over the last couple of days."

Rachael listened intensely as Luke relayed some details he'd missed earlier. He also added the details of his conversation with his uncle.

"So that's everything to date, and now I don't know what to do. Was there a reason for my nightmares? Was there some supernatural or spiritual force that was guiding me to a story that could be the saviour for Skip's newspaper? What about Skip's diner? Was seeing that just a coincidence or a sign of confirmation that I'm on the right path? Is the whole bus and Linderman thing something I should just leave in the past, as Uncle Errol said? I don't want to upset him, but then again, I can't help but feel he was discreetly encouraging me to find out more? I have so many questions, Rachael, but no answerers. And I just don't know what I should do."

"Well, if you're asking me, I think you need to find all the answers, and you won't find them unless you dig a little deeper. But listen to yourself; you'll know the right thing to do."

Their post-party bedroom activities had left Luke mentally and physically depleted, so although he'd planned to go home, he instead drifted off into an unintentional sleep. Luke woke up and turned to see that Rachael's alarm clock indicated it was three thirty-seven. As he lay quietly next to her, it became apparent that a peaceful mind is an imperative characteristic for a relaxed body. Rachael's bed was very comfortable, and the warmth of her body laying close to him was comforting beyond words. But what he needed to do was clear his mind of the many frustrating questions he had.

Prioritising the other tasks he needed to address was the first step in formulating a plan. First, there was his current assignment, and Skip had given him a deadline of four p.m. Monday for its completion. It was a topic that epitomised what was behind the demise of *The Eye*. Long gone were the days when hot news could wait for the printing process. Now it was 2019, and unless you had an exclusive scoop on a topic tantalising enough to make people buy a printed paper, the chances were people would skip the purchase and find any information they wanted from another source on their computers. However, it was a story, and Skip had a deadline. So any plans to visit the Linderman house would have to work around the article. Luke realised that if he could finish the story on

Sunday, it might take his mind off obsessing about the house and give him the time to think things over.

Two hours later, Luke was back in his apartment with newfound motivation to finish the article as quickly as possible. He set about the task enthusiastically. It would never be his best journalism by any measure, but by midday, and with another twenty-eight hours till his deadline, the bulk of the article had been completed. With the task well under control, the logistics of going to the house that afternoon became a realistic option, and it would soon become an option that Luke could no longer put off.

Although his car engine was running, it just seemed appropriate for Luke to sit for a few moments. Perhaps it was an opportunity to reflect on the situation and maybe even get a bit of godly intervention to get his timing right. Whatever the reason, the pause led to an episode of self-doubt related to the wisdom of making this trip. Luke was not one for talking aloud to himself, but there is a time and place for everything, and this was one of those times. In a strange way, in the privacy of his car, talking to himself actually made things a little clearer.

"I knew I was going to end up doing this, didn't I? So why didn't I just head out earlier? I could've already been there, had a look at the place, and be on my way back. But now, by the time I get there, it could be dark, so I probably won't see much. Then there's the drive back. I'd be lucky to get in bed by midnight.

"So tell me, Luke, why am I doing this? Is it the nightmares? Is it the potential for a story? Is it because of Uncle Errol's reaction? Or is it all three? I know that this is just going to fizzle out, but I need to do it so I can move on. So, then, come on, Luke. Let's get this over with."

He realised that there was a long drive ahead with his decision to go to the house, which meant there was no time left to waste.

"Go now, or don't go at all," Luke told himself firmly. Then he placed the car in gear and sped off.

The driveway off the narrow back road was hard to find, and it was really more a case of luck than skill, given that there was no indication the drive would lead to anything more than a farm shed. The steel gate that eventually blocked vehicular access meant any further progress would have to be made on foot. Ironically, the sign attached to the gate that left no confusion about the fact that this was private property provided the necessary footing to clear the hurdle of the gate. As his feet touched the ground on the other side, Luke noted that the rest of the fence line would have proved more challenging. Now that he was over the gate, his heart raced with the increasing sense of anticipation as he proceeded up the steeply curved driveway.

Up to that point, there'd been no sign of the house, its location hidden by contours in the land and the foliage of the surrounding trees. At the final turn in the driveway, however, the camouflage all dropped away, and the full view of the building ahead stopped its latest visitor in his tracks, leaving him speechless.

Luke could only stare. He was totally captivated by the intimidating grandeur of the now exposed house. Feeling himself drawn in by the building's charms, Luke stopped to focus on the majestic façade. It was the first aspect of the house that grabbed your attention, and it took a few minutes to really comprehend the skill and craftsmanship that had to have gone into its construction. Luke was no expert by any means, but he'd never seen anything like this magnificent structure.

The building's clifftop peninsula location provided almost complete privacy from prying eyes as its layout in relation to the surrounding woodlands deliberately made very little of its outline visible until that final turn in the driveway. With only one way in and out, it would have been easy to be just a few yards down the road and not realise there was any building, even a tiny one, around, let alone a large mansion positioned less than half a mile away.

Time had done the house no favours; years of neglect had left most of the paintwork deeply faded, peeling or non-existent, which in turn had exposed much of the woodwork to being ravaged from exposure to the elements.

The house had been built in the early twentieth century by Eric Linderman's father, Ralph. After his parents' deaths, Eric had completed a long and expensive refurbishment. The builders and craftsmen he'd brought over from Germany continued the authentic styling in the renovations. Easily seen as mere extravagance, the specialised skills required for Eric's vision were not his only reasons for importing the labour. There was another, not so innocent, reason. The house was to hold secrets known only to Eric, his wife, Edith, and his brother, Peter. What the house hid was not information that Eric wanted the locals to know.

Luke continued to stare in awe. He couldn't help making comparisons to *The Great Gatsby* movies he'd recently seen and the conversations he and Rachael had as they left the cinema, when they'd walked hand in hand and discussed what life must've been like in such times for those with unimaginable wealth.

Now standing right in front of his eyes was a building that no doubt saw such extravagance.

The limited information Luke had found about this particular home spoke of the amazing parties that were held there in the late *1930s and early '40s. Yes, it wasn't the same decade as The* Great Gatsby, but the grandeur would've been the same.

The now long since boarded-up windows would back then have been crystal clear and open, spilling the light and sounds of a jazz band playing inside to give arriving guests a hint of what they could expect. Guests would most likely would've been greeted on arrival by smartly dressed staff ready to take their coats and hats, whilst other staff would be circulating to ensure empty hands got filled with hors d'oeuvres and crystal glasses filled with the finest French champagne.

The elite of society would have circulated as the comfort of chatting with lifelong friends was exchanged for conversations with potential political, social or business contacts. Old money would mingle only with old money; if the reputation was already established, there was no need to impress. Young playboys would circulate among the various groups, checking for potential conquests, perhaps an aspiring starlet keen to be Hollywood's next leading lady, who could be wooed into bed with tales of influence and industry contacts.

Luke closed his eyes for a moment. It was easy to picture in his mind's eye a convoy of luxurious cars, each with bespoke handcrafted coachwork, slowly making their way up the drive and stopping, one by one, outside the magnificent and massive oak doors. With their well-financed passengers now in the care of the master of the house, each chauffeur would proceed to move their car to its allocated parking space to allow for the unloading of the next vehicle's precious cargo. Such events might have happened eighty years earlier, but Luke could still feel the atmosphere, smell the aromas of exquisitely prepared foods mingled with rare French perfumes, and taste the bubbles of champagne that escaped the crystal flutes and wafted on the evening breeze.

Chapter 16
(March 1940)

If you lived in Widow's Creek, Kentucky, there was one thing that was certain, regardless of whether you were black, white, old or young. The chances were that you were poor, your parents had been poor and your children would grow up to be poor. Most Widow's Creek residents struggled all their lives to make a living on the local farms that made up the community. Most were just getting by on what they could rear or grow. Many of the area's 200 or so residents had long since resigned themselves to scraping out a meagre existence in this godforsaken part of the country.

As frugally as they were forced to live, at least whatever they did have was wholly theirs. Walking away was a choice a few people had made, but the paltry values of their farms, if there was any value at all, hardly constituted a good start to a new life outside of the familiar here, which they'd always known and felt relatively safe in.

Otis Jennings was a big man with a big smile. He was one of those few who'd made a successful life away from the barren family farm in Widow's Creek. He'd called it home for most of his life, growing up on the farm where his brother now attempted to eke out an existence for himself, his wife and their children. Otis's escape came in the form of the United States Army. After enlisting, Otis trained as a logistics driver, and it turned out to be something he excelled at.

It had come to the attention of Otis's superiors that the six-foot-five-inch, 290-pound African American man affectionately called Oatey by his buddies could skilfully drive any vehicle he was put in charge of, including the ability to delicately manoeuvre even the biggest of military vehicles with the precision of a watchmaker. Otis had another skill that cemented the positive reputation he had gained—he had an inner compass so accurate that he rarely required the use of a map, no matter how unfamiliar the terrain.

When Otis was discharged, he was given an opportunity that would change his life forever. Friends of his commanding officer required a personal chauffer, someone who was not only a good driver but could also double as a personal bodyguard should the need arise. With his impeccable driving skills, physical stature and ability to handle himself well in combat situations, Otis fully met all the criteria. He was invited to apply for the job, and his commanding officer's personal recommendation sealed the deal of his employment.

As employers, Harold and Morgate Griffin were well liked by those who worked for them. The Griffins had a theory that if you looked after your staff, then your staff would look after you. Otis was paid well, and having few expenses, he was able to send a good portion of his wages back to his brother's family in Widow's Creek. Otis got to travel to interesting places and enjoyed all the perks of association with the Griffins. Because he took his responsibilities seriously, he was able to provide his employers a feeling of complete care. Harold and Morgate knew that Otis would not only safely deliver them to their destination, but also had the skill and physical prowess to handle and make right any difficult or dangerous situation in which they might find themselves.

As the tyres of the dark blue 1938 Chrysler Imperial crunched the first bits of gravel that formed the driveway to the Linderman house, Otis prepared to give his employers the entrance they would expect and that he thought they deserved. It was all about the timing, and that was completely up to him. He watched the maroon Rolls Royce ahead of them deliver its guests, and Otis realised he had to allow its occupants time to exit and be greeted. He was determined that his passengers would not suffer the indignity of having to wait after Otis pulled to a stop; their hosts must be ready to greet them at that moment.

Slowing to little more than a walking pace, Otis guided the two-and-a-quarter-ton machine gently up the short rise that preceded the sharp right-hand turn toward the house.

Upon turning the corner, the magnificent estate came suddenly into view. In even the worst of circumstances, this house provided a visual spectacle, but now, even more so than usual, as their hosts had expended significant efforts to produce an Irish theme for this St Patrick's Day event. Wooden figures painted as leprechauns lined the final yards of the driveway, whilst green lights had been installed to highlight the house's façade, producing an eerie, surreal effect.

Otis had timed the arrival perfectly. The Rolls was just starting to move forward as Otis approached the drop-off point directly in front of the main entrance stairway. There would be no waiting, as the reception committee was ready and waiting to give the Griffins the full arrival fanfare.

As the footman opened the rear door, the Griffins were serenaded by a short Irish jig. Like the footman, both the fiddler and the accordion player had been hired specifically for this occasion, and each guest was greeted with a unique twenty- to thirty-second tune that set the mood for the rest of the evening.

As the butler led the Griffins up the steps, a figure came forward from the doorway to greet them. It was their host, Eric Linderman. Eric's warm, friendly smile and firm handshake left each of his guests feeling special as they were led away into the serenity of the reception area. Then it was Edith's turn to set the mood as she circulated among and even paired up some of the guests, all the while using her natural charms to the fullest extent.

With his passengers safely out of the car, Otis engaged first gear and manoeuvred the blue saloon forward and around to the side of the house, where a waiting parking attendant directed him to execute a turn to permit the car to be parked at an angle alongside and facing the driveway. This arrangement of vehicles would allow each driver to safely remove their car at any time without blocking any other vehicle from entering or exiting the area. Once clear of the car, Otis was directed by the attendant to the chauffeurs' waiting area. It was a cool, clear night, and Otis inhaled deeply, letting the fresh air fill his lungs. He could detect the faint and distant salt of sea air. This side of the house led down to what Otis assumed was an adjacent garage due to the design of the doors fronting that part of the building. Having a general interest in vehicles, Otis took note of the vehicles that were already parked. The opulent examples of luxury were exactly what he expected to see on an occasion such as this.

Looking down towards the garage, he couldn't help but wonder what sort of vehicles the home's owner had parked inside.

The interior of the chauffeurs' room was considerably warmer than the air outside. It was a large room holding several leather couches and offering a selection of newspapers. Some sandwiches and an ample supply of freshly ground and brewed coffee had been placed on a table in the middle of the room.

A few guests were staying the night, so their drivers were shown to the modest staff sleeping quarters. Most, however, just like Otis, would be driving their charges home after the party. For some, it would be early, but for most, the departure would be well into the early hours of the morning. Otis knew it would be many hours before he could enjoy the luxury of his own bed, but he was quite happy thanks to the generous salary the Griffins paid him, along with an extra allowance if he worked past midnight. Tonight would provide even more money that he could send back to his family. The fresh coffee would be a welcome friend as he struck up a conversation with another driver.

As large as the Linderman house was, there were no staff members actually living on the immediate premises. The house's only occupants were Eric, Edith and Eric's younger reclusive brother, Peter. Eric was very close to and protective of his younger brother and respected his wishes to keep a very low profile whenever guests were in the home. Eric had never hidden Peter's existence, but because few people were able to understand the concept of chronic shyness, Eric found it best to only mention Peter if he was specifically asked.

The Lindermans had only two permanent full-time staff, Mr and Mrs Best. The Bests lived in the property's cottage, which was a mere 200 yards from the main house, but completely unseen from it. That was thanks to careful positioning so that neither home could be seen from the other, along with the thick woodland that lay between the two buildings.

Leighton and Amelia Best had worked in the Linderman household for over twenty-five years. They were amongst a number of staff who had originally worked and lived in the house when Eric's parents were alive. But following their deaths and the renovations carried out by Eric and Edith, only the Bests remained, and they had been moved to the newly built cottage. Each morning, the Bests arrived for work at exactly seven.

Amelia Best was the Lindermans' cook, whilst Leighton looked after the day to day running of the household. Consulting with Eric, Leighton Best would organise the cleaning and gardening staff as needed, whilst a collection of trusted contractors would be commissioned whenever painting or other maintenance was required.

A much more demanding task was sourcing the extra service and catering staff required to help out at the parties that the Lindermans were hosting on an increasingly frequent basis. A butler, wait staff and housekeeping staff were needed to prepare and return to normal the bedrooms that overnight guests used, to name but a few of the extra people that had to be hired. Leighton Best had the contacts and made it his personal quest that everyone he hired lived up to what was expected of them. From the moment they arrived to set up, Leighton coordinated and carefully observed his charges, ready to step in should the required level of service not be achieved. Anybody not rising to meet expectations would never be hired again.

Like her husband, Amelia kept a close eye on any temporary staff hired for food preparation. The kitchen was her domain, and everything that left its four walls had to pass her personal inspection.

Most guests were unaware that the majority of staff were only hired for the occasion. Explaining why no staff lived on site could lead to difficult questions; therefore, the subject only arose if the Lindermans were directly asked.

Edith had planned to perfection all of their prior parties, but on this occasion, she could not take credit for the idea of a St Patrick's Day theme. That honour went to Kathleen O'Connor, an acquaintance of Irish ancestry who Edith had met several months earlier.

1940 was one of the rare years that St Patrick's Day did not fall on March the 17th due to a clash with Palm Sunday. Edith Linderman had a sense of hesitancy about hosting a celebration on a day that was not officially recognised. However, after consultation with Kathleen and other acquaintances' she had come to the conclusion that most guest would probably not be too concerned and a party held on Saturday the 16th would ensure the attendees were quite jolly by the time the clock struck midnight.

. At that time, Eric would set off some green fireworks, and Edith would ensure the Irish whisky flowed freely. For the guests, the evening would be a time to relax and socialise. They would be completely unaware of the true reasons for the Lindermans' hospitality.

Harold and Morgate needed little encouragement to wander around the room, champagne glasses in hand. There were old friends to catch up with and other captains of industry or influential figures to meet. Like their hosts, they were both very social people. However, that was where the similarities ended.

On the other side of the house, Otis had settled into one of the large chairs, its soft green leather covering gently cradled around his large frame; this was a luxury that he was not accustomed to. Otis had cut short his initial conversation with another chauffer when the man started smoking. Cigarette smoke was something that Otis did not enjoy; it was, however, a perceived luxury that most of the other drivers engaged in and as such, something that was hard to keep away from. His attention was now focussed on an article in the local paper. The comfort of the waiting area, with its soft furnishings and ambient lighting, was far more pleasant than what he or any of the other drivers would normally expect. The location would usually be very basic, and often, the chauffeurs were actually expected to wait in their vehicles. A blanket, a torch and lukewarm coffee were always tucked away in the trunk for just such occasions.

Otis was completely unfamiliar with the couple entertaining his employers, but he was sure that anyone who provided an area like this for staff could not be bad. Whoever he was, he must be a caring individual, and if asked by his employers how his evening had been, he would certainly convey that fact. As plush as the interior of the Imperial had been when it left the factory, the Griffins had invested in the skills of the master coachbuilders Mason & Kirkbridge to bring the comfort of the vehicle's interior up to a level that would be hard to surpass. A thick glass and wooden panel now separated the driver's compartment from the rear. That, along with over 150 pounds of felt sound deadening and the thick shag pile carpet, ensured that any ambient noise present in the cabin whilst driving was kept to a level that would exceed the expectations of any self-identified person of importance. As part of the car's upgrade,

Mason & Kirkbridge had also replaced the original upholstery. Rebuilding the seats saw the craftsmen encasing the now upgraded padding in the finest deer skin leather, and the result was a level of depth and softness that guaranteed it wouldn't be very far into the four-hour drive home before both Harold and Morgate would be fast asleep, cocooned in their personal world of tranquil opulence.

Otis knew he had an important job to do, and no person or circumstance would stop him from doing that job with excellence. He would deliver the Griffins home safely and with minimal disturbance. Some of the other drivers had taken the opportunity to have a short sleep, but Otis preferred to stay awake. He sat quietly as he absorbed the information in the article. Aware that it would be a long drive back, he knew he had to be fully alert, so for now, he would rest, read and wait.

Chapter 17
(September 2019)

"Hold it right there." The deep voice was authoritative and startled Luke out of his mental comparisons to *The Great Gatsby* house.

The voice rang out again. "Slowly raise your hands, or I will shoot first and ask questions later."

"Don't shoot! I'll fully cooperate." Luke slowly raised his hands, extending his fingers as he did so to show that he wasn't holding anything.

A large figure emerged from the cover of shadows among the trees. He looked scruffy and unshaven, but was wearing a uniform that identified him as a security guard.

"What is your name? And what are you doing here?"

"My name is Luke, and I was just driving by and decided to stop for a quick look. I love old buildings and was fascinated by the quick glimpse I got of the house as I drove by."

The guard's cold expression made Luke realise just how unconvincing his answer was.

"No one just drives by here. Show me some identification, but take it out slowly. No quick moves, now."

Reaching towards his back pocket, Luke slowly and carefully retrieved his wallet and opened it to remove his driver's licence, which he passed to the guard. He was aware that any false moves could be met with a gunshot.

An additional voice startled Luke as a second guard approached from behind.

"His car is empty, and he's on his own."

With his gun still menacingly trained on Luke, the first guard nodded to acknowledge the second guard before casting his eyes downward to look at the picture on the licence. There was a moment of uneasy silence before the guard spoke again.

"This is private property. Why would you think you have the right to just walk in?"

"I am sorry. I clearly made a mistake and would be happy to leave quietly."

"I think that is a good idea. I know who you are now, so think twice about returning, because if I ever see you here again, things will go very differently."

The guard passed the licence back to Luke, his unspoken facial gesture indicating that Luke should immediately proceed back down the driveway. Turning to leave, Luke now caught a glimpse of the second guard in his peripheral vision, but he chose not to make eye contact. He just continued walking briskly towards his car.

Back on the main road, Luke pulled over at the first convenient safe spot. His heart was pounding and his hands shook. He was also craving a big drink of water to quench his extremely dry mouth. Luckily, he always kept at least one bottle of water in the back of his car.

The day had been ridiculously long; Luke knew he should have left home earlier. Looking at his watch he realised that if he had left first thing after getting home, he would have been back already and making progress on Skip's article. Two motels within the space of three days was not budget friendly, but still spooked by his encounter with the security guards and worn out from the events of the last twenty-four hours, he did not need Rachael to tell him what he needed to do. He was too tired and shaken to safely drive home, and common sense dictated his decision.

Thirty-five minutes down the road, there was a twenty-four-hour diner with cheap accommodations out back that beckoned to the weary driver. Although tired and hungry, the first items on Luke's agenda were to call both Rachael and Skip.

Luke made the call to Rachael first and told her everything that had happened over the past day, including the trip to the Linderman mansion. But the one fact that he consciously omitted was the minor detail of the armed guard challenging him. Instead, he elected to say that he'd noticed there were guards and decided to go no further. But even that toned down version of events caused Rachael to express concern for his safety. Aware that he'd learned as much as he reasonably could and not wanting to worry her further, Luke promised he would re-evaluate the situation and not do anything dangerous.

Skip was also very keen to hear from Luke and was initially concerned about Luke's ability to meet his deadline. But Luke's reassurance that the article would be delivered by four p.m. the next day was a relief to Skip and set a good tone for the rest of the conversation.

Although he had no idea where chasing the bus was going to lead him, his journalistic instincts nevertheless told Luke that some degree of print-worthy content would come from it, maybe only suitable for a small column on the last page, but then again, it wasn't total fantasy to think it might be front page headline material. As excited as he was, Luke still did not want to give too much away. There was a fine line between keeping Skip interested and leading his boss into thinking that he had something that he did not at that point. Luke chose his words carefully.

"I've still been chasing the story about the old bus, and I believe it's worth pursuing. I've had several interesting leads, but they've all raised more questions than they answered."

Luke's words got Skip's full attention. "So, is this the one in a million exclusive you're going to get me?"

"Well, I'm not committing myself to such a bold statement, but you know how the game is played. You follow ten leads, and nine will lead to a dead end, but the one lead opens the door to an awesome story. I'm chasing a lead that's out there and still in the unknown, so I'd rather not say too much about it right now. So I'll just see where it ends up."

"OK. I can understand you don't want to give too much away, but it if starts taking you away from the rest of your workload or affects your deadlines, then you need to tell me all, and if I consider it worth chasing, I'll reallocate you the time. If not, though, then it's something you have to either put away or follow up on it in your own time."

A big bowl of beef nachos and a cup of strong coffee helped calm the tapeworm that had been growling in his belly for the last several hours. A hot shower in the small but clean motel room helped wrap up bedtime needs, so even though it wasn't late, Luke was asleep before he knew it.

Looking at the bedside alarm clock's bright red digits, Luke could clearly read 3;27, and he realised the same clock had shown 2;54 when he first awoke for a toilet stop and a glass of water. Now, only thirty-three minutes later, despite being exhausted, he was nonetheless wide awake. It could have been the strange bed or maybe the soft foam pillow that didn't offer the same cranial support that his own latex pillow did. Perhaps it was the spiciness of the nachos or even the stimulating effect of that coffee. Although they were all potential contributing factors, the true culprit was easy to identify. The overwhelming reason he couldn't sleep was the fact that, once again, there was too much going on in his mind.

Eventually considering himself defeated, Luke decided to finish his assignment for Skip, a task that took him through to five after five. He now had a sense of relief; even with the long drive ahead, there was now no rush to get back as quickly as possible. He'd have plenty of time to send the file from home, and Skip would assume that Luke had finished it up in his apartment that morning. As necessary as sleep was, Luke was tempted to watch some YouTube videos, and a quick search for 1930s' buses yielded a selection of hits, many showing vehicles designed much like the one that was responsible for him being in this strange bed. But it was always, as he'd expected, not the bus in question. As the clock ticked slowly towards six, Luke found that YouTube had taken him to a collection of topics unrelated to buses. His eyelids were beginning to droop, and sleep would have taken hold had he not spotted an old mansion in one clip.

It wasn't the same place, but it was nonetheless very similar to the Lindermans' house. The video was one in a series called *Kent's Secret World*, in which the host, Kent Clark, carried out urban explorations of abandoned factories, government buildings and old private residences. Kent Clark's credentials made reference to his background as an architect and structural engineer after spending time in the armed forces. A passion for old abandoned buildings had led Kent to now identify as a full-time urban explorer. Intrigue and tiredness battled it out in Luke's head, but drowsiness snuck up with such deceit that Luke soon drifted off, his tablet still playing the last YouTube clip that his conscience mind recalled seeing.

It was loud voices that finally broke the hold tiredness had commanded. Luke's neighbours for the night, who had up till that time been very quiet, were now departing their room with all the grace of an excited herd of elephants trapped in a store that sold fine crystal. A cacophony of clanging, banging and very loud talking made Luke thankful they were not his full-time neighbours. The bedside clock brightly displayed eight thirty, and he suddenly remembered the notice in the reception area boldly stating that all guests had to be vacated by nine thirty or penalties would be charged to their account. An hour would be enough time for a quick hot shower and a replay of one of Kent's YouTube videos whilst the tablet recharged. There was one particular item that needed to be checked before hitting the road again.

The end of each YouTube clip referenced Kent Clark's website, a place where fans could get Kent's latest updates and submit potential locations for Kent to check out. The intrigue was too much, and with just a few clicks, Luke was soon looking at a professional website with links to each of the YouTube clips.

Luke found himself drawn into the website's content. Kent was obviously endowed with a degree of humour, and his opening statement boldly informed visitors that they should make note that his name was Kent Clark, whilst the man who worked at the *Daily Planet* was Clark Kent, so any email making reference to Superman would not be answered. He added that he'd already received more than his fair share of bullying when he was at school.

Further reading informed Luke that Kent was continuously on the lookout for new places to explore and was always open to receiving ideas. Fans were invited to email him details about any potentially suitable building, including where it was located and why it would be an interesting place for him to visit. Luke was tempted to fire off an email immediately, but with his watch now showing nine twenty-six, it would have to be done later.

The diner had served up just the right breakfast to prepare a body for a long drive, and he'd washed it down with the strong coffee his body craved. The drive home was long with the familiarity of each hill, tree and house prompting a feeling of déjà vu. There was no way he could have safely made the trip last night. As the miles ticked by, Kent's website and the invitation to contact him consumed more and more of Luke's thoughts.

Luke composed his words until he believed that he couldn't possibly say anything to make the Linderman mansion more appealing as a potential place to visit, that is, without telling outright lies.

Pulling his car over into a lay-by, Luke wrote and sent the email right away.

Chapter 18
(March 1940)

Edith was both a social queen and the perfect hostess; she could captivate and manipulate an audience without even trying. Nonetheless, the St Patrick's Day party was going to fully test her skills at manipulating guests and discreetly influencing who talked with whom as she and her husband circulated among the visitors.

To most of the party's attendees, the Lindermans were generous hosts. It was obvious that they were networking with the movers and shakers to their advantage, but that was something all of the guests would have done had the roles been reversed. Therefore, that fact in and of itself would raise no suspicion. Who could have guessed, however, that the charming couple's hospitality had sinister undertones?

There were two types of social events held at the Linderman house. There were the big gala parties like this one, and there were smaller, more intimate events where only two to six people would be invited. The purpose of the former was to divide people into two groups: those who could be easily manipulated, and those who could not or weren't worth the effort. Only the first group would be invited back at an appropriate time.

As they worked their way around the room, both Eric and Edith carefully manipulated the topics of their guests' conversations, being sure to include the inevitable discussions about what was happening in Europe. When participating in these, the Lindermans made the case that the conflict was one that America would be best served by keeping out of. This topic allowed them to rapidly determine who agreed with their views and who believed that America wasn't doing enough to help the Allies. In addition, there was always a third group of people who believed that it would actually be in America's best interest to side with Nazi Germany. After all, those people would reason, Europe had many spoils of war, and dividing them between Germany and America could make certain groups or individuals very rich and powerful. The tricky part was that people who held those views generally chose not to air their ideas publicly. They were usually identified instead not by what they said, but rather by what they didn't say.

The Lindermans believed that everybody had weaknesses that could be exploited; it was just a matter of how well hidden they kept their secret self. The primary purpose of the evening was not to celebrate Ireland's patron saint but, rather, to look for any clues to those weaknesses in their guests and determine any that could, under the right circumstances, possibly be exploited. Just as lovers share pillow talk, finding people's true inner feelings required that everybody feel relaxed.

The Lindermans' own pillow talk would prove extremely interesting, as they would compare notes about the evening. Sometimes, it was the difference between what a man said and what his wife said about him that might provide the salient clue. Other times, it might be the way that one person reacted to another. With this in mind, it was not missed by Eric that Randal J Pilkington politely accepted finger food from the two female servers, but he became much more animated when the young male server with the name badge Rolf brought around the miniature sandwiches. In addition, Eric noted how his guest turned to follow Rolf with his eyes as the server moved away to offer the treats to other guests.

And then there was Cyril Parkman-Moss, whose reactions to Rolf and the slim female server with the name badge Annie were friendly, but quite neutral, whilst the fuller figured server with the more than ample breasts, Nicola, evoked a completely different reaction. As he accepted the savoury offering, Cyril was totally unaware that he was thanking her cleavage rather than the woman herself. Cyril was a breast man, and Eric had noted it.

The most interesting contact of the evening was by far Geoffrey DeVilliers. Geoffrey was a very powerful man, and having something on him would be invaluable. The conversation with the DeVilliers started out on the topic of the virtues of private schooling as compared to a public school education. That had, in turn, led to the subject of discipline, which in turn brought up stories of corporal punishment, in particular, the time honoured art of caning.

That point in the conversation was where the subject matter prompted Geoffrey's wife, Enid, to leave the conversation, allowing her husband to recount a couple of stories about punishment administered in his schooldays. One recollection in particular was when a group of boys, including Geoffrey, were paraded in front of the entire school and, one by one, had to pull down their trousers, bend over a wooden chair and accept six strokes of the cane. As he privately recalled his envious anticipation whilst awaiting his turn, it was not what Geoffrey said so much as the expression on his face as he relayed the story that caught Eric's attention. To Eric, it was painfully obvious that the thought of the incident conjured up a range of emotions. Geoffrey had started to get noticeably fidgety, and his face had turned several shades of red darker than it had been before.

With contacts going all the way to the top in Washington and at the highest levels of American industry, Geoffrey DeVilliers was an extremely influential man who could be of immense value to the Lindermans. Mr and Mrs DeVilliers would most definitely be invited back.

The Lindermans knew that not everyone in attendance that evening would be what they considered valuable, but everyone at the party had a purpose. There were those like Randolph Cummings, whose own contacts necessitated an invitation. A full-time philanderer who lived off his inherited wealth, Randolph epitomised the term playboy. With bottomless pockets and without the limitations of marriage, Randolph was free to live every red-blooded man's dream. An endless succession of starlets and heiresses shared his bed. Making money was never one of Randolph's goals because he already had enough to sustain his lifestyle. Rather, what drove the man was the quest to continually increase his already long list of sexual conquests. In his company, married men would be filled with envy and jealousy, but in a conservative society, they knew their reputations were too important to be put at risk. The occasional liaison with a lady of the night was the best they could hope for.

Randolph, however, revelled in embellishing scandals; in fact, it was expected of him. Had he really bedded both the mother and daughter? Which powerful man's wife was the latest to succumb to his charms? Unlike the others, scandal enhanced Randolph's reputation rather than diminishing it.

Randolph would have seemed of little use to the Lindermans except that he had multitudes of contacts, and there were those in his social circle who associated with him solely in the hopes of accessing one of the many women Randolph had ready access to.

Then there was Chester Wilmington, who was an associate of Randolph's, and it was through Randolph that the Lindermans gained access to this very powerful and influential individual. Chester was the polar opposite of Randolph, and although often in Randolph's company, Chester would make it abundantly clear that he was married and would not partake of any extramarital affairs.

Although giving the appearance of moral righteousness, in reality, Chester was no different from his associate. Instead, his was a case of the unthinkable consequences of getting caught. Chester Wilmington's wife came from a well respected East Coast family with a powerful heritage, and barely a day passed without Agnes Willmington reminding him that should she ever be embarrassed by a scandal, she and her family would ensure her husband's complete destruction morally, financially and socially.

Chester had been married since his late teens, so boredom and complacency had long ago set into his marriage. With the couple now sleeping in separate rooms and his conjugal rights consigned to any form of legitimacy only on his birthday, Chester was terribly jealous of Randolph's playboy lifestyle. Chester now found himself, not by choice, living out his own sexual fantasies through the exploits of a man who was both friend and nemesis. There were nights when Chester would awaken alone in his bed, unable to sleep for tossing and turning whilst fantasising about the young blonde lady that he saw Randolph leaving with that evening. Time after time, this scenario would play out, and Chester eventually found himself heading down to the cellar in his lustful rage, where he would set upon the leather punching bag he called Dolf, sometimes until his knuckles bled. Yet the following days would see him helping Randolph secure contact details for his next planned conquest.

Randolph knew the power he had over Chester, but the Cummings' money was new, so it didn't carry the same weight as established wealth. Randolph's father, Wilmot, had made some good financial decisions prior to the Great Depression, and he had ensured that the family's modest money was readily accessible at a time when most people were desperate to sell whatever they had left. Ruthless and with a steel-plated conscience, Wilmot Cummings was ready, when the economy failed, to step in and purchase enormous swathes of real estate, most of it vastly below its true value. Then he would sell it back later at grossly inflated prices. After Wilmot's death, Randolph was the beneficiary of what would be considered a fortune by even his wealthiest peers.

But nonetheless, the newness of the Cummings' money barred him from the automatic right to fully integrate with the East Coast's established communities of wealth that Chester was a part of. There were even some who found the Cummings' fortune vulgar and despicably distasteful.

Despite never having had to work a day in his life for all that he had, Randolph was painfully jealous of Chester's full acceptance in society, something Randolph craved. Knowing the level of power that he had over such an influential man him helped Randolph feel powerful himself. The relationship between Randolph Cummings and Chester Willmington was complex and bizarre; despite the power and wealth each of them had, Randolph needed Chester as much as Chester needed him.

It soon became clear to Eric that Chester Willmington could be a trophy prize, although his capture came with many challenges. Petrified that any hint of scandal would bring his wife to make good on her promise to destroy him, Chester never allowed himself to be alone in the company of any woman who was not his wife or a close family member. He made sure there was always at least one other person present who could verify that any conversation had been completely above board and beyond reproach.

Eric smiled as he conversed with the two men. This was going to be a challenge that required all of the skill and manipulation that he and Edith could collectively muster. But Chester would be theirs, and his friend Randolph would unknowingly play a vital part in the plan.

Although substantial, the Linderman assets were not unlimited. Events like this party required a great expenditure of effort and money, and like any other investment, they needed to produce positive returns. So when guests like the Griffins were identified as being of little value, further invitations would not be readily forthcoming, unless, of course, particular circumstances dictated otherwise.

Any unwelcome discussion on the subject of staff at the house would result in Eric explaining that he found it more convenient not to have staff living in the house, adding that it allowed them to walk around naked at night if they so chose, which always provoked an outburst of laughter. Eric would then explain to his audience that his relationship with the Bests was of such value that he trusted them implicitly to organise everything.

Both explanations were realistic and, in fact, true. But they didn't tell the whole truth. The Linderman house was home to many secrets that despite being well hidden would result in unthinkable consequences should they ever be discovered by the prying eyes of anyone else. The Lindermans trusted the discretion of the Bests, whose loyalty was incomparable. For their part, the Bests knew that not everything was as it seemed. They were aware of late night visits by strange, unmarked vehicles and other unexplained activity, but they had no reason to question the activities of their employers. Whatever happened when they were not there was none of their business.

Chapter 19
(Late September 2019)

It was two weeks to the day before Luke's inbox presented a reply from Kent@kentssecretworld.com. Without even checking what other email had arrived, Luke's immediately positioned the curser to open the reply. Each one of the previous thirteen days had begun with an air of expectation, followed by an anticlimactic disappointment when everything but Kent's reply presented itself for reading. Subconsciously, Luke held his breath as he digested the words.

Thank you for your submission of potential locations. I endeavour to check each recommendation for suitability; however, there are a variety of reasons why many locations are not viable, including but not limited to the degree of interest that could be generated among viewers, access restrictions, legal issues and time constraints.

Unfortunately, the building/buildings you identified is not suitable for Kent's Secret World. I do, however, thank you for your submission. If you like what you see on my channel, please hit the subscribe button and don't forget to tell your friends. Many thanks and happy exploring, Kent.

The first indication that he was looking at a generic reply was the plural context of the first sentence. The reply itself had been disappointing enough as it was without a doubt a rejection, But the fact that it was most likely the exact same email that a multitude of people had received left Luke feeling more gutted each time he read the words again, each time a bit slower just in case he'd missed something on the many prior passes that he knew was not there and would not magically appear. As Luke came to grips with the realisation that his submission had been completely dismissed, he couldn't help but question the dismissal of his scenario.

How could he possibly not be interested? I know he would be if he saw the house in person and felt its presence. Of course, he doesn't have the association with the bus. But if only he would go there, he'd feel it and want to explore the place.

Feelings of disappointment, intrigue, potential, excitement, justification and determination all blended into a casserole of thoughts over the next hour and a half. Aided by two cups of coffee to clear his head, Luke went to work, and the keystrokes made by his fingers flying over the keyboard culminated in what he hoped would not be seen as begging.

Dear Kent,

Thank you for your email. I fully understand that you must get many suggestions for locations, with most being unsuitable for the reasons you described in your reply.

I would not be sending this if I did not believe with all my heart that this place should not be so easily dismissed. As an investigative journalist, I am provided many leads, most of which lead only to dead ends.

But if I don't investigate those that hold even the faintest glimmer of hope, then I would not get the results that I do. An unexplainable set of circumstances have led me to the position I now find myself in with respect to this location, and I know with complete certainty that there is much more there than first meets the eye.

Please reconsider your decision, as I believe investigating this place is very much in both of our best interests. I look forward to your response.

Luke Spitz

Kent's reply was nearly instantaneous, and this time, it was not a generic one.

Dear Luke,

I stand by my decision not to investigate further at this point. However, the sincerity of your email has piqued my curiosity.

I do offer another service that I don't openly advertise. I can provide a drone-based scope of the property in question. I will check out the property to confirm its suitability, and if I move forward, I will send a copy of the drone footage to you. If I decide for any reason to upload the video content or carry out a Kent Clark investigation, then your money is fully refundable. The price depends on a number of factors, including accessibility and the distance I have to travel. In this case, the fee comes to a total of $1,200.

Please note that I am not a spying service, I do not engage in any form of illegal activity, and I am only interested in genuinely abandoned buildings. If I find the building is knowingly inhabited or you are engaging my services for any illegal purposes, I will abort the mission and the money will not be refunded.

If after reading this, you want to proceed, please fill out and return the attached form, which stipulates the full list of terms and conditions.

Thanking you, Kent

Luke pondered the thought of handing over what would amount to a sizeable chunk of his meagre savings.

What would Rachael think? I'm in my late twenties, and all I have to show for myself is an old car and less than 2k in the bank after I pay Kent. When she finds out how little I'm worth, will she still consider me long-term boyfriend material? Or will she just think of me as someone for a bit of fun until Mr Successful comes along?

Then again, this could be my only chance to find the answers I need. If I don't do this, I might always wonder what if! And that would be true regardless of whether I marry Rachael or not.

When he was a young boy, Luke's dad had often talked with him about there being no such things as coincidences. He would tell Luke that all things happen as part of God's master plan, and sometimes, you have to stand back and look at what is really happening in the bigger picture. Luke was too young to understand at the time, but as he grew older, his mother would repeat what her late husband had said to him.

"So what is really happening?" Luke asked himself aloud.

The nightmares, the bus, the house, Uncle Errol, Kent Clark's video and his offer; they're all part of a big jigsaw puzzle with some missing pieces that I have to find.

With his newfound clarity about the situation, it was obvious to Luke that there was no way he could let this opportunity pass by. A feeling inside also provoked the thought that once Kent saw the house, Kent would, like Luke, become captivated to the point he would want to upload the footage and he'd refund Luke's money. That idea helped to justify the decision, and Luke found himself filling out the order form right away.

An acknowledgement email arrived soon afterwards, containing details for transferring the money and a brief note clarifying that once the money had been received, a suitable date would be assigned and could be up to three weeks away. However, the footage would be sent as soon as it was obtained.

Two long weeks followed for Luke, but knowing that he had a lot to make up for with Skip, he immersed himself in work. The distraction also helped him not to think about the house as the days slowly passed. Things were still going well in Luke's love life, and with no more nightmares, he became relaxed enough to spend an increasing number of nights with the love of his life. Luke now truly felt they were a long-term couple.

Fifteen days after the money had been transferred, an email appeared from Kent, as promised.

Dear Luke,

Attached is a link that will take you to the footage of the building in question. I have to be open and honest in saying that I found filming this property intriguing. There are some aspects of the building that just cross all design boundaries, and even with my knowledge of construction, they surprised me. The house certainly appears to have been abandoned for quite some time, and although initially tempted, I will not be uploading the imagery or carrying out an exploratory investigation. I have nonetheless decided to give you a partial refund of $300, which I just transferred to your account.

Thanking you for your business, Kent

Luke's hands trembled as he began watching the video at the provided link.

After opening with a shot of the south cliff face taken from the Chesapeake Bay side, the drone elevated to just above the treeline. As the gyroscope stabilised, the powerful lens progressively zoomed in to focus on various parts of the house. The now boarded-up windows and ornate roof trim identified a building whose magnificence was hidden under decades of neglect. The drone made a 270-degree sweep of the house from the south-west to the south-east, always using the zoom to get close before retracting and repositioning. However, no footage had been taken from the east side, so all views of the front of the house were taken at an angle. It was seventeen minutes of professional quality filming that gave Luke a good understanding of the outside of the house and its surroundings, showing much that would not be visible from ground level. The footage had provoked a degree of excitement that only served to underscore the mystery of what lay within.

Errol answered the door and exclaimed, "Well, this is a surprise, Luke! Come on in and tell me what brings you out at night to see your favourite uncle?"

Errol's comment contained a bit of family tongue-in-cheek humour, but underneath the comedy, there was a serious question.

"I hope you don't mind the visit, but I have something I must show you. I only received it a couple of hours ago, and I've watched it three or four times already. But I must share it with you. It's on my laptop."

Errol said nothing, but appeared to be deep in thought as the video played.

"Can you play it once more, please?"

Luke obliged, and as the seventeen minutes passed, Errol once again said nothing. Even after the video had finished playing, no words left his mouth for what was an excruciatingly long time.

"So, let me get this straight. You paid twelve hundred dollars to get this man Kent to film this for you? I told you that nothing good could come of this, it was all so long ago."

"It was actually only nine hundred. He refunded three. I know what you told me, but I also know that things happen for a reason. And this all started with my nightmares and led me to the house, so I can't let it go. And there's also your reaction when I first told you. I believe you also want to know what is inside that place."

Errol once again remained silent until Luke moved around in order to make direct eye contact with his old uncle, which finally broke the silence.

"Will this man film inside the house? If so, you must contact him and offer him money. After you've spoken to him, let me know how much he wants, and I'll transfer the money to you."

"How much should I offer him?"

"I trust you to work out a price that's fair to everyone, Luke. Just let me know the details."

The change in Uncle Errol's attitude towards finding out more about the house filled Luke with a justified enthusiasm that made the words for this email come easily. This time, he wasn't just writing for himself; now, he included his beloved uncle.

Dear Kent,

Thank you for the video footage that I received earlier today.

I am going to get straight to the point. I would like to commission you to do an internal exploration of the building. I'm aware that you have already stated you are not interested, but to use a Hollywood-inspired phrase, I want to make you an offer you can't refuse. In addition to a monetary offer, I believe that what lies inside that building will be of overwhelming interest to both of us. And I somehow think you are already aware of this.

I look forward to your reply. Luke

The closing of the laptop lid signalled the closure of Luke's long day. All that was left to do before bed was a phone call to Rachael to keep her updated.

The constant checking of his private email the next day yielded no reply, and Luke committed to his latest deadline for the less than thrilling article that Skip wanted a follow-up on.

Still, I know I'm going to have the story that beats all stories. One that will make this trivial nonsense look pathetic. It could even be the story that saves the paper. I can't wait to see the look on Skip's face when I've finally put together all the bits and pieces and know what I'm dealing with.

Finding a still empty inbox prior to leaving work was disappointing, but upon his arrival home, another check provoked an air of excitement. There was a reply. The twenty words of Kent's response were completely noncommittal, with no mention of his price or even whether or not he was interested. It was just an invitation to meet.

Meet me at the LouLou Café on the corner of Mainview and Hunter in Richardsville tomorrow at 7:30 when it opens.

Luke had a restless night; thoughts of the drone footage played in his mind on a continual loop. As dramatic as the footage was, it came nowhere close to duplicating the feeling that Luke had when he saw the place in person. As the time ticked by, Luke came to an additional realisation that that he had to be part of Kent's mission.

A pre-bedtime check of driving times told Luke that he could expect a journey of just under three hours. Adding in enough time to grab a coffee on his way out of town and allowing extra time for unexpected hold-ups, he set an alarm that brutally tore him from his fitful sleep at three thirty in the morning.

His seven fifteen arrival at the café's deserted car park meant Luke had enough time to make a quick call to Skip's work number to leave a message.

"Hi, Skip. Luke here. I'm following a lead on the story I told you about, and I'm currently a few hours away. I will be in this afternoon, and I'll catch up on all my other projects before their deadlines. Bye for now."

At seven twenty-five, the door to the café snapped open and the 'Open for Business' sign was displayed.

Right. I'll be the first inside, ready and waiting for Kent.

Much to Luke's surprise, although he'd seen no one else enter the restaurant, when he walked in, he saw he was being watched by the man sitting at a table on the other side of the room. A nodding gesture indicated that he was the man Luke had come to see.

"Hi. I'm Luke. I guess you must be Kent."

Luke's outstretched hand was met with a firm handshake.

"OK then, Luke. You're serious. You never can tell with people."

"Sorry, I'm not sure what you mean," Luke replied, puzzled.

"A long drive early in the morning on very short notice. If you weren't serious about your proposal, you would have tried to make this meeting another time. I've already ordered two coffees, so I guess I assumed you would show."

"Yes, it was an early start. But this is important. I have to know what is inside that house. There's a big mystery surrounding its past, and I need to find out what it is. So, what's your price?"

"Now you're assuming that I am interested."

"As you already pointed out, if you weren't, you wouldn't be here."

"Actually, Luke, I'm here to find out the facts. Until I know enough to be happy, I will make no commitments. I don't do anything illegal. There are others out there who do similar things and might take on sketchy work, but they are amateurs with no military training. I served ten years in the army as a demolition expert. Anybody can blow up a building, but if you want to demolish part of a structure without damaging the rest, or if there are surrounding buildings that have to be undamaged, you need to be intimate with how different sorts of buildings are constructed. That, Luke, is what I do best. I don't demolish buildings any more. Instead, I explore them and appreciate each one for what it is.

"I never do anything that might put my site at risk. My sponsors would walk away, and I will not get into any situation where I could be accused of trespassing. I might give the impression that I just walk into abandoned places, but in reality, I am very careful and always do my surveillance and due diligence. This building is abandoned, but there's a security presence. That's why there was no drone footage taken from the front. Once I spotted the guards, I made sure that I kept back and used the zoom instead to get closer looks. There will have to be an extremely special reason why I would do this, and I'm not talking just money. So now, tell me what that special reason is."

Kent looked Luke squarely in the eye. It was an awkward few moments, and the arrival of coffee gave Luke a welcomed opportunity to compose himself before answering.

"We both know there is definitely a special reason. If there hadn't been, I would never have emailed you, and if you didn't know that, you wouldn't have replied. My dad always told me that there's no such things as coincidences. So if it wasn't a set of non-coincidences that led me to that house, then what was it? I think you also realise there's something very unusual about that place. Something has aroused your curiosity. Destiny brought us both here, and we both know something is going to happen, one way or another. So my question to you is what's your price?"

"Ten thousand dollars," Kent replied without so much as a beat.

"I'm willing to offer you five, but you have to bring me along."

"I can tell you right now, that's not going to happen. I work alone so I can react to a changing situation quickly. I don't mean to be rude, but having you tag along would be a serious hindrance."

"I understand your reluctance, but it's not negotiable. I have to see inside that place. I'll do everything that you ask of me, and do my best to not be a liability. I can help you find that place's secrets. I'm no idiot, and you can count on my complete discretion with everything you tell me."

This time, Kent paused before replying. "I know I'm going to regret this. but six thousand and I'll take you along, provided you agree to all of the following. I say from where and exactly when we go, and that might be on very short notice. You will do everything exactly as I say to, so if I tell you to quickly lie down and hold your breath, then that's exactly what you will do. I will do my best to get us inside, but if things get dangerous and we have to abandon the mission for any reason, then the money is non-refundable. You have to be happy with that."

"I agree. Now, let's shake on it to make it official."

Kent still felt that he was making a huge mistake, but he held out his hand to seal the deal.

"Well, then, you'd better have a look at the full video that shows the security and where we will access. We will arrive by dinghy, then climb the cliff face. There appears to be a path cut into the rock face, but if it's not passable, I'll endeavour to find another entry point. Assuming we ascend there, on the way up, I'll want to check out a spot on the cliff that looks like a cave. This will not be just a stroll up the driveway and waltzing in through the front door, so at any point, I might abandon the mission for safety or security reasons, and in that case, as I've already stated, there will be no refund."

Luke nodded approvingly. Now he had to break the news to his uncle that it came with a six thousand dollar price tag. What there would be no mention of, however, was that Luke would be going along on the expedition.

Chapter 20
(July 1940)

From the moment the three men met that evening, the conversation, like millions of other conversations across the country, had centred on how the war in Europe was progressing, particularly the consequences of the recent fall of Paris to the seemingly unstoppable Nazi war machine. Ten months into the hostilities, the recent defeat at Dunkirk, the fall of Norway and Germany's penetration into Russia all signalled to some Americans a disaster waiting to happen if the United States got inevitably drawn in. But to others, it was a regional issue far from the safe borders of continental America.

Randal J Pilkington and Byron Boyd—or BB, as he was known to his friends—had a lot in common. Both were powerful industrialists and men of influence in both American industry and within the president's administration. Both men had busy schedules, and their private lives seldom crossed paths. So it was with the anticipation of an enjoyable evening that on this warm July evening, they were two of the three figures drinking whisky whilst watching the waves crash against the headland on the other side of the bay.

It was not the first time that Randal and BB had visited the home of their host, Eric Linderman. But it was the first time the three men had been together just by themselves. Edith Linderman had organised a trip for Mary Pilkington, Felicity Boyd and herself to visit a friend's beach house on the South Carolina coast, leaving the three men to enjoy some undisturbed time together.

Randal was a man who liked to direct the conversation, and his host wisely and strategically allowed him to do just that, giving only enough input to nudge the subject matter in the direction Eric wanted it to go. The conversation slowly became more open as the effects of the whisky and the dissolved HCF that had been discreetly placed in their glasses kicked in.

Byron was a quiet man; but his laid-back personality was one that must never be taken as a sign of weakness. Many of his adversaries had learned that lesson too late, much to their detriment. Byron liked to listen; it helped him gauge the people around him and find their weaknesses. He was a man who could be deadly ruthless if the situation required it. Eric knew he had to tread carefully if he was to beat BB at his own game. Fortunately, Eric had one thing working in his favour. Both of these men had a common weakness, something Eric had figured out in their previous conversations and that Eric would now make work to his advantage.

"With the serenity of this location, it's hard to put into perspective all that's going on in Europe," Randal stated.

"You're absolutely correct about that, Randal. My parents knew they had found the perfect spot to build this house on all those years ago. However, it does get quite cold in the winter. The wind just blows up from the sea and hits hard. But I find that wind can bring peace to the soul if you let it, and peace is something we should strive to preserve."

"Make the most of it, Eric. There won't be peace if England falls, because then, Hitler will set his eyes on us."

Eric replied evenly, "There is some merit in what you say, Randal. But personally, I believe that's a highly unlikely scenario. Even if Hitler conquers England, it will cost him dearly, and he won't have the resources or the will to cross the Atlantic afterwards. Now that Churchill has the reins, England will be a lot harder to beat, and they still have Europe's best navy. The chaos that would ensue from such a conflict would leave both economies depleted, which is not sustainable for either side. The inevitable result would be a godsend for any American business looking to help rebuild and charging a healthy price for their services, of course. I say let them be. We need to stay right where we are, totally out of it until the dust has settled. Then, we can walk in and pick up the pieces. It's important that we resist the calls of those who cannot see the implications of going to war. America must remain strong, but neutral."

"I hope you're right, Eric," BB joined in. "I hear many others say that we should keep out whilst they destroy each other, but with the atrocities being reported on a daily basis, there is a growing call to step in. It's no secret that FDR wants war. It's in his personal interest."

"His personal interest, maybe. But it's in the country's best interests not to go to war. We must remember that the news outlets have their own agendas, and FDR is using that fact for his campaign. One day, BB, when Americans like you and me own half of Europe, you might come over and give me a big pat on the back, telling me how right I was."

"Eric, please don't be offended by my next question, but you make no secret of you and your wife's German heritage. So one cannot help but wonder if you have other reasons for your strong views on keeping America out of the conflict when many politicians are calling for us to join the Allies right away."

"I'm not offended at all. In fact, I'm quite glad you raised the question, as others may not have the courage to ask. A lack of transparency starts rumours, so I'm pleased that you can hear the truth right from my lips. Edith and I were both born in Germany, and we both came to America at an early age. I am proud to have German blood in my veins, but let me be quite clear that I am also a proud American, and my loyalties lie one hundred percent with the United States. I do not want to see America go to war with Germany, or any other nation, and I would like to see a peaceful end to the conflict in Europe. The biggest casualties of war are civilians, and whether they are American, German, French or British, millions of innocent people will lose their lives."

Eric paused for a few moments before continuing.

"OK, gentlemen. I must confess that even though everything I just said is undeniably true, you've probably guessed that I also have a financial interest in keeping us out of the war. And, yes, I do stand to lose a lot of money if we should get drawn into the conflict. So let's hope the unthinkable does not happen. Gents, please join me in a toast." Eric raised his glass as he continued, "To America. Long may she stand strong. And also to peace in Europe."

Randal and BB joined their host in raising their half-empty whisky glasses. As the three glasses lowered, Eric Linderman moved to change the course of the evening.

"Gentlemen, I have arranged some entertainment. Would you like to follow me?"

After being led through several doorways and down a set of steep steps, Randal's amazement was genuine when the three men finally stood facing a purpose-built stage. "You and your house are both full of surprises, Eric. The last thing I ever expected to see was an auditorium with full stage under your house."

"We use this venue to host special functions. The stage can be removed to turn the area into one big open space, too."

Eric ushered his guests to two leather armchairs located right in front of the stage, which was raised to about twelve inches above the floor.

"When you said you'd arranged some entertainment, I thought maybe you had a movie to show us. Now I feel like I'm walking into a Broadway show, am I right?" Randal waited for Eric's reply with eager anticipation.

"A show, yes. But Broadway inspired? Probably not."

A bottle of Scotland's finest had soon been used to top off their glasses as Randal and BB prepared themselves for whatever Eric had planned.

Eric clapped his hands and called out, "Let's start, boys."

No sooner had the words left his mouth than a young man moved onstage from behind a curtain. He was carrying a record, which he placed on a gramophone already positioned to one side of the stage. It was the young man's clothes, attire consisting of only a pair of woman's knickers, black thigh-high stockings held up by a garter belt, and a leather vest, that made Eric's guests gasp.

As the gramophone needle started relaying the sound of an upbeat Cab Calloway number, the young man was joined by five similarly attired young men who proceeded to dance with each other erotically.

When the young men started rubbing against each other, Randal suddenly rose from his seat. "What is the meaning of this disgusting nonsense, Eric? This is utterly outrageous!"

Eric motioned to the first young man to stop the music and then he turned to face his shocked guests. "Gentlemen, please. I have a reputation to uphold, and as such, there is no way I would have gone to all the effort and expense of putting on this show if I'd thought for one moment that you would not enjoy it. I am a man of great perception, and maybe, just maybe, I might know you better than you know yourselves. Let me assure you that no one is going to walk in on us. What happens on this side of that locked door will be known only by us and the young men on the stage. And with their profession, they are most certainly not going to share anything about what they get up to. I promise you one hundred percent privacy and an opportunity to relax and unwind.

"I believe you both have certain thoughts you share only with your inner selves, thoughts that life prohibits you from acting on. You're not alone. Everyone, young and old, male and female, has thoughts of things that arouse them, but so very, very few people are privileged enough to act on those thoughts. So tell me, gentlemen, do either of you really want this performance to stop?"

There was total silence as a mixture of embarrassment, lust, expectation and fear combined to leave even Randal speechless.

"I thought not. So please, my friends, sit back, relax and enjoy the show."

BB now turned to address Randal. "Eric has obviously gone to a great deal of effort and expense to arrange all of this, and I think it would be rude of us not to watch his presentation. I'll reserve my judgement until I have seen the whole production."

The show continued, as the young men danced and rubbed against each other in time with the music. It was not a production choreographed to high standards by any means. Its main purpose was not to portray a sense of quality but rather to provide homosexual erotica, which it did well. Its victims were left intoxicated by their own sexual deviances they had spent so much time repressing.

Both Randal and BB were so captivated by the activities onstage that they had failed to notice that Eric Linderman had moved off to one side of the stage. And he was not watching the production; rather, his attention was trained on the reactions of his guests. The truth was that Eric Linderman was disgusted by what was being displayed, and in fact, he found the whole concept quite repugnant. But there was a bigger picture to keep in mind, and he could not let his personal feelings get in the way of entrapping his victims.

Within fifteen minutes, it was all over, and Randal and BB both sat awkwardly in their chairs neither knowing quite how to respond to something that they had enjoyed, but should not have.

After giving his guests a moment to reflect, Eric broke the silence. "Gentlemen, I hope you enjoyed the show, but don't be disappointed. The show is not over. In fact, for the two of you, the evening has only just begun. The six young men are now at your disposal for a private showing. At the back of the stage are two separate private areas where they are willing to entertain you. There are six of them and two of you, so that is three each, unless you want to make other arrangements."

Randal protested. "Watching this sort of activity is one thing, Eric, but participating in it is a completely different ballgame. If my involvement in these sorts of activities ever came to light, it would ruin my private, public and business lives."

"I fully understand your concerns, but you must realise it is just as much in my interest that my gift to you remains a well-guarded secret. This room has three entrances, and all of them are locked from the outside. You can get out, but not back in unless you are let in from the inside or you have the master key, of which there is only one, and I have it. Your chauffeurs are staying in the servants' wing on the other side of the house and will see or hear nothing."

"Eric, you say this is your gift to us. In my experience, one gift requires the giving of a gift in return. Tell me, Eric, if we were to partake of this gift, what would we be indebted to you for?"

"My dear friend, shame on you. My gift to you is a symbol of our friendship and requires nothing in return. I am sure there will be times in the future when we will each have the opportunity to help the other, and I am sure there will come a time when you will be in a position to help me with some problem I might have. But there are no debts owed, and if in the future, I ask for your help and you are unable to give it, there will be no hard feelings."

"One more question for you, Eric. If we're such good friends and you believe that you know so much about us, then I feel at a big disadvantage, not knowing what makes you function. You say everybody has secret desires buried deep inside. So then, share with us what yours are, as I believe yours are different from mine or BB's."

"Oh yes, Randal, mine are very different from yours and probably those of most other people, too. I am very lucky in having a beautiful wife who serves all my manly needs. My obsession is on a different level, not a physical act, but more an emotional experience. Seeing and feeling someone's total guilt and shame is to draw on a level that rises above sexual satisfaction."

"Do you mean us? Are you doing this for your own gratification?"

"No, most definitely not. Please, let me explain in more detail what I am talking about. Berlin during the Weimar period after the war was a very sexually open society. Cabarets openly exalted the virtues of lesbian and homosexual behaviour. It should therefore come as no surprise that during the Depression and with the onslaught of hyperinflation, many Berliners of all types turned to selling themselves in all manner of sexual services. The word spread amongst the wealthy throughout Europe, and they would come to visit and partake of the services not available at normal brothels. One street, for example, had pregnant women offering sexual services. At one end, there were the women who were barely pregnant, and as you travelled down the road, the woman got progressively farther into their pregnancies until finally, at the other end, there were those just about to give birth.

"Men, women, boys and girls, there was something and someone for everybody's tastes. There was another service offered by some desperate men who had no other way to feed their starving children. They called it das Familienerlebnis, or as we would say, 'the family experience.' For a price, a father would let you have any sort of sexual depravity with himself, his wife, his sons and daughters, or even the whole family.

"Oh to be there, not to partake, but rather to feel the atmosphere and see the pain on the man's face as he broke down the most sacred duty of any father, that of protecting his family. Can you imagine his pain as he wished there was any other way, wondering if his wife would ever forgive him. Can you imagine the look in the eyes of his children that pleaded, 'Father, why are you allowing this to happen? Save me from this nightmare.' Imagine the shame he felt as he allowed himself to be abused in front of his family. Could he live with himself after that? Could he ever expect respect from his children again? The atmosphere in the room would be electric; the thought sends a shiver down my spine.

"So, gentlemen, now you know my secret. I leave you in the company of these young men who I am sure will look after your needs. I do ask, however, that you retire to your bedrooms before four o'clock. I have arranged transportation for these entertainers to leave here at four forty-five, before it gets light. You must understand that in their line of work, discretion is just as important for them as it is for you. There will be a wake-up call made to your rooms at eight thirty, and breakfast will be served in the dining room at nine fifteen."

Eric knew he had to leave quickly before there any more excuses could be made to delay the liaisons he had organised for his guests.

"Is there anything I have missed? I think not. So, gentlemen, I will see you for breakfast at nine fifteen. Enjoy the rest of your night."

Briskly exiting through the door they had entered from, Eric Linderman closed the door behind him firmly and let out a sigh of relief. He knew the lustful desires of those two men of influence and high standing would get the better of them, and from this night onwards, he owned them both.

As the bedroom door slowly latched closed, Eric turned and made his way to the edge of the bed where, after sitting down, he clasped his hands to his face.

"What's wrong? Did they not take the bait?"

"It's OK. They each made a quite pathetic attempt at pretending they were not interested, but it was not convincing. They were both consumed with their lustful thoughts. They have no idea how much they're going to wish they'd never come here tonight."

"Then our plans are falling into place, so what is wrong? And don't tell me nothing as I can see something is deeply troubling you."

Edith placed the book she had been reading firmly onto the bedside table before positioning herself behind her husband in a spot that allowed her to rub Eric's shoulders. The pressure of her hands and fingers working into his shoulder, her fingernails digging deep into his aching muscles, caused a combination of pain and pleasure that caused Eric to groan in ecstasy as a shiver tracked down his body.

"Oh my God, that feels so nice."

"Tell me what's wrong, or I will stop. Are you sure everything is going to plan with our guests downstairs?"

"Yes. They are falling deep into the trap. So deep, in fact, that they will never be able to climb out, and soon, we will own them. The problem is that I sometimes wonder if I am doing the right thing. I have allowed unnatural acts to take place in my house. In fact, I have not only encouraged those acts, but I have financed them as well. What I have allowed to take place in my house goes against everything that the Führer's new Europe stands for."

"You are correct, but just as German soldiers are giving up their lives for what is right, we have to give up the innocence of our lives for the greater good. A machine is made up of many parts, each with its own purpose. Take out one part, and the machine will not work as it should. We are just a small part of the machine of change. Imagine the pride we will feel when the war is won and we are invited to Berlin to be personally thanked for doing our part. You will make me the happiest woman in the world. We must not concern ourselves with what is happening downstairs; when Peter has edited the film, those two men will be ours."

"That is the problem, Edith. When my parents died, I promised that I would look after Peter for as long as we both live, and that is a promise I will never break. Taking care of my brother is not just about giving him a warm, dry home and three meals a day. It's about looking after his moral and mental health as well. I walked out of that basement just now knowing that I did not have to witness what was going to happen, but I left Peter there having to see everything. What sort of brother am I?"

Edith increased the pressure of her fingers as she worked on the muscles in Eric's shoulders in an effort to calm her husband.

"Am I asking too much of him?" Eric asked.

"Don't underestimate your brother. He is much stronger than you give him credit for. You of all people should realise he is a wise man; he knows that everything we are doing is for the good of a victorious German Reich and a better world for all. Your brother would do anything for you, but he also knows right from wrong, and I know he is happy to do this for you and for Germany."

"You are right Thank you, Edith. What would I do without your support and understanding?"

"Keep strong, my husband. The Führer would be so proud of you for your sacrifices."

Eric moved his position on the bed and allowed his head to sink between his wife's soft breasts. There was something magical about her ability to calm his mind in the midst of a storm, and such was the serenity of her words that Eric had soon dozed off.

Two sharp tones from the buzzer on Eric's side of the bed brought him back from his tranquillity. He looked at the clock and saw the hands indicated it was just after three thirty. The two tones were a signal from Peter that their guests had departed from the basement.

With his ear positioned to his now slightly ajar bedroom door, Eric heard the unmistakable clunk of a guest's bedroom door closing. It was now safe for him to return to the basement.

The entertainers barely acknowledged Eric's presence as he walked back into the underground room. The events of the evening were purely a business arrangement, and the group had been paid well. They had come to do a job, and now, having fulfilled their obligations and having been at the Lindermans' for over thirteen hours, they were clearly tired and keen to get their equipment sorted and leave.

Eric felt very uncomfortable in their presence; sitting on a chair at the far wall, he was aware of avoiding eye contact with any of the men.

"We are ready now."

Those four words got Eric's attention. Standing up and making his way to the small tunnel that led to a secluded part of the grounds, he secured the door open before ushering the troupe through the tunnel to the outside and their transport. From the outside, the vehicle looked like any delivery truck that would commonly be seen on a public road. Inside, however, were two rows of seats and an area for their equipment. In their line of work, any arrival or departure from a venue required absolute discretion.

Satisfied that the truck and its cargo was making its way off the grounds of his estate, Eric allowed the solid door to close behind him. The firm clunk of the one-way latch reassured him that it was now safe to converse with his brother.

Chapter 21
(October 2019)

As the waves slowly, but steadily increased in height, Luke's hands gripped tighter. His left hand had hold of the grab rope that was an integral part of the inflatable dinghy's outer construction, whilst his right firmly clutched the handle of the waterproof box that contained Kent's drone. It had been made abundantly clear by the man who was currently busy guiding the small boat through the waves that should the drone be lost overboard, the expedition would be over, with no refunds. In a perfect scenario, Luke would have both hands grasping Kent's precious drone or firmly securing himself inside the inflatable.

With no life jacket, Luke was aware that if he got tossed into the cold water, it could mean the end of his life. It wouldn't matter whether the sea was ten or one hundred feet deep at that point. As long as it was over his head, he would be relying on his extremely limited swimming skills, which might keep him afloat for a time but would not allow him to swim through the waves towards the safety of the distant shore if Kent lost sight of him.

Because the dinghy's small size didn't allow it to cut through the water, each wave crest caused the adjacent trough to hit the aluminium base with increasing intensity. Luke felt his eyes sting as the wind-driven particles of salt spray relentlessly pounded his face. Any reassurance came only from the look on his companion's face; there was no sign of fear, just a ruthless determination to get to their destination.

Telling himself that if Kent wasn't worried, then he shouldn't be either, Luke closed his eyes in a vain attempt to calm his nerves. The intensity of the hold Luke had on the dinghy rope and the box had combined with the coolness of the sea breeze and was starting to take a toll. Both hands had numbed, but despite the pain, there was no way he was going to relax the grip he had on the dinghy.

It had been approximately twenty minutes since they had left the security of the sheltered bay that was the closest practical departure point Kent had been able to identify from a combination of Google Earth and surveillance from his drone. The drive to the bay was via an old four-wheel drive path that tested Kent's Jeep Cherokee to its limits. Having elected to place the dinghy on his home-built roof carrier required quite a bit of additional effort in preparing it for the water, but it was a wise choice as the state of the track was such that towing the small trailer would have made the difference between getting through to the launching point and never making it there.

As the swell showed no signs of decreasing, Luke tried not to think of all the possible consequences of the inflatable getting tipped over. His life was totally at the mercy of a man who clearly hadn't wanted him tagging along in the first place. Kent was a man who liked to operate on his own. With his military training, he could well and truly look after himself and saw other people as a liability. However, against his better judgement, money had muddied his decision. Kent had, of course, set some very strict criteria for Luke to accompany him. There was looking after the drone, naturally. Luke had also been instructed to follow all directions without question. If Kent decided the mission had to be aborted, then he had his reasons for doing so, and there would be no backtalk about it from Luke. Both men felt uneasy about their relationship, but Luke had come to the realisation that he had to trust the man who was in control of the mission.

A sudden release of the throttle brought the twenty horsepower Yamaha down to an idle. Turning to Luke, Kent now spoke his first words since they'd left the shoreline.

"That was a bit rough on the other side of the headland. I nearly decided to abort, but we're almost there now, so pass me the box with the drone… carefully."

Luke watched with anticipation as Kent removed and unfolded his expensive toy in preparation for its flight.

So he also thought the sea was rough. At least he carried on, but what is he going to do with the drone?

Kent must have noticed the quizzical expression on Luke's face.

"As you can see, it's impossible to work out where exactly is the best place for us to land. I know it's approximately over there, so the easiest thing to do is send the drone up with the thermo running, and once I spot the location, I can hold it there and give us a bearing to follow."

Luke nodded approvingly, pretending he fully understood what Kent was doing.

After a few minutes of staring at the screen that had kept him fully engrossed since releasing the drone, Kent issued a sudden exclamation of relief. "Got it! I'll lock its position."

Kent was now following the indicator on the tracker that he'd removed from the waterproof backpack. Tracing the signal from the drone, Kent moved ever closer to the rock face where the waves were crashing.

"Over there, Luke. Get ready to jump when I get you close enough."

Aware that any miscalculation would result in him landing in the water, Luke summoned every ounce of his inner strength to focus on his legs and the jump they had to execute to propel him onto the rock face.

Once they were safely onshore and the rope Kent had thrown Luke was secured around a rock, the men lifted the dingy and its cargo out of the water and placed them high enough that any rogue waves would not dislodge it. The drone had now served its purpose and was returned to the box and stowed onboard.

"Follow me carefully and quietly, and if I say to get back to the dinghy, you get back here as fast as possible with no questions asked. Is that perfectly clear?"

Luke nodded before starting to ascend what was effectively a roughly cut walkway up the steep side of the cliff.

An earlier drizzling rain had combined with the moss on the rock surface to make the path slippery so that each step presented an opportunity for, at best, a sprained ankle. The mossy surface also released a smell that gave Luke the feeling that he was descending into a cave rather than ascending a cliff face.

Kent's raised hand brought Luke to a welcomed halt. Had they kept walking ,the area that had captured Kent's attention would have been easily missed by Luke. But in all fairness, had Kent not already known about the cave from his initial drone footage, he too might have missed the small pathway around an overhanging rock and into the recessed area that had been carved about ten feet into the rock. The illumination from

Kent's torch now exposed the secret cut-out. At the very end was a solid steel door approximately four feet wide and with no exposed hinges or handles. Kent tapped the corroded exterior, and the tone indicated it was a heavy gauge steel. Whatever it led to, any attempts to open it would have to be made from the inside.

A shake of Kent's head and a finger pointed upwards told Luke that they were going to continue upwards on the path.

Before long, the top of the ridge was just over their heads. Once again, Kent's raised hand indicated that Luke should stop. Kent moved slowly forward and raised his head to just above ground level. After a quick scan in all directions, he returned and whispered, "It looks all clear, but I'm not taking any chances. I'm going to have a quick scout around and plant these." Kent showed Luke the two small devices has just removed from his backpack.

"These will produce a lot of bright flame and noise without the dangerous release of energy that comes with explosives. I can set them off from my phone, and if necessary, they can provide a distraction that will give us time to escape. Hopefully, we won't need to use them, but if you hear any noise or commotion, head straight back to the dinghy and wait for me there. Now, stay here. Once I've made sure that all is clear up top, I'll come back to get you. Do not come up until I give you the all clear, no matter how long I've been gone. And don't make any noise whilst you're waiting. Have I made myself perfectly clear?"

The eye-to-eye stare told Luke that doing anything other than he'd just been instructed to do was not an option. "Perfectly clear!" he confirmed.

The ten or so minutes before Kent returned felt like an hour as Luke's ears strained to hear the faintest of noises. Temptation eventually got the better of him, and he slowly moved up to a position that allowed him to slowly raise his head enough to get a first peek of the house. Although the house and its grounds sat on a peninsula, their ascent up the cliff had brought them to a position about fifty yards from the house. The first twenty-five yards was the wooded area that surrounded the house on the clifftop.

Kent must be overly cautious. I could stand up and start jumping around and the security guys would never see me as long as I didn't make a noise. So why did he want me to stay below the ridge? Is he coming back to get me? Or is he going to just look around for himself? Maybe I should walk over. No, if I do that, he'll abort the mission. I have to trust him.

Making his way back down to where he'd been told to wait, Luke realised just how much he had to trust Kent. The guards were armed, and he knew they would surely recognise him from his previous altercation. He was also aware that despite Kent being more than capable of handling himself in a conflict situation, that was the very last thing that he would want. Kent's life now revolved around his explorations and his YouTube channel. Conflict with armed guards or the involvement of police could put his whole business, and life, at risk. It would be Kent's priority to return Luke safely, and he could not afford for Luke to get hurt whilst in his care. With that thought, he knew that whatever Kent was doing, Luke had to trust him.

The sudden sound of Kent's voice spooked Luke.

"It's all clear. Follow me and keep low. The first part is wooded, and just before we get to the clearing, I'll get you into position behind a tree. Then I'll dash across and open the side door I just unlocked. When I signal you, it'll be your turn. Run quickly, but quietly. I will close the door behind you. Understood?"

Luke nodded.

"OK, then. Let's go."

The door closing behind Luke was a tremendous relief after his short but intense dash. Luke paused to catch his breath. The stale mustiness of the air in the house was the first thing to hit his senses. It was a natural reaction to want to go around and open all the door and windows. But that was obviously not an option, so the smell was something they'd have to get to used to.

Even with their eyes now fully dilated, the boarded-up windows on the lower floor made the interior of the house only barely visible. Kent produced two small aluminium torches from a pocket and then adjusted the settings before handing one to Luke. The light they emitted was not very bright and was a dark red, like an old photo developing room. Kent then passed his charge a pair of goggles.

"Put these on. They'll help convert the non-refracting light from the torches. They're military grade and work well once your eyes adjust to them. The important thing is that if the guards happen to pass by then they won't be able to see the light coming from the outside. Only the lower windows are boarded up, so we have to remember not to draw attention to ourselves, right?"

The two men spent the next ninety minutes walking through each room of the house. All three levels still contained a lot of furniture, but everything, even the beds, had been covered with dust sheets. The rooms were all checked out, one by one, as they made their way from top to bottom. The final room to investigate was the cellar. The subterranean cavern was accessed through a door close to the back of the kitchen. The concrete steps going down into the dark void were steep, and the overpowering smell of mould was a reminder of how long it had been since anyone had been down there, let alone lit the furnace.

The large green cast-iron contraption that was the centrepiece of this area prompted a sense of amazement in Kent.

"'How the hell did they get it down here?" he whispered, more to himself than Luke. "Keep your torch on night mode, Luke. I know we're below ground, but that chute leads to the outside, and I'm not sure it's light proof."

Spending the next seven or eight minutes examining the furnace, its boiler and the multitude of knobs and levers that controlled the beast, Kent was both captivated and puzzled. For some reason, he felt compelled to explain to Luke in great detail how it functioned. Luke, meanwhile, did his best to try to keep pace with a subject he had difficulty grasping.

Kent was wrapping up on part of his lesson. "And that, Luke, is how the hot water is sent to any of the five circuits to heat different parts of the house. But what gets me is the furnace itself."

"It just looks like a furnace to me. What's strange about it?"

"Do you see those gas tubes with the nozzles on either side? Well, they rotate. When they're pointed up, with this flame director installed, they will shoot the flame up and over the boiler tubes, then up through to the chimney whilst a fan blows outside air in from below. Nothing strange about that, but watch this."

Kent carefully moved the triangular shaped device perched between the two flame tubes and nudged it partly out before rotating the flame tubes until their nozzles faced each other.

"I guess it was designed to save gas. You could put tree branches in here and fire up the gas flame until they were afire, then turn the gas off. If you wanted to, you could even use it to burn your rubbish. Most unusual, but I guess it must have worked."

With each room now explored, the men made their way back to the first room they saw, the reception area.

"So how long do you think it's been empty?" Luke asked. "Seventy to eighty years maybe?"

"Well, Luke, some rooms quite possibly. But some other rooms haven't been vacated quite so long. Did you see the paper dated December 1999 with the headline about the millennium bug?"

"No, I didn't."

"It was in one of the bedrooms. That's less than twenty years ago."

Twenty years sounded so much less exciting than eighty.

"Now I have a question for you, Luke. What is unusual about the room we're in right now?"

It seemed such an unfair question. Luke knew nothing about buildings or construction. And here was a man who had been a specialist in structural demolition in the armed forces and followed that with a career in civil engineering. *Add to that his personal passion for old buildings, and you've got a full-on expert.* Yet here he was, asking Luke about oddities in a building that seemed perfectly normal to him.

"Sorry, Kent. You'll have to tell me."

"Well, apart from the fact that the basic design is just so unusual—it's like a cross of retro Bavarian and gothic German with some American and a slight English twist—I was actually asking the question specifically with reference to this room, which spans the entire width of the house. There are no load-bearing walls to take the weight off the two upper stories. So now look at the thickness of the outside walls. They're twice as thick as I would expect them to be. All of the load in this part of the house is transferred through the floors to the exterior walls, and I can see only one explanation for that."

"Which is?"

"I suspect there's a large open area under this room that is totally separate from the cellar where the furnace is located. But there's no sign of an entrance anywhere. I didn't want to have to do this, but the intrigue has got the better of me."

Kent removed several tools from his backpack. The first was a battery-powered drill into which he installed a long, thin bit. A few minutes later, he was swapping that bit for an even longer one as he attempted to drill through the second layer he'd encountered about twenty-four inches below the hole he'd made in the floorboard. When finished, the small hole would be discreetly covered by the carpet he had temporarily pulled back.

The next tool removed from Kent's backpack was a long, semi-flexible probe that he inserted in the hole after connecting it to a small electric box housing a display screen. The tool was in fact an ultrasonic probe that emitted pulses at different frequencies as Kent rotated the sensor's direction and adjusted a knob that changed the probe's angle relative to the vertical plane. Slowly, a picture of what lay below them emerged on the screen. Even Luke was able to determine the layout of the cavity as the screen built the image of a large rectangular space containing a collection of unidentifiable objects.

"I knew it! There's a room below. It's big, but not quite the full size of this room by the looks of it. I can confirm that once we get in there."

With his tools packed up and the carpet returned to its original position, there was one more job to do before they tried to find the entrance. A laser measurer soon told Kent the interior dimensions of the reception room, which he noted on a pad with a pencil. With all his technical equipment, Luke thought using such a retro means of recording seemed quite out of place.

Kent knew where the room was located, but accessing it proved to be a frustrating obstacle, and after half an hour, he was ready for a different approach.

"Wait right here and don't move till I return," he commanded.

After first checking that all was clear, Kent soon disappeared out the door they had entered through, leaving his companion to wonder just what he had planned. Ten minutes later, Kent returned and quickly let himself in. He finally gave Luke an explanation.

"By my calculations, the end of the garage aligns closely with the end of whatever is down there, just like the back door. That was a Zweissmann lock. They are bloody good locks, some of the best ever made, but they're no match for my skills."

It was the first time Luke had seen this man so obviously impressed with his own talents crack a smile.

"Now, follow me. We're heading straight down the side of the house to the doorway that leads into the garage. We'll gently close the house door behind us, but won't lock it just in case we have to come back. The garage door is closed, but as I said, it's unlocked. Are you ready?"

Luke nodded.

Once again, Luke's mind was put at ease when the garage door closed behind them. He was aware that his heart was pounding, but Luke attempted to look unfazed by the experience.

"The garage goes all the way across the building, and by the look of things, it has vehicle access from both sides. But we need to check down at this end."

Kent indicated they should move to the east end of the building. However, his concentration was interrupted by the first of several vehicles, their shapes distinguishable under the dust cloths covering them. Lifting the first cover back a couple of feet exposed the distinctive grille of an old Mercedes.

"Holy shit! This looks like it's been just left where it is for the last eight decades. I have no idea what this would go for today, but I imagine that to a collector, it'd be a worth a lot."

The dim light of the torches identified the Mercedes as the first of four vehicles that had been stored in the garage under covers. There were three cars and a fourth, much bigger vehicle that was parked against the far wall of the garage to the right, where they were heading.

Luke's throat went dry and he struggled to swallow. There was no need for Kent to lift the cover for him to know what lay underneath. He knew exactly what the three letter badge on the grille would be. Suddenly, to his horror, the evil chugging sound from his nightmares resonated in his head, and overcome with terror, Luke was suddenly unable to move. He knew exactly what was under that last cover, and now he found himself trapped with it in the garage of this bizarre house. How was he going to escape?

Chapter 22
(1941)

"This way, gentlemen."

The open palmed invitation was authoritative but gave a sense of expectation. The three politically powerful men obliged as they started to walk in the indicated direction. Their evening had till now been a time of eating, drinking and the airing of economic and political views. Without their wives present, the discussions had been robust and at times joyfully vocal as the wine and the port loosened inhibitions and exposed their true inner selves.

Eric Linderman had not wasted any opportunity to explain the advantages of America staying neutral in a conflict that had no place in their world, though his comments were very tactfully executed.

Throughout the evening, there had been talk of an entertainment event that Eric Linderman had planned for his guests, one that apparently would be unforgettable.

With the serving staff now dismissed, the house had a feeling of emptiness.

"Eric, are we going to see this show or whatever it is that you have been alluding to all evening? Because apart from our chauffeurs around the back, I don't think anyone else is here. You haven't been teasing us now, have you? Maybe it's just a movie you have to screen."

"Victor, I do not tease my friends or guests. If I said that I have some live entertainment for you, then that is exactly what I will provide."

Victor Linden was an inspiring politician, handsome, charming and from a well-established background. Victor had the world at his feet, married to the perfect wife and father of two perfect children, with a perfect list of impeccable qualifications. Getting him to visit was a coup for Eric.

Like all his victims, Eric's first objective was to form a bond that could help influence decisions. But should that not develop into a situation that was beneficial, then Eric wanted to hold the Ace of Spades in his hand, and he was ready to play his cards tonight to make sure that he was holding that card.

Victor's pairing with his two fellow guests, Arlo Laidlaw and Franklin J Munroe, was not just a random selection of souls. Eric had researched his guests well, and although Victor was going to be a hard nut to crack, Eric hoped that the influences of the other two men, both with reputations for wayward behaviour, might help Victor let down his guard enough to allow the woman—who came with her own reputation of being able to charm her way into any man's bed—to work her magic. Having incriminating footage of Arlo Laidlaw and Franklin J Munroe would be useful, but having something over Victor Linden would put Eric's plan into a whole different league.

Now seated in front of the mini stage, Victor was wary of the situation he found himself in. He was a man heading for great political heights, and any hint of inappropriate behaviour could ruin his future.

What if Eric's hints indicate we're going to witness a display that a man in my position shouldn't be seen at?

Seeing the doubt in his guest's expression, Eric reassured him that nobody else would know about the evening, and along with the peer pressure from his companions, it put Victor at ease.

Unbeknownst to him at the time, Victor's concerns about seeing something discrediting would hold true. However, as common sense slowly became overruled by primitive human urges, he would walk away seeing the evening as nothing more than well-deserved innocent fun. Had he known the real purpose of the events that brought him to this situation, he would never have accepted the invitation.

Even as a young girl, Rose Appleyard knew the art of manipulating men. Bowing her head down whilst looking up with wide open eyes, her softly spoken words, "I'm sorry, Daddy," would have Rose be forgiven for all sorts of misdemeanours without the slightest punishment from her elderly father, whilst her mother would shake her head in despair as her husband administered a verbal warning that would have been little more than, "Well, don't do it again, Rose."

Growing up, Rose learned to perfect her feminine charms to get what she wanted from life. Boys would help her with her schoolwork and her chores for little more than a cheeky smile.

Although never short of male admirers, in her early twenties, Rose found herself alone following the death of both her mum and dad. Her parents had hoped to see Rose married and settled down; but they had realised that their only daughter was too free-spirited to be confined to a life of marriage. As Rose gained maturity her Mother had noticed her daughter's behaviour towards other attractive women her age was not dissimilar to the enthusiastic approach she had towards the company of handsome men. Jean Appleyard had wisely decided that it was best not to say anything to her husband or to Rose herself, in turn taking her suspicions to her grave.

Alone and without a purpose in her life, Rose's big break came when she was spotted dancing in a local play by Maggie McLaren, or Ma, as she was known by all her friends and acquaintances.

Ma was on the lookout for a suitable replacement girl in her high-end entertainment business.

The minute Ma spotted Rose, she knew that she had to have this woman in her service, for Rose was special and Ma knew it. Sure, Rose was beautiful; no one would ever deny that. But so were thousands of other young ladies. What Rose had went far beyond looks alone; maybe it was the seemingly childlike innocence, or perhaps it was her ability to draw people in with her eyes, right up until her prey felt one with his captor. Whatever it was, it made Rose very dangerous because no man could resist her charms.

Ma's cabaret act was not your run-of-the-mill act. Their shows were never advertised. Attendance meant that you had the right contacts needed to secure their services, and for good reason. The troupe could be easily described as starting with extremely risqué and moving on from there. Their shows ran from mild to wild, and what their clients received depended on who the audience was and how much they were willing to pay for a performance.

For this evening, the client had paid handsomely and expected the full show for his guests. The client's proviso was, however, that unlike his guests, he was not to become part of the show as it was a present for his friends and his friends only. Eric, never one to be caught out, did have a backup plan in the event that any of the other men insisted he get up on stage. If necessary, Eric would look down and quietly whisper that he had a current medical issue down below but was happy for them to go ahead without him. Eric had used this ploy in the past, and it always evoked words of sympathy. Plus, nobody had ever questioned him as to what the medical issue actually was.

As she waited for the curtain to open, Rose had a rough idea of how the evening would unfold. She would start the cabaret act with the other five girls dressed only in very revealing costumes. After a while, the dancing would become more sensual and eventually progress to the girls erotically caressing and performing sexual acts on each other.

At the right time, someone from the audience would be invited on stage. The girls were experts at what they did, and it would always be the man who would offer the least resistance who was asked first. Generally, his friends would vocally encourage his participation before they, in turn, would put up a false pretence of reluctance to participate, while in reality, they would be extremely keen. Soon, the participants would be filled with uncontrollable lust as the women would undress them before intimately engaging with their audience. Rose had been instructed to pay particular attention to Victor. With a perfect family image to preserve, he would be the hardest to get to yield to the opportunity presented to him. Rose, however, was confident; after all, she had never failed yet to get the desired results.

For Rose, what she participated in on stage was just an evening's work, and with Victor being both handsome and charming, it made her work that much more pleasurable. However, had she known the real purpose of the events that brought her to this situation, events that could have seen her face splashed over the covers of various newspapers and labelled as the femme fatale who brought down America's most aspiring politician, she would never have consented to come to the house, let alone carry out her performance.

Chapter 23
(October 2019)

Luke's reluctance to get any closer to the end of the garage was quite apparent to Kent, who had become concerned that his client had started to freak out, which was the last thing he needed.

"What is the problem, Luke?" he asked quietly but reassuringly.

"Nothing."

"Then just wait there. Don't move and don't make a noise. I am going to check out that vent in the wall. I just have a sneaking suspicion that there might be an entrance."

With Kent now checking the far wall, Luke was forced to face his demons alone. At least, that was how it felt to him regardless of the fact that Kent was in fact just on the other side of the cloth covered vehicle.

Kent's figure suddenly appeared from behind the bus and walked back to where Luke was standing.

"I was right. There's a vent shaft that leads to a passage. It has to be a way in or out, maybe an emergency fire exit for whatever is down there. So, are you coming with me, or do we head back to the dinghy?"

Luke, however, remained exactly where he was. To get to where Kent was indicating, he had to first walk in front of the beast and then between it and the wall of the house.

"OK, we're going to abandon this right now. I can't have you freak out on me."

Luke shook his head from side to side. He knew this was his one and only chance to discover what had brought him here, and he couldn't afford to blow it. With a deep breath and using every ounce of his inner strength, he moved forward, all the time making sure not to make eye contact with the bus or its dust cover.

"Lead the way, Kent."

Although still concerned about Luke's potential risk to their mission, Kent's intrigue at the whole situation had got the better of him. He knew he could abandon the mission and come back by himself at a later date and Luke would be totally unaware, but there was something down there, and Kent wanted to know exactly what it was.

Kent suggested it would be a good idea to secure the steel grill behind them just in case they exited via a different route. After doing that, the two explorers carefully descended the steel ladder that was located directly behind. A short distance along the passageway that was at the bottom of the ladder, they found further progress was blocked by a solid door, its closure secured by two locks. Kent removed his lock picking kit from the pouch on his belt before turning to Luke.

"What you see on TV, where a lock is opened in barely a second, is not always true, certainly not for quality locks like these."

Seven long minutes passed before both locks were conquered and the door opened. Once through the door, Kent made sure that he was happy that the door could easily be opened from the inside before he allowed it to close. Aware that Luke had noted his assessment of the door, Kent felt obliged to explain his reasoning.

"I once read about an English urban explorer who was investigating a long abandoned mental asylum in rural Belgium. After entering one of the rooms on the upper level, he realised just in time that the solid door was spring loaded in the closed direction, and with no internal mechanism it could only be opened from the outside. The article went on to note that with the room's thick walls and barred windows, the explorer realised his chances of getting out should the door have latched shut, were probably nil."

This, however, was not a time for stories and Kent ushered his nervous companion onward. The passage continued for approximately another twenty feet before a second ladder took them downwards a further six feet. The area they now found themselves in ended with what appeared to be a doorway, but if it was a doorway, there were no visible handles or locks.

"Well, I'll be darned, Luke. This door has spring-loaded latches, so if I give a solid push, like this…"

Kent didn't finish his sentence as the door had sprung open into the large dark void that lay beyond.

As their light sources illuminated the large room, the two men stared in amazement. The air was overwhelmingly musty, far worse than the house itself, as they ventured forward into the dark unknown.

"I don't think anybody has been here for at least eighty years."

"I would be inclined to agree with you, Luke."

Turning his attention to the door they entered through, Kent again checked that it could be opened from inside and in the process noted that when closed, it appeared to be a wall panel.

"Well, Luke, I guess our point of entry is a secret exit for emergencies, but not actually the main entry to down here. That is still for me to find."

Both men were overwhelmed with excitement as they slowly started piecing together the layout and contents of the room.

A platform elevated a small amount over the floor level was packed with much-used furniture. The stage and whatever was presented on it seemed to be the main purpose of the room; there were pull-across dividers running on overhead tracks that could separate different areas behind the main stage, presumably for changing and preparation by the performers.

"You keep looking around, Luke, but be careful and don't make a noise. I am going to find the main exit into the house, and I think that I know where to start looking."

It wasn't long before a tap on Luke's shoulder indicated that Kent wanted him to follow to the now open doorway and stairs that led back up into the house.

An upper door opened into a hallway in the house, the same hallway that the two men had walked down less than an hour ago. Kent spoke quietly to his fellow explorer.

"I can't believe I didn't figure this out when we were in the house. This upper door can only be opened from below, and when it's closed, nobody would know a door was even there, let alone that it leads down to a lower basement. There will be a device somewhere that releases the door lock from the house. Maybe it's behind a hidden panel, but it could take a while to find. You go on the other side and slowly open and close the lock until I say stop. I'm going to listen for the locking mechanism operating."

Kent put his ear to the wall as he indicated for Luke to close the door. It only took three operations of the door mechanism before Luke was greeted by thumbs up from a smiling Kent.

"OK, Luke. Now we have that sorted, let's check out the rest of the basement as we are starting to run out of time."

On the far end of the underground room were two toilets, a shower and a changing room that was adjacent to a doorway. Just like the other door that led into the house, this door could only be opened from the inside. The door opened easily as Kent jammed some wood in front of the open entrance to keep it that way whilst they checked where it led to. The small passage ended in what resembled a well disguised pillbox whose concrete structure stood adjacent to a secluded part of the estate. This area was accessible to automobiles by a small left hand turn just before where the driveway turned right to enter the grounds. It appeared that this was somewhere that vehicles could stop to deposit or collect people, presumably from the concealed entrance.

Returning back inside the main room, the men found and opened yet another door. This one was unlocked and located about two-thirds of the way down the wall from the stage. The room within had only the door as entrance, with no windows in any of the four walls which were, along with the floor and ceiling, constructed of solid reinforced concrete. It was not hard to figure out that this was a storeroom; its contents, however, defied explanation: different sorts of wooden and steel contraptions identified themselves in the light of their torches. Bending over to check some of the leather straps that were attached to the devices at various points, Kent turned to his companion, the perplexed look on his face quite apparent.

"Well, Luke, if I didn't know better, I would swear we were in a medieval torture chamber rather than a storeroom. And now I'm really beginning to wonder what else we will find hidden."

On the other side of the main room and almost directly opposite the storeroom was yet another doorway. This one, unlike the one that led to the pill box, could be opened from both sides. The door opened easily, allowing the two men to proceed along the concrete tunnel that was behind. The passageway was about thirty feet long and descended as it made its way to the second, but this time steel door. A large central handle acted against a spring to pull two steel bolts from their containment housings. Despite the age of the door and its locking mechanism, its operation was as smooth as the day it was installed.

"I know what's behind here; turn your light off." Kent uttered his request as he started to slowly allow the door to open. "I knew it."

The comment was spoken quietly and had a tone of satisfaction as the door swung open to reveal the location on the cliff face that they had examined on the way up.

"This is how we are going to leave, Luke. Hold the door open and whatever you do, don't let it close, if you do, it will spring shut and lock automatically and the only way back in will be through the house."

Luke obliged, holding the door open as Kent made his way to the pathway. Soon returning, Kent signalled they would head back into the underground room as he checked his watch.

"Well, that makes our exit a lot easier and saves time; we will call it one-hour maximum, OK?"

Kent started to examine the large room's interior with renewed enthusiasm.

An expression of puzzlement came over him as he first used his laser measurer to take internal measurements then went around placing his ear to the walls as he gently tapped them.

"Can I ask what you are doing?"

"These walls are not load bearing and don't form the exterior walls of the house, either. This room is twelve feet narrower than the room above; I suspect there's a U-shaped passageway that surrounds this room, and I am going to find it. In fact, I think I know where to start looking."

Heading back to their initial entrance point to the room, Kent opened the false panel and stepped into the void at the bottom of the ladder. After a bit of gentle pushing, an additional false panel to the left of the ladder sprang open.

Luke stared in amazement as Kent stepped into the darkness behind the once hidden door, his torch illuminating the surprise that lay inside.

A passageway extended down the side of the room. It was a void approximately five feet wide on one side, the solid concrete exterior wall braced every few feet with steel beams that ran up to and underneath the ceiling. Looking down the void identified a number of long unused still and movie cameras, their lenses aimed at glass panels on the internal wall.

"What is this, Kent, some sort of movie set up for projecting images?"

"No, Luke. These are movie cameras, not projectors. See? They look into the main room."

Luke felt stupid. He had just initially assumed it was part of the entertainment set up, but Kent's words had now made the obvious apparent. Kent followed up with his assessment of what they had found so far.

"I expect these viewing panes line up exactly with the mirrors on the wall inside; they will be one-way mirrors, and whatever was going on in there could have been filmed from in here without anybody in there even knowing. I would have to make an educated guess that there was some sort of illegal activity taking place here. The people would either enter the room from the portal in the garden or the hidden entrance in the house, with the doorway to the cliff and the one to the garage being emergency escape routes."

"That sounds like a good assessment so let's try and work out what was actually happening here."

This time, Luke led the way as they backtracked to their starting point. Heading in the opposite direction, the two men noted what they had initially missed. The passageway had an intersection just inside the door, and the new passage did an almost 360-degree turn and circulated around the back of the shaft that had the access ladder before straightening up and passing a locked doorway halfway down on the left side before continuing on to make a right turn into a passageway on the other side of the room.

"There we go, Luke. As expected, the outer wall of the other side of the building and the same supporting beams along with the same false wall set up between this and the inside of the room. And look, more cameras. These would see the back of the stage. Why would you have cameras on this side unless you were a pervert filming the actors getting dressed?"

"Maybe we should try to open that other door that we passed."

"Exactly what I was intending to do, but first, I want to have a look down the end of this passage. It appears longer than the other side. Bloody Shillmann locks," Kent muttered as he fiddled to get the lock-pick in the right configuration.

"These are better than half the stuff you can buy today."

Finally, to both his and Luke's relief, there was a small click as the lock sprung. For over eighty years, it had guarded whatever was behind the door, but now, just like the others, it had succumbed to Kent's skilful hands.

On one side of the room boxes upon boxes were stacked on rusting steel shelving. On the other side, a leather seat sat in front of a sturdy wood table whose top held a writing pad, writing implements and a desk lamp covered in dust. Above the desk was a long wooden shelf containing steel canisters. Luke realised immediately that they held film.

A flag hung from the end wall behind the seat; it was red with a white circle in the middle. Inside the white circle was something that the very sight of caused a chill to run down Luke's spine. It was a black swastika, a symbol of hatred, fear and destruction. With shaking hands, he used his phone to take a few photographs of the room's contents.

"We need to go now, Luke."

Kent had a strange look on his face as he gestured towards the door.

As uncomfortable as he was in this evil place, Luke knew he had finally found the holy grail of his quest, and now he was being asked to leave.

"I mean it, Luke. We must leave now. This mission follows my rules, and we have talked about how this works." Kent's words had a firm and authoritarian tone.

"OK, but I need to take a few samples of what's here."

"I will not take anything, and I do not condone illegal acts of theft. That is not what I am about."

"It's not theft so much as my research. I have been led here to this room that has not been accessed since goodness knows when. I don't think anybody knows this place even exists. I have to know what is here. Aren't you curious?"

"I am walking out the door for two minutes. What I don't see in that time, I have no knowledge of. But after two minutes, I will be locking the door regardless of which side you're on. And if I see you holding anything, I will not be happy and I'll make you return the item."

A few hastily gathered folders out of some of the top boxes, along with a single reel of film was all Luke could fit into his small rucksack as Kent walked out of the doorway for his agreed two minutes.

"Is everything back where you found it?"

"Yes."

"Then we need to go right now. We'll exit via the tunnel and close all the doors behind us. Don't leave anything behind. Once we're outside, you will quietly head back down to the dinghy. I will need to go retrieve my distraction devices and lock the door to the house, so follow any hand signals I might give you. Do you understand?"

Luke nodded approvingly as they made their way back to their exit point. The firm closing of the steel door behind them was a realisation that the adventure was nearly over.

"The gear, thanks."

Kent's statement along with his outstretched hand was a reference to returning both the torch and the glasses. The time at the house had become so all consuming that Luke failed to be aware that he was still wearing Kent's treasured toys.

"I don't want them getting covered with saltwater spray. They are very expensive, and you can't exactly just go buy another set at Walmart."

Chapter 24
(1940)

The four doors of the dark green Lincoln opened simultaneously as the vehicle came to a halt, its speedy entry into the grounds indicating that the four men inside were aware that they were running late. The driver looked up towards the man positioned on the top step just outside the entrance way; it was quite clear that the two men knew each other well.

A wave and a greeting came from the man on the step.

"Just leave your car there, Simon, you're the last, no one else will be coming."

Simon's hand gesture acknowledged the comment as he and his three passengers closed their doors and proceeded up the stairs.

"It's good to see you, Eric."

"And you too, Simon"

Simon pointed towards his fellow travellers. "You know Lyle and Stefan. And this is a colleague of mine, Linton Green."

Eric extended a warm handshake to the two men who he already knew, before turning to the man he had not met before.

"I am Eric Linderman, welcome to my house."

Simon was aware of the uneasiness in Eric's expression and decided to interject.

"Linton is a good man. You have my personal assurance he thinks just like we do."

"Well, Linton, there isn't much of a better recommendation than a personal one from Simon; I hope you have an enjoyable and enlightening evening."

"Thank you, Eric. I have heard many good things about you and just like Simon said, you will find that we have much in common."

A welcoming glass of champagne or whisky was soon offered to the new arrivals by Leighton Best as the men followed their host into the reception hall to join the eleven other guests who were all fully engaged in various conversations.

With the last of Best's duties now complete, Eric Linderman was keen to release his help and get the meeting underway.

"That will be all for tonight, thanks, Leighton."

Aware that there should be no hesitation in his departure, Leighton collected his coat and hat in preparation to make the short trip to join his wife in the estate cottage.

Satisfied that his trusted staff member was now on his way back to his cottage, Eric entered the reception room in preparation to get the evening's event under way. The air was filled with excited chatter. Fully aware that there was much to get through, Eric Linderman knew that as the host of the event he had a reason to get the formalities underway.

"Gentlemen, may I have your attention please?"

His voice was powerful and authoritative and immediately commanded an air of respect. Eric now stood emotionless and upright until all the chatter had turned to complete silence. It was a trick he had observed and learned from the man that he admired most in the world. If it worked getting the attention of a crowd numbering in the tens of thousands, then it was going to be successful in a room filled only with sixteen men. Finally, when he had everyone's attention, he spoke.

"Thank you, gentlemen. If you need to top up your drinks or go to the bathroom which you will find signposted from the hallway, then please do so now, and when you are ready please make your way to one of the seats in front of the lectern as we will be starting our formalities in exactly five minutes."

Eric's outstretched hands indicated firstly to the wooden drinks table located to his left just in front of the window. A lace tablecloth made the transition between its top surface and its contents which consisted of several champagne bottles chilling in ice buckets, a collection of three different types of whisky, a container of ice and a selection of appropriate drinking vessels. Secondly, his hand indicated the direction that the bathroom was, through the doorway from which they had entered. Finally, Eric gestured towards the seats that had been positioned around the elevated lectern at the other end of the room. It would be from this spot that he and two others would address the eager attendees this evening.

With the precise timing of a Swiss watch the elapse five minutes was once again signalled by Eric's words, this time from the lectern whose slight elevation raised the speaker approximately six inches, just enough for him to maintain dominance over the crowd.

"First may I say thank you all for making the journey out to my house on this cold and rainy evening. I know that for some of you it has been a long journey. I hope everybody now has a drink. There is more champagne and whisky on the table. Please feel to help yourselves. Later in the evening my beautiful wife Edith will be serving a light German style supper for us.

"Tonight my home is your home, and I will be doing everything I can to make this an enjoyable time. Later we have an amazing guest speaker, Klaus Schoombie, whom we are very privileged to have here this evening. Following my own few words, our friend Ethan Katley will be giving us an update of what is happening in Europe. No, not the version altered for the American public but rather a true and accurate portrayal from German news sources.

"Before we hear from our other two speakers I have been given the privilege of telling you a little bit about myself.

"Some of you I have known for a while, others I have just met for the first time today. For the former I apologise if you have heard this before and for the latter I will start with the basics.

"My name is Eric Heinz Linderman, and I was born in Stuttgart fifty-four years ago. When I was eleven, my family moved to America where my father used his German skills combined with hard work to make a very successful life for himself and his family in our new home. I stand here this evening both as a proud German, my country of birth, and as a proud American, the country I now call home.

"I love to read and none more than a good history book. We can learn so much about our future from looking back at what has happened in the past.

"Empires rise and fall; it is all part of mankind's progression. The Assyrians, the Persians, the Greeks, the Romans, the Ottomans to name but a few and more recently the British have risen and made their mark on the world with their cultures before starting the process of fading away into history.

"Now, as the sun begins to set on what is left of the British realm, we see the rise of the next and most powerful empire that has ever ruled, yes, gentlemen the German Reich.

"A realm unlike any other, Germany will learn from mistakes of others in history. Germany will never be the first empire but, my friends, I tell you, it will be the first thousand year empire."

Eric's slamming of his fists on the lectern, timed to match the increased volume emphasising the end of his sentence, ignited a round of applause.

"So what makes the advancement of Germany different from every other country? My friends, there are lots of answers to this question, but I am only going to mention two.

"Firstly, there is German technology. Europe was stunned by the advance of the German Army. The Blitzkrieg offensive could not have happened with the speed that it did without having the best army backed up with the best military equipment. Germany has the best bombers, the best fighter aircraft, the best tanks, the best guns and on the water she has the best ships and submarines.

"German technology, however, is not only about war. Once the war is won the German people will live in the most technologically advanced nation in the world. The Führer has plans for every German family to own a car, whilst superbly engineered Autobahns will allow seamless travel between city centres. Germany will have the fastest and best railway network in the world. German aircraft will rule the skies and make flying between countries as simple as driving to your neighbour down the road. The German housewife will have technology that will make any person a good cook and the list goes on and on.

"Some of you were lucky enough to have been collected from the station by my own bus and I must thank my good friend Herman for doing the driving tonight. Why would I own a bus, you may ask? I won't bore you with the full story, but I will say after having the opportunity to travel in a OMD vehicle I was so impressed by the ride that I had to have one myself.

"In my garage, I also have three cars, two Mercedes and one Auto Union. Why three cars? Because each one is different and unique in its own way, however, they all have one thing in common: faultless German technology and craftsmanship. I don't think that there is a single person alive who could argue that Germany does not lead the way in all aspects of modern technology so now I move on to the second example of what makes Germany unstoppable.

"Picture this scenario, gentleman. Any other country that had the indignities of the Treaty of Versailles imposed on it would have crawled into a burrow, only occasionally sticking its head out to see if it was safe.

"But no, my friends, not Germany. When she was down, injured and raped of her dignity, she licked her wounds and stood back up on her feet determined never to be in that position again, and now, little more than twenty years later, she stands as the world's most powerful country as her former aggressors tremble in fear.

"That, my friends, is German resilience, which, along with German technology, will combine to make Germany unstoppable.

"America is now at a crossroad. We could do what many of our misinformed politicians are calling for and go to war on the side of England and her allies, or we could do the right thing and remain neutral.

"Let me be clear, I am not asking for us to go to war on the side of Germany either. Germany is strong enough to do what it needs to do in Europe on its own. What I am calling for is neutrality, which means being completely neutral, so no more Atlantic convoys, no more clandestine help or the passing of sensitive information to the British and French.

"Germany will acquire all of Europe, including England, it is just a matter of time, so America needs to choose. Are we going to be a friend? Or are we going to be an enemy of the world's greatest empire?

"There would be many misguided people in our country who would hear me say these words and accuse me of being anti-American. Oh how wrong they would be.

"I have this wondrous vision, a vision so intense that it brings tears to my eyes. A world weakened by war will allow the unimpeded rise of a second and compatible empire, the American empire. I see Germany and America standing side by side and together like twin brothers who together will rule the world.

"Canada, weakened by its obligations to the British Empire and its pointless struggle, will not be able to stop a northern expansion by the United States. Just as Austria welcomed the German advancement,

Canadians will line the streets to welcome us as they look for stability and strong leadership.

"On our southern border we will be able to finish what we started in the Spanish American war. Soon everything north of Colombia will be part of the new one-hundred-states America.

"As wondrous as this is, there is more to my vision than just a redistribution of borders; it is also about the economic power that both Germany and America will hold over the rest of the world. Let me explain.

"The destruction of the British economy will come as a direct result of their inevitable humiliating loss. England will not be able to hold onto her colonies, who in turn will look for independence. These emerging countries will need help and financial guidance to get started and, gentlemen, as some of you will already realise, the dollar can be a greater weapon than the gun. Loans will become harder and harder for emerging nations to repay and with strategic assets as their security, American corporations will eventually control of many of the world's mineral and wealth assets."

Eric paused for a moment, partly because the intensity of his speech had left him emotionally drained and secondly because he wanted to slow the pace of his speech down, allowing him to stress the next and most important words. Finally the moment was right for him to continue.

"I realise that we might all be here for different reasons.

"There are those of us who have both German and American blood and ancestry and would be devastated at seeing hostilities between these two great nations.

"There are those of us who support Hitler's policy of freeing Germany from the tyranny that was imposed on it by the Treaty of Versailles.

"There are those of us who support Hitler's views on the cleansing of Europe and advancement of Nazi principles.

"There are those of us who can see problems with our own political direction and look to Germany for guidance.

"There are those of us who see the rise of Germany as an opportunity for America to expand its own borders and economy.

"There are those of us who realise that Germany leads the world in technology, science, medicine and all the fields that can benefit mankind.

"There are those of us who see the eventual integration of Europe into the German empire as a godsend for American business as we help build the economies of the defeated nations.

"And there are those of us who see what is happening in Europe as part of mankind's destiny.

"For me, all of the above reasons apply. For you maybe it's just one or two but regardless of your motivation for being here tonight, we are all looking for the same outcome.

"I plead with you, we all need to do our part to make sure our great country does not side with England and its allies and be drawn into a conflict that is not America's to fight. Even as we speak, hundreds of thousands of tons of American supplies are heading eastward on Atlantic convoys, but it does not need to be like this.

"Many don't share the views of our president; we must make sure people see beyond the lies and keep America out of what is only a European conflict. Keeping America out of this war will save tens of thousands of American lives and stop the conflict dragging on and taking the lives of millions of innocent civilians.

"Thankfully not everybody has been blinded by the lies and exaggerations that the public are being exposed to or been tempted by the quick financial gains of siding with the English.

"I think it goes without saying that we must be careful as to who we speak to with, there are many corrupted by anti-German lies. But if we don't speak up for what is right and just, then who will? Gentleman, we have a moral obligation to let the truth be known.

"My friends, war is not pleasant, but I think we are all old enough to know that sometimes we have to walk through the mud and the thorns to find the cool refreshing water of the flowing river. And when this war is over what a beautiful river we will be refreshing in.

"Thank you, gentlemen, for listening to both my story and my vision."

Eric's final words were the catalyst for the audience to stand up and applaud. As the applause finally dissipated, Eric stretched out his hands to indicate for the guests to resume their seated positions.

"Gentlemen, your gratitude has humbled me, but this evening is not about me. Tonight we come to hear our guest speaker and what a privilege it will be to hear from Klaus Schoombie, a man from the German consul who has personally met the Führer not once but three times.

"But before we hear from Herr Schoombie we have our regular update from Ethan Katley as he enlightens us with recent news from Germany I know Ethan's perspective is always a favourite of these meetings as, like you, I strive to hear the truth. Please welcome our good friend Ethan."

Another round of applause followed allowing Eric to make his way to back to his seat as the attention of the room was now focussed on the tall, slim, blond man making his way towards the lectern.

Chapter 25
(October 2019)

Aware that all the documents were written in German, Luke was keen to sit down and start converting the written text to English. Earl White was the name on the outside of the old cream coloured folder that Luke had decided to look at first; it was a name that would appear repeatedly in the text, leading Luke to believe the contents of the file were exclusively about that person. The written content was very neatly laid out, but the style of the handwriting was beyond what his scanning programme could master, and the task proved excruciatingly slow.

A few minutes online found the likeliest candidate. Earl Maxwell White was an American industrialist. Born in New York in 1885, Earl rose to become a major force in the American steel industry and, from the one clear online photo, was a man of immense prominence at the time.

Luke stopped to look over the photos that were also in the file. He had viewed them several times already but each sighting of the content still surprised him just as much as the first time that he saw the man humiliatingly shown in the images.

The text may have been all in German but pictures, as the old saying goes, speak a thousand words and depravity is the same in any language. Could this man be Earl White? There was certainly a resemblance to the picture of the man on the internet. Assuming that they were one of the same, did he know that he was being photographed whilst engaged in the incriminating activities that the photos showed?

Several of the photographs showed the man dressed normally from his waist up, that was apart from the lead that was attached to a dog collar around his neck. Below his waistline, however, the man was naked except for a pair of woman's stockings held up by a garter belt whilst his genitalia were fully exposed. Another set of photos from the collection showed the same man this time with his upper clothes removed leaving him now dressed only in the same stockings and garter belt as the previous set of photos. In this second set of images the man was positioned on all fours on the floor whilst a large woman sat on his back like she was riding a horse. To complete the bizarre theme the woman was fully dressed in equestrian attire complete with riding helmet and a riding crop in her hand.

Luke had researched enough scandals in his career to realise that by today's standards the content, although truly weird, was very mild. What could now be obtained with just the click of a mouse would make this actually look quite comical, but in 1940s conservative America, photos like these would have destroyed a person's career had they had ever come to light. These images were quite clearly intended for the purpose of blackmail, so why then would a man of such stature allow himself to be photographed in such compromising positions? The answer was obvious: he wouldn't. These images were deceitfully obtained and non-consensual.

Turning his attention to the film canister, Luke carefully prised the rusty lid from the steel container. As expected, a reel of film lay within. Carefully unrolling a few feet and examining the picture contained on a single image gave very little away. Luke was aware of a local business where old films could be digitally transferred at a reasonable price but discovering its full content was a job that would have to wait.

Luke's original plan to convert the documents and digest the contents before seeing his uncle did not make sense any more. Uncle Errol was fluent in German and letting him read the documents as they were written made for a much better plan. The ensuing phone call got the immediate attention of his uncle and once Luke had conveyed the fact that he had objects of interest from the house to be viewed, Errol could not hide his expectations of seeing them with the utmost of urgency.

The contents led to a strange reaction from his initially excited uncle. Errol, however, would not share his thoughts or even acknowledge Luke as he became captivated by what was in front of him. After about twenty minutes, slowly looking up from above his glasses, Errol broke the deafening silence.

"So then, you're telling me that you also went to the house. That was not the plan; I thought it was just going to be your friend Kent."

"Actually he is not my friend; this was purely just a business deal. All of what has happened was because of my dream, and all the leads that I have followed have been mine, so do you honestly think I was going to let him go without me?"

Errol looked at his nephew disapprovingly for a few moments. "How did you get past the security guards?"

A question suddenly turned into a shocking realisation for Luke.

"How did you know there were security guards? Oh my God, you have been there, haven't you?"

Errol said nothing but it was obvious that he was familiar with the house. Finally he replied to his nephew's question.

"It was a long time ago and I do not wish to talk about it at this point of time. You, however, must tell me every detail of what happened on your trip there, including everything you saw both inside and outside of the building. Afterwards I will tell you what I have read."

Luke sat back in the chair that up until now he had placed himself on the front of. Now relaxed as he could be under the circumstances, Luke, as methodically as he could, recited the night's events, right from the moment he got into Kent's small inflatable dingy till they returned back safely to shore. Errol listened intently and at times took notes. Eventually it was his turn to talk about what he had read from the files he had been given.

"You are not stupid, Luke. I am sure you have figured most of this already. It appears that Eric Linderman was keeping collections of incriminating evidence on a variety of people. Each file has a lot of information on the person's character and seems to concentrate on their weaknesses, especially the things that could be used against them if evidence of those activities were obtained. There was a lot of meaningless information that was written in some sort of code. I assume given time I could work out what all that meant.

"Additionally there was information about that person's use to Eric Linderman, information about their personal and public lives, their business contacts, and the political influence that they had. I assume Linderman was planning to blackmail various people in order to influence America's attitude to the war."

"Did you specifically recognise any of the names? From the limited time I have spent researching some of the obvious names, it appears they were people of influence at the time. It does not matter if you didn't as I am going to do some in depth research on them to see what I can find; I just haven't had the opportunity yet."

"Sorry, Luke, I did not recognise any of the names."

Errol looked directly at Luke for a few moments before continuing.

"You want your story and I want to know everything that was happening at that house. To give us both what we want we need to acquire more of the information that was stored in that room. We must cooperate, but more importantly we must be careful."

Errol took a deep breath before continuing.

"Luke, I realise that if I ask you to persuade Kent to go back and retrieve the rest of what is down there, then you would insist on going back as well, therefore it is something that I am very hesitant to do. As reluctant as I am to ask you, I know that this whole scenario requires just as much closure for me as it does for you, so against my better judgement I am asking you but only on the provision that you do not put yourselves in any danger?"

"Closure for you?"

"Yes, but I cannot tell you anything more at the moment, so please be patient."

"I know he will be hesitant, but I have my suspicion that despite what he might say he is planning to go back anyway, but by himself and without telling me, in which case we will never see anything else of what remains there. Maybe the temptation of money could persuade him, I can only ask."

"Then we must get the rest of what we can regardless of cost. Luke, I have seen enough of life to know that every man has his price; you will need to find out what Kent's is."

"What shall I offer him? I know he will ask for much more than last time and I can't agree to an amount not knowing what you are willing to pay."

"Luke, you are a wise young man. I trust once again you will come to a fair price. Whatever you agree to pay him, I will honour that amount and pay it."

"I really wish you would give me a figure."

"Offer him what you need to, and I will transfer that amount to you. When you are there, you must get as much as you can get, documents, photos, the movie film canisters and whatever else seems relevant and if you can, take photos, everything will help put the picture together."

"For me it was all about my dreams and the corresponding course of events, but I still don't know why do you want all this information, did you also have nightmares? Or do you know one of his victims?"

"Not now, Luke, as I said be patient. I promise that I will tell you all, but not now. Do what you can with Kent and in the meantime leave this all with me so I can do my bit by studying all the material in detail. I think I am stating the obvious by saying this, but neither you nor Kent must tell anyone what you have found already, or what we are planning to do."

The voice on the other end of the phone initially did not sound happy to be receiving the call.

"Yes, Luke, what do you want?"

Although Kent's phone greeting was not as welcoming as Luke would have liked it was how it was, and Luke was going to get straight to the point.

"Hello, Kent, I need to return to the house, and I am willing to pay you accordingly."

"Sorry, Luke I am not interested, I should never have given you my number, thanks for calling, goodbye."

"Wait, Kent… Are you sure that you are not interested, because I think that you are."

"OK, I will play along with your games, Luke, so why do you think that?"

"Firstly, you answered my call when you could have ignored it. Secondly, you genuinely found the house interesting with all its surprises and thirdly, I know you are planning to go back without me, so when you go back why not take me and get paid for it?"

"So then what makes you think I am going back?"

"Simple really, why else would you have wanted to find out how to access the basement from inside if you were not planning to go back? You didn't need to know to exit the house."

"Maybe I was just interested in how the mechanism worked. Even if I was interested you could not afford me."

"So you are interested?"

"I never said that, but if and only if I was, it would be at least twenty-five k."

"I will see you for coffee tomorrow morning, you know where and you know when."

As Luke put his finger on the end call icon the reality of the last few minutes sank in, He had controlled the conversation and put Kent on the back foot. Hopefully tomorrow morning he could keep the same momentum. Tonight, however, would be an early night for he now had an early alarm and long drive awaiting him in the morning.

"So you are here then, Kent."

"Likewise yourself, Luke. I am surprised that you can afford twenty-five thousand."

"I am willing to offer you ten thousand."

"Well, I said twenty-five, and that was if and only if, I was interested, so I guess we have both had a wasted morning coming here."

"No, Kent, I don't think I have. You see I don't believe that you really expected me to pay twenty-five k. I am willing to offer you ten thousand, no negotiation. I need to get as many of those remaining documents as I can and you want to go back and explore more, goodness knows what else is there. This way you get to have your second exploration and with ten thousand tax free in your pocket, is that not a win-win for us both?"

Luke paused for a moment, hoping Kent would not butt in and break his verbal stride.

"And by the way, if you don't agree then I will be going back by myself: I will hire somebody else to take me there and back by boat. I can't pick a lock but by God I will find a way of breaking in, and if I am caught and the police get involved, then I would be forced to tell the truth, you know about being here before with you and that situation would not be good for either of us."

Kent looked blankly at Luke; this was not the same person he had first dealt with. Luke could see Kent was planning his next tactical move, but he was unprepared for Kent's question.

"I am not about stealing stuff. You would have seen from my videos that I never take anything that does not belong to me. So cut the crap and just tell me exactly what was in the files that you took the other day?"

Caught off guard and finding himself now having to think on his feet, Luke's mouth went into bullshit mode as he told Kent what he wanted to hear whilst fully aware, that he needed to keep it realistic.

"Family documents, there was an issue many years ago that split my family in two, a division that still exists to this day, two plus generations later. I believe the blame lies not with anyone in my family but rather with another person, someone associated with this house. I want to heal old family wounds if I can, but I do need those documents."

"I guess with the Nazi flag there, and your family obviously being Jewish, I can see why whoever was there may have had an issue with your relatives."

Kent now looked Luke directly in the eye.

"Are you telling me the whole truth, Luke?"

For a man who showed little emotion, Kent appeared genuinely sympathetic, but it was sympathy based on a partial lie and now Luke felt extremely uncomfortable as he confirmed the false statement. Guilt prompted him to suddenly increase his offer to Kent.

"I will pay you fifteen thousand if you agree."

"You said ten thousand before, and I will agree to that, but only on my terms; Just like last time we go when I say go and we leave when I say leave and I have the right to abandon the visit any time I feel we need to retreat or take cover. I will not be removing anything from the house. You can take the small rucksack you took before and you can only take what you can put inside with the zipper closed. But only the files that you need to sort your family issue and nothing else. I want the ten thousand in my account by midnight tonight and additionally this will be the last time ever, and I mean ever, that we will go there. Afterwards our association is over so no more contact unless I initiate it. In fact if anybody was to ask, we have never met. Do you agree fully?"

"I agree."

The long drive back was an opportunity to reflect on the lies that Luke had told Kent.

If this all comes out in the open when the story is published then Kent will know it had nothing to do with my family and I don't think he will be very happy. But what choice did I have. Nothing that I write will make any mention of his name and anyway, he will have his ten thousand.

No matter how hard Luke tried to rephrase his words to justify the situation, he could not overcome the guilt of lying to Kent.

Chapter 26
(February 1941)

It had been eleven months since Eric Linderman had first met Geoffrey DeVilliers back on Saturday, 16 March, at his St Patricks Day party. The evening of the sixteenth had not been a time for in depth conversations; it was rather an opportunity for making contacts and to work out who was of enough value to spend the time and effort to manipulate. Eric knew only too well that popularity was a very fickle subject; one week your place and event was the place to be seen, the next week you could be yesterday's news. Eric and his wife, Edith, had to work hard; their house had to be a fun place that people wanted to come back to.

Geoffrey was not a man of big physical stature, but he was a big man in the world of influencing politicians. A secured friendship with him was of the utmost importance; in fact he was probably the number one person that Eric needed to get on side with that evening.

The two struck an initial bond that evening that saw Geoffrey returning to Eric's estate in October later that year for a more informal party of six guests and their wife's. It was at this event that Eric cunningly allowed Geoffrey to let his guard down just enough for Eric to see an opening into his heavily guarded thoughts. The conversation had started on the subject of private schools and how it was not just the academic advantages, but the self-discipline and higher personal standards that pupils set themselves that made them better people. As the conversation progressed, a bit of careful manipulation by Eric found the topic of conversation focussed on the punishments administered by various private schools, in particular caning.

Now a further four months on, Geoffrey DeVilliers and his wife Betty had accepted Eric's third invitation to visit. This time it was just the two couples and now Eric was preparing to take a big chance. If he got it right then Geoffrey DeVilliers would be his, but if he got it wrong, then Eric could lose everything that he had worked for.

Waiting until a fourth visit just to be sure would have been the safe option but Eric did not have the luxury of time on his side. Geoffrey DeVilliers was a busy man, and any further visits were not guaranteed or there was the possibility that Geoffrey might insist that the Linderman's visit them, something that would be a waste of time. Eric knew tonight was the night that he had to make his move.

As the four figures sat around the large table, the conversation flowed as freely as the wine. Eric was using all his skills to mirror Geoffrey, that is, without making things to obvious. Eric's efforts were well executed as Geoffrey found himself feeling more and more comfortable with the man who apparently saw life in the same way that he did.

Dessert followed the main course which in turn which in turn was followed by coffee and a glass of fine port.

As planned, Edith initiated the split between the men and women, inviting Betty to view some of her fine needlework in the sewing room. This was now the cue for Eric to invite Geoffrey to the front library for a drink of Eric's favourite McDrumond's, and it was here that Eric made his move to get the conversation back on track.

"I think it will be a very different world that we live in if we get involved with the war, and I am not just talking about the obvious effect that war and its casualties will have on our country, but rather the change in social attitudes."

"It's almost as if you read my mind, Eric. I can see exactly what is going to happen: women will end up working as if it was a normal situation. Long gone will be the days of the home wife caring for the children. Men will also return from overseas after having been exposed to lesser cultures; it will water down the good name of the American man. America needs good leaders of industry and good leadership, and this comes from good self-discipline."

Eric was quick to reinforce Geoffrey's thoughts.

"And self-discipline starts from discipline at school. It not only teaches you right from wrong, but also that for every action there is a consequence, a good action gets a good consequence and the same with bad."

"Yes, we talked about this last time, Eric."

"You are right, we did, and that got me thinking about how I am the man that I am today because I was disciplined at school. For us it was the cane and that meant a visit to Mr Karl, the deputy head teacher and the man who administered it. A call to Mr Karl's office inevitably meant between one and twelve strokes, depending on the nature of the offence. I learned just how important personal grooming was. It was one stroke if your tie was not done correctly, two strokes for dirty shoes that were not polished and two strokes if you were caught with your shirt not tucked in. Any ripped clothing incurred three strokes. Then of course there were the serious offences: swearing, fighting, talking back, not completing homework or being late for class without a good reason, everything had its repercussions. There always seemed to be a boy in Mr Karl's office bending over ready to receive the cane."

Eric was carefully watching the expression on Geoffrey's face as he finished his sentence and he was not disappointed; it was exactly the expression that he was hoping for.

"Well, Eric, for me it was Mr Anderson. At about six foot six, he was a terrifyingly large man, with snow white hair and of Scandinavian heritage. Everyone was scared of him. Mr Anderson was a man you definitely didn't want to get on the wrong side of.

"Like your Mr Karl, our Mr Anderson was the administrator of the cane. Our school limited the punishment to twelve strokes, but in saying that Eric Mr Anderson wielded the cane with such ferocity that I think twelve of his strokes would equate to about fifteen of any normal man."

"Tell me, Geoffrey, were there any boys at your school that you hated? I had this boy in my class, Bobby Sinclair was his name, and he was a nasty character. Bobby always seemed to get away with things by putting the blame onto others. I think a good quarter of my punishment was a result of his actions, it just seemed so unfair at the time."

"Yes, there is always one like that and for me it was Freddy Smith, he was so cunning. None of the boys at the school were poor by any means, but Freddy's parents were so unbelievably wealthy that he thought that he was above everybody else and consequently could get away with anything, and somehow he just seemed to do just that. When Mr Anderson appeared at your class door I always used to wish that it was Freddy's name that he was going to call out, but it was usually someone else. I remember that evil grin of satisfaction Freddy would have every time someone else got called up for something that he had done."

Eric sighed and took another sip of whisky before replying.

"Life is so funny at times, Geoffrey, in some ways life is a continuation of one generation to the next. Take for example a skilled craftsman, perhaps a furniture maker in a family business. The grandfather teaches the son the skills that he needs, and then the son grows up, has his own children and then passes these skills on to the grandson who will, in turn, pass the information to his son and so on through life. But when we relate that to the Mr Karls or Mr Andersons of this world, we realise that they knew that they were passing on a good sense of values, the same that were passed down to them, and that they were values that would help that person later in life. Unfortunately we or the rest of his pupils don't get a chance to pass that on ourselves.

"Sometimes I have fantasised about caning Bobby Sinclair, hoping that it would turn him into a better person. Do you ever think about doing the same to Freddy Smith?"

Geoffrey looked a bit embarrassed but decided since Eric had been honest so should he.

"I have never really thought about it but since you mentioned it, perhaps I actually do."

"I knew it: we are alike."

Both men laughed suddenly; for Geoffrey it was safe to open up.

"So tell me, Geoffrey, if Freddy Smith were here today, would you have any issues with caning him?"

"No, I don't think I would. In fact it would be a very rewarding experience."

"I thought that might be your answer. Please follow me down to a part of the house that very few are privileged to see."

As they entered the downstairs room Geoffrey could not help but express his amazement.

"This room it's large enough to hold a party and I would have had no idea that it existed. Tell me, Eric, what is behind that curtain?"

"Funny you should ask, let me introduce you to an acquaintance of mine."

Eric pulled back the curtain to reveal a man tied to a wooden frame; the contraption was designed to position the man slightly bent forward with his arms and legs firmly attached to the frame with leather straps rendering him unable to move. The sight of the restrained man caught Geoffrey totally off guard.

"Eric, what is this all about?"

"I can't give you Freddy Smith, but I can give you the next best thing. This man's name is Clarence, and he is a true masochist, he absolutely loves being caned. In fact he often actually pays people to cane him, so when a friend told me about him I thought this could be a win-win situation. You can cane your Freddy Smith substitute and Clarence won't need to pay for it."

"I am not sure about this, Eric, it's all wrong; there is a big difference between talking about things and actually carrying these fantasies out."

"That's a shame. I promised Clarence that you would be keen, now he will be disappointed. If you were to help him out with what he is hoping for then nobody will ever find out. You are perfectly safe here. It is a soundproof area and Clarence is certainly not going to tell."

Geoffrey looked towards the bound and gagged man, totally unaware that his cooperative nature was primarily due to the fact that he had been heavily drugged. The young man was not struggling so he must be happy and as Eric had said, who was going to know?"

"OK then, I will do it for him. I would hate to disappoint him if it's really what he wants."

"I knew you would. Here, take this."

Eric passed Geoffrey a cane. It was long and flexible, with one end bound in leather to act as a handgrip. Geoffrey took the cane and examined it, before testing its flexibility; slowly and deliberately he bent it back and forth. Eric realised this was a delaying tactic whilst he took in the situation, and he had to act quickly before Geoffrey changed his mind.

"I imagine that it is just like the one Mr Anderson used on you."

"Yes, it is similar, from what I can remember."

"Well it's the one Clarence particularly likes, so please go ahead, give Clarence what he wants."

Geoffrey positioned himself behind the young man before raising the cane to execute the hit. As the cane came down it was apparent that he had subconsciously slowed the momentum of the implement down before the point of impact which considerably decreased the force of the cane against the young man's trousers.

"How did that feel, Geoffrey?"

"Actually it felt quite strange."

"I know why it didn't feel special, it was because you were not committed. Think of yourself on the golf course. You are about to drive down the fairway. You raise your club, line up the target and execute the shot. As the club comes all the way towards the golf ball you keep the maximum energy of the swing as you follow through and therefore completing the shot as it was meant to be played. What you don't do is slow the club just before the moment of impact. It's the same here; you need to follow through. That is what Clarence wants."

Realising his subconscious reluctance to execute the task with maximum force, Geoffrey just nodded to acknowledge Eric's observations.

"One other thing, did Mr Anderson cane you through your trousers? Because I had to pull mine down. Mr Karl used to say he wasn't here to damage a school uniform."

"Yes, I had to as pull my trousers down as well."

"Then I think you should do the same, pull his trousers down."

Geoffrey willingly obliged as he found himself filled with an unexpected but heightened sexual arousal. Eric, well aware that he was now fully in control of the situation, passed Geoffrey a pen.

"Write Freddy Smith on his underpants, you need to be sure that you know who you are caning."

Once again Geoffrey obliged before smiling; seeing that name made the experience all the more real. As he executed the second stroke Geoffrey found himself again involuntarily pulling back just before the moment of impact and once again Eric found himself having to provide the encouragement needed for Geoffrey's third stroke.

This time Geoffrey followed through all the way, as he spoke out: "You need to be punished, Freddy."

Geoffrey had broken the barrier that lay between reality and a dark aspect of his mind. There would be no more holding back. A surge of adrenalin pulsed through his veins at the sound of the impact as the fourth and fifth blows were executed with violent enthusiasm.

"I think that is enough. I don't want to injure him."

"You won't, Geoffrey. I used to get up to twelve strokes and I survived. Clarence told me he enjoys either twelve really hard strokes or up to fifteen medium ones, and by my count, that's only three hard and two medium. You have a way to go yet."

After another three full-force hits, Geoffrey stopped again.

"Geoffrey, I really think you need to show the school how Freddy is being punished for all those things that he did at your expense. Pull down his underpants and show the school the marks on his bum, pretend you are doing this in front of the school assembly."

The situation had become a macabre role play that Geoffrey had allowed himself to be drawn right into. Reality had faded into the acting out of the revenge fantasy and common sense had long since departed Geoffrey's mind as he pulled the young man's underpants down and lifted his shirt to clearly show the red welts that were starting to form on his bare skin. Stepping back he turned to face the imaginary school audience, totally unaware he was now looking directly into the lens of a camera.

"Great, now finish the caning, make it thirteen, because two were only soft."

Geoffrey nodded and went to pull the man's underpants back up.

"No, make it on the bare flesh as that is what Clarence likes."

The five remaining strokes were administered enthusiastically as Geoffrey counted them out

"Nine... ten... eleven... twelve... thirteen... That's it, Freddy. Your punishment is complete."

There was both a sense of satisfaction and a heightened sexual arousal was still present as Geoffrey turned to face his host. Eric, however, had not yet finished with the manipulation of his guest.

"Rub your hands over the welts; you will be able to feel the pain that Freddy is feeling."

A very unconvincing, "No," from Geoffrey told Eric what he had suspected.

"Go on, do it, feel the pain you have inflicted. He deserved it and you will never have another chance to feel how you have punished him for all those things he did. I know that you want to."

Eric's permission now overruled any reluctance that Geoffrey had to carrying out the remainder of the bizarre fantasy. Slowly and carefully Geoffrey slid his right hand over the raised red marks on the skin of his victim. He could feel each one, and knew each one was the result of his actions and a punishment for a person long removed from his life. As Geoffrey slowly caressed each raised mark, it felt so wrong but also so good. A few hours ago he would never have dreamt this would have happened but now it was all real.

Now filled with mixed emotions of excitement and concern about what he had just done, Geoffrey's mind intertwined with the sheer perversity of the situation, and hidden pathways into the dark corners of his mind opened up as he felt overwhelmed with the ongoing sexual arousal, a type of arousal that he had never felt before. Apart from his long suffering wife, Geoffrey had sexually indulged with an amassed collection of prostitutes over the years, some possessing quite unique skills, but nothing had ever made him feel like he did at this point of time. It was so wrong but because it was wrong it was right. Suddenly Geoffrey realised that he could bear it no longer.

"Is there a bathroom handy?"

Eric pointed down to the other end of the room, prompting Geoffrey to walk briskly down in the indicated direction. It was approximately ten minutes later when Geoffrey returned. He was red in the face completely flustered and obviously deeply embarrassed.

"Where's Clarence?"

The man was now not around and the frame that he was tied to was visibly empty.

"I untied him he and he left; he appeared to be very happy and said it was just what he needed."

"Oh, I didn't realise I was away that long."

"No problem. Come upstairs. I think we could both do with a good whisky before we rejoin the ladies."

It was two a.m. when Eric and Peter descended the stairs to the lower room. Geoffrey and Betty's room for the night was on the second floor and at the back of the house. After closing the door to the downstairs room Eric knew that nothing that was about to happen would be heard by his guest.

The two brothers pushed the empty frame to the side of the room and back out of view before opening the door to an adjacent room, and dragging out the original wooden frame which still contained the unconscious body of the young man. Carefully placing the frame in the original position that it had been previously located, they were now ready to carry out the second part of their sick plan.

During the whisky session a few hours earlier, Eric had secretly indicated to Peter to turn up the library heating, something that had prompted Geoffrey to remove his distinctive diamond patterned cardigan, the same cardigan that Eric now had in his possession and was proceeding to put on.

Eric indicated to his brother positioned behind the one-way glass mirror. "Are you ready, Peter?"

Peter nodded to himself before proceeding to position the movie camera so that only an arm in the distinctive cardigan was visible. The clatter from the camera's Geneva cam indicated the apparatus was now rolling through its yards of still unexposed film. Eric now continued to administer the beating on the helpless victim at the same rate that Geoffrey had but with a now heightened ferocity that soon started to split the skin of the helpless victim as the wounds intersected. The continued impacts soon sent splatters of blood flying as raw flesh was now exposed.

Finally, Eric stopped the macabre assault, stepping back to allow Peter to focus the cameras lens on the raw torn flesh that once was smooth skin.

"Now look what you have done, Geoffrey. You are a naughty boy and really did take this too far."

Eric laughed at his own macabre joke. Happy that Peter would have completed his filming, he stepped forward, checking for signs of life from the victim who had long passed out from the overwhelming pain. The opening and closing of a door indicated Peter was now back in the main room.

"Seems he is still alive, Peter. Some of these Jews are just so hard to kill. I don't think he will still be alive tomorrow when we come to clean up this mess. We can't afford to take any chances. Just in case, I will do him a favour end his miserable life now."

A nearby pillow smothered the last faint signs of life out of the young man as Eric turned to Peter.

"Well, brother, that is one less Jew on the Earth. It's good we are able to help our Führer cleanse the Earth of animals like him, isn't it?"

Peter nodded but said nothing.

"Well, I wasn't lying when I told Geoffrey that Clarence or whatever this Jew boy's name is, would not be telling anybody what happened. Now it's bedtime, Peter. Sleep well, we have a lot of cleaning up to do down here in the morning after Geoffrey leaves."

Eric looked at the cardigan that he had now removed.

"Oh shit."

Peter looked down to notice that the cardigan had marks from several splatters of blood; bed would have to wait till they had this unexpected issue sorted.

Sliding between the sheets on the left hand side of the bed, Eric Linderman was pleased to finally be in bed. It had been a long day and now all he wanted before going to sleep was some intimate time with his beautiful wife. As he started to talk about their plans for the following morning, his right hand slowly slid down to caress his wife's inner thigh.

Instead of allowing his fingers to work their magic, Edith turned, moving Eric's hand away in the process before interrupting her husband's words for her own.

"I have been thinking even when the war in Europe is over and Germany stands victorious, you do realise that we will still have a big part to play."

Eric realised that this was one of his wife's prophetic moments; she was a deep thinker and now was one of those times that she needed to share her thoughts. Eric knew that if he was going to have any chance of making love to his wife it would only be after a deep and meaningful discussion.

"I guess you are correct but what specifically are you referring to?"

"All those years ago when the winds of change started in the Fatherland, we realised like many other good Germans that it would take war to cleanse Europe. Remember how we both realised that America must never be an enemy, that is, until Europe had been cleansed and the Fatherland had time to rebuild its strength. How right we were in the plans that we made to help this happen.

"And now that war is upon us, as our Führer starts the liberation of Europe our timing is critical. Once we start to act upon what we have there is no going back."

"When do you think we should make our move? Do we have enough evidence on enough people? Or do we wait longer? I trust your intellect, Edith, you have always been right."

"Not yet, Eric. I believe we can still gather more material for once our secret is exposed our lives will be very different. I hope that we will never have to use what we have, diplomacy is always the best option, but what we have will be our insurance policy in case the mood starts to swing the wrong way."

"That is exactly what I was hoping you would say, Edith. Hopefully, after the victory, the Führer decides not to attack America but rather live side by side?"

"That will not happen, Eric. Once the war is won do you think the Führer will tolerate the excesses of American capitalism with its lust for wealth, greed and self-indulgence? Lack of self-control will be the downfall of America. Look at Pilkington and Boyd, two men willing to sacrifice all they have for a couple of hours of unnatural lust. Americans are weak. Those who are strong will be led by the weak and their strength will mean nothing.

"I have no doubt about a final victory for Germany, we just have to look at how Europe is falling to its knees, but as I said before we will still have a big part to play. We need to know who to pursue and who to keep for when the inevitable happens and the Fatherland fights for control of America. Tomorrow I think we should revaluate our master plan, look at what we already have and how we can best use it just in case the political mood in Washington starts to change."

"As always, my dear wife, you are right. I tell everyone I love America and Germany equally but that is not true, and I feel bad each time I say those untrue words. You know where my true loyalties lie and when the inevitable happens everyone will have to pick a side, then I will show my true loyalties."

Edith started to laugh, noting that her husband looked concerned as if her humour was initiated by something that he had said.

"I am not laughing at you, it's just a thought crossed my mind. Americans will be told that they are fighting for their country but unlike Germans they will find themselves fighting and dying for the powerful industrialists. American soldiers will look up to the mighty German onslaught which will be fighting for their true convictions."

Chapter 27
(Early November 2019)

Although the water was calmer, the boat trip from the departure point at the beach to the base of the cliff face seemed somehow a lot longer than Luke remembered. But now with the dinghy safely secured and the two men ready to make the ascent, Kent felt obliged to go over the rules one last time.

Luke listened intently to what he had already heard more than once before.

"Are you quite clear then?"

"Yes, fully understood. There is one thing though—can we enter the basement via the garage like we did before? We have explored the house and the basement room, but we have only had a quick look at what was in the garage, we could have missed something important."

Although planning to enter via the internal passageway from the house that he now knew how to access the lower room, Kent surprisingly seemed receptive to the idea as Luke's suggestion made perfect sense. Luke, however, had a totally different reason for wanting to enter via the garage. He had unfinished business with what lay under the large dust cover.

With their prior knowledge of the grounds and the building layout, accessing the garage was a much quicker task the second time around. With the door closed behind them Kent started to make his way around what was a well packed area. Many of the garage's contents drew his attention. Apart from the cars there was in one corner a collection of old furniture including a couple of wardrobes packed tightly with clothes. In addition to checking the contents of the garage, Kent was also checking for any signs of other hidden entrances or compartments.

With Kent still engrossed with his discoveries Luke saw the opportunity to slip away to the other end adjacent to the house and close to their intended entrance to the basement.

For Luke the last couple of days had seen much soul searching; he knew he must put an end to the fear that still lingered inside and confronting your demons head on was only one way to do that. Despite the fact that it would be a challenge easier said than done, this would also be the last time ever that he would have the opportunity to carry out what he needed to do.

As he approached his adversary Luke listened intently for any sounds of life from what he knew was just an imamate object. The silence was both calming and overwhelming, no evil hissing or chugging, just silence in its purest form.

Empowered with a new sense of confidence, Luke moved forward slowly to within inches of the covered contraption. The dust cover, after sitting untouched for decades, was noticeably stiff and almost moulded over the easily distinguishable front of the fenders and grill.

Lifting the dust cover it was no surprise to see the six headlights that stared back at him like the eyes of a giant insect watching him from its lair. Raising the cover a little further exposed the rest of the once shiny grille and the badge proudly displaying the initials of its manufacturer, OMD.

It would have been all too easy to place the cover back or to just look away, but rather drawing from all of his inner strength Luke, stared back at the once pinnacle of German automotive engineering before stepping forward to place both hands on its grille.

"I know you drew me here for a reason and I also know you can't hurt me as you are nothing more than a collection of metal parts. I am not scared of you any more, so I call a truce."

Hearing a noise behind him Luke turned sharply to see that Kent had been observing his actions.

"What the hell are you doing, Luke? You are not going to go stupid on me, are you? Because if you are losing it, then we are out of here."

"No, not at all, it's something that I just had to do but it's all sorted now. I think we should move on now, I want to use my time wisely."

"Wait."

Kent's words halted Luke in his tracks.

"So this then is the bus that terrified you. Now, it appears you are not scared of it any more, according to what I just heard you say that is, so prove it."

"What do you mean?"

"I mean prove you are not scared of it, by going inside."

"That's not necessary, Kent."

Kent put his finger to his lips to indicate that Luke was starting to speak to loudly, before replying quietly.

"But, Luke, I think it is, and anyway, I would like to see inside it myself."

Kent proceeded to lift up the dust cover that hid the right-hand side exposing its chrome and glass doorway. Just like the adjacent three cars, the dustsheets had kept the vehicle clean and to a degree protected. However, time itself still serves a punishment to all things mechanical.

Turning the chrome handle that was positioned aft of the doorway, Kent proceeded to push on the centre of the bi-folding entranceway. To his surprise, in a testament to the skill of the long-departed German engineers, the door slid open with ease, exposing the cabin's interior to fresh air for the first time in many decades.

"In you go then, Luke:"

Kent spoke quietly but firmly as he indicated for his charge to proceed in. Hoping that his guide would have taken the lead and gone in first would have been too much to ask as Luke's foot took the weight of his body on the first step. A version of his first dream played out in his thoughts as the potential consequences of what could happen if the door would close behind him, presented itself.

No that is silly, Luke boldly told himself. *And anyway, I have made a truce with it, the bus wanted me here and I came. It knows I am here to find what it wants me to find, so why would it do anything that might stop me. And it can't drive off, it's in an enclosed garage.*

Luke turned to check that Kent was still behind him; fortunately for him, unlike his dream Kent was and he was indicating for Luke to go fully in.

Luke knew exactly how the interior would be, and behind the stale air was the sight of once proud luxury. The leather seats still looked comfortable despite being covered with a thin layer of mouldy grime.

"This is just amazing, it's like new, I bet if it was all cleaned up there would be very little work required to make it a collector's dream."

After walking to the front to check the driver's compartment Kent returned.

"Stay inside, I am going out and just shutting the door for a moment."

"No, I will come out too."

"Trust me on this, Luke. I have been in many dangerous situations, and I have seen fear in men's eyes. The only way to beat fear is to face it head on, so do this or we are not going in the house."

Luke was stunned with the ultimatum; he had paid this man a lot of money for a specific purpose and now he was threatening to renege on the deal.

"I mean it, Luke."

Kent placed his hand on Luke's shoulder.

"I know you have made a truce with your fear, something represented by this vehicle, but you haven't conquered it, I am putting my trust in you because if you freak out we could both get discovered. Don't let me down, Luke."

And with that Kent stepped backwards onto the garage floor, closing the door behind him. There was a brief moment when Luke could feel himself getting ready to scream then nothing, absolutely nothing; there was no chugging sound, no indication of the bus moving, and it was just like being in any normal suburban bus.

As Kent pushed the door back open he looked directly at Luke. Kent was a hard, tough man but for a brief moment Luke saw softness in his eyes as he softly spoke.

"Good man, Luke, I knew you could conquer it."

After a brief pause in which Luke could tell the previous sentence was not complete, Kent spoke again.

"Many years ago an old man helped me conquer a life limiting fear that I had. Perhaps one day you can pass it on and do the same for somebody else."

"Thanks," was the only word that Luke could mutter; it was a word that seemed far too inadequate for what his companion had just done.

"OK, Luke, let's get this closed up and recovered. I have a policy of whenever possible, leaving things how I found them. It might be abandoned but it still does not belong to us and there is someone who will have legal claim to all of this. Treat other people's property the way we would want them to treat ours."

Just like their entry into the garage, opening the remaining locks that stood between them and the basement proved to be a much easier task for Kent the second time round. Once inside the lower room Luke was now anxious to get back into the annex room containing all the documents, but with the hidden passageway and a locked door between him and the room, his itinerary in the basement he was still at Kent's mercy.

"I want to check out what is under all those covers behind the stage area and also see if I can have a look under the stage. You just never know what might be waiting to be found in this strange place."

The removal of the dust sheets exposed a collection of items including chairs, more wardrobes filled with clothes, lots of partitions and even mannequins when suddenly Kent's attention was drawn to a wooden frame about seven feet high. Adjacent to it on the floor was another part which could clearly be affixed to the first part to form a cross like structure. Steel rings were bolted to the wooden frame at various locations and onto each ring was attached a leather strap. Kent moved over to whisper to Luke.

"Look at this, Luke, it's like some sort of medieval torture device that someone could be tied to and beaten. With all the items we saw in the storeroom last time and now this! I would really like to think that had another purpose. Logic, however, tells me there was probably some bad shit happening down here, and that makes me very uncomfortable. With this family situation that you are trying to sort out, whoever it was that caused the trouble that split your family must have been an evil bastard. I just hope you know what you are doing. Sometimes things from the past are not worth the trouble of trying to fix. What I am saying is be careful; when it comes to this place there is something terribly wrong and I am getting some very bad vibes."

Luke cringed; there was no way that he could tell Kent his reason for being here had nothing to do with a split family situation.

Disappointingly a small door in the back of the stage assembly only confirmed that it was modular and was both movable and adjustable without being part of the room.

"Nothing there, Luke, nevertheless it was worth a look, eh! I know what you're here for so let's get you in that room."

Until now Kent had kept a close eye on his companion and consequently Luke fully expected Kent to follow him inside.

"I have a wedge to put under the door so that it won't close. I'm going to go back up top as there are a few things I want to check out again. I will leave you to do your research and I will be back down in about fifteen minutes. Do not under any circumstances leave this room, I need to know where to find you. Oh and one last thing, don't forget I never steal stuff so don't let me see anything in your hands when I get back."

Luke knew exactly what Kent meant. The rucksack was not very large. There was absolutely no way he would get everything in, and he had only fifteen minutes to work out what those few items would be. The remaining items could at best only be photographed.

Kent's return saw his companion staring into a doorway hidden behind the desk. Luke had his selected documents and had just finished repacking the boxes after photographing their contents when he had dropped his torch. Bending down to retrieve it he noticed that the illumination of the torch's beam had highlighted an unlocked doorway. Although the door was small it opened into a large cut-out section of dirt behind the room they were in.

Moving a shocked Luke aside, Kent positioned himself to look in. Some wooden battens were positioned to keep a number of wooden boxes from the dampness of the ground; each box was about three feet long, approximately eighteen inches wide, and about eighteen inches high. Each box was painted black and on the top in white paint was crudely painted a Star of David with either the words Jude-F or Jude-M.

Neither man spoke; there was a cold feeling emanating from the space as they stared inwards. It was a feeling that sent a shiver down their spines as neither would dare to mention to what could be contained within each box.

"Close that door, put the desk back and quickly put everything back as you found it. We are getting the hell out of here now."

Kent's words brought a feeling of relief to Luke. He had what he needed and now wanted to be anywhere except in this house. Grabbing his rucksack, he prepared to follow his guide firstly into the passageway then, after removing the wedge and locking the door, they followed the passage into the main underground room, and from there to the cliff face accessing tunnel.

With the steel door now closed behind there was an initial sense of relief. This, however, was short lived as Kent hesitated, whilst a look of horror now filled his face.

"Shit, shit, shit!"

"What's wrong?"

Kent was a man who never made mistakes in his military career—a mistake could be the difference between life and death—but now totally thrown by what he had seen he had done something worthy of a novice: he had left his camera bag inside the room. Kent knew exactly where it was, but its retrieval required access back into the house and back down into the basement. Kent could not believe that he had done something so stupid as he continued to curse himself.

"I have to go back, you proceed on to the dinghy and wait for me. I am going back inside and into the basement again, and after I have re-closed the tunnel door I will still need to go up and retrieve my distraction devices. Then we get the hell out of this godforsaken place. So go, wait for me quietly and do not move away from the dinghy as I won't be long, understood?"

"Yes, Kent, all understood."

Barely at the dinghy, Luke suddenly turned around to the sounds of shouting followed by three gunshots which in turn were followed by two explosions that for a split second illuminated the dark cliff top.

Adrenalin fired Luke's heart to burst into an unsustainable rhythm as he grabbed the dinghy and with superhuman strength threw it into the water. This proved to be a good decision as an exasperated Kent rushed down the path and dived straight in. With the motor now powering them away from the shore, the sound of gunshots could still be heard.

Chapter 28

"I am sorry, Uncle, but this is all I have. Kent would only let me take a backpack and there was only so much that I could carry out of the house in it. Kent refused to take anything himself so it was only what I could fit inside. There is so much more there including lots of canisters of film, but they were very heavy. I took some more files that appear related to individual people. I obviously can't read German but assuming they relate to the images that are on the photographs that were with them, then it is going to make for some interesting reading. Just like Earl White's photos, most of the images can only be described as either extremely bizarre or pornographic. With the limited time I had I was able to find some documents that appeared to be more general. Hopefully these files will hold clues, but I do have some photos as well."

"Luke, calm down, take a deep breath and speak slower."

Errol took the box that his nephew had put the contents of the backpack into; walking into his dining room he carefully placed the box on the solid oak table that proudly stood as the centrepiece of the large room. Saying nothing, he removed the lid and took out one cardboard folder before opening it and examining its contents.

Luke waited eagerly for any response; would Uncle Errol now share the true meaning of what information he was looking for? If all this information was just incriminating blackmail material on a bunch of people, all of whom would have died a number of years ago, then how would that be of concern to a man who would have been just a boy at the time? There was, however, no response as his uncle carefully skimmed over several pages before returning the contents to the file and repeating the procedure with a second cardboard envelope. After what seemed a very long time, Errol broke his concentration as he turned to his nephew.

"This is everything that you have, is that correct?"

"Yes it is, you have everything that I was able to take on both my first and second visit, apart from the photos. I will send those to your email later. There was a lot more there but unfortunately there will not be any more visits to collect anything else as we ran into some trouble."

"Trouble, what happened?"

Errol looked deeply concerned at the use of the T word; his facial expression told Luke he demanded an answer. Luke knew that he had no choice but to relay the details.

"As we left Kent realised he had left some of his gear in the room under the house. He was preparing to go back when he was disturbed by one of the security guards, We managed to get away safely but Kent was concerned that if found, the gear could be traced back to him. But I think even if someone got into the house they would not be able to access the lower rooms. I don't know if Kent will ever go back to get his gear, but I can say with one hundred percent certainty that he will not be taking me, no matter how much money I offer him."

"So do they know who you were?"

"No, we got away, but it was close, Luckily Kent had placed a couple of small explosive devices up top that he was able to activate remotely with his phone. It gave enough time to give us a head start. Afterwards Kent told me that's why he would only let me take a small backpack."

"Well let's hope you are right then. Now you must go as I have much work to do. It is going to be a long night for me. You must tell no one about this yet, come back at six tomorrow evening when we can go over what we are going to do."

"One thing before I go, I found something else under the house."

Luke took a deep breath before continuing#, aware that his words could cause his uncle great distress.

Seeing Skip at work presented Luke with a dilemma: should he say anything yet or wait for the full story from his uncle that evening? Luke decided to hold off until he had all the details on what exactly he had collected.

Uncle Errol was very sombre as he opened the door. Although keen to hear what his uncle had read, Luke realised he should not appear to be excited as something was deeply troubling his uncle.

"I will make us a coffee."

On his return Errol carefully placed two cups and matching saucers onto the table before emptying the contents of the coffee jug and the small jug of cream.

Errol looked Luke directly in the eye before commencing that which he had been preparing all day.

"You know me as an old man, but I was young once just like you are now. Going even further back I was once a young, frightened boy. You probably won't know this but we both share a sad coincidence. I also lost my father when I was young, in fact, at a very similar age to you, but unlike you my sister did know her dad. I was three and Ruth was two when my father died. Unfortunately he had a lot of debt to his name, so when his creditors started lining up to take any assets that they could, my mum was left with basically nothing except the clothes that she and her children were wearing. My mother was a proud woman but was forced to concede that her only option was to move back in with her parents.

"My grandparents did not have a lot of money and my mother worked hard to put food on the table for the four of us. Then one day, she never came home. It was a cold day in October 1941, and I had only just turned four. At that age, I only have limited memories, but I was old enough to remember watching my grandparents stare at the meal that was waiting for her on the table. The meal that got colder and colder as it stood waiting to be eaten, but it never was. I also remember the large police officer putting me on his knee as he said things that I really did not fully understand.

"I was fourteen when my nan died almost exactly a year after my pop left this world; it was the first time that I had no one to look after me.

"That was the point when I vowed that I would look after my sister Ruth. For as long as she lived on God's green Earth, I would make sure she had a roof over her head, and that holds just as true today.

"My nan and pop had instilled good work and life ethics in me, and I was determined to rise above what life had thrown at me. Hard work and a good attitude to life helped me gain respect and set my life in a positive direction. I remember my pop telling me that no matter what the situation, if you leave somewhere in a better condition than when you found it then life will always reward you, maybe not straight away but one day. Luke, his words were true, life did give me back what I put in plus interest.

"When I was twenty-two, fate intervened into my life. I had quite by chance befriended an elderly ex police officer, Joe 'Tortoise' Turner. Joe was known as Tortoise because he never rushed into things, rather he was slow and methodical, and this always got him his results. One thing led to another as he shared the story about a collection of unsolved disappearances of people in the early forties, one of them being my mother.

"From what Tortoise told, me plus my own research done a long time ago, I discovered that over an eighteen-month period from June nineteen-forty to December nineteen-forty-one there were fourteen people of Jewish heritage who went unaccountably missing, male and female, all aged between seventeen and thirty-five, and all within a two hundred mile radius of the Lindermans' house.

"We talked, we shared, and I became obsessed with finding out what had happened to my mum and the others, Joe's suspicions had fallen on Eric Linderman at the time, but he could never prove anything. In fact he had found himself blocked at the highest levels from following through any further."

"The files I gave you, have they proved anything?"

"Not directly with regards to my mother but after reading what you gave me my level of suspicion could now not be any higher.

"Let me start by telling you everything that I now know. I have already told you that both Eric and Edith Linderman were born in Germany and although they came to the States when they were young, they both maintained a strong association with their German heritage. Evidently from the moment they met they were inseparable, right up to dying together. After marrying Edith, Eric moved her into the family home with his parents and Eric's reclusive young brother Peter.

"After his parents died, Eric spent a long time totally refurbishing the family home with most of the labourers coming over from Germany to work on the house. It would not be hard to conclude that the secrets that they built into the refurbished house went back to Germany with them and remained unknown to anyone else, except by those who were invited down and even then they would only be privy to part of what the house contained.

"I think you would also have read that Eric and Edith were extreme extroverts and nobody was outside their ability to be charmed by them. Slowly and surely they would have expanded their social circle to include some very rich, powerful and influential people. Nobody turned down an invitation to the Lindermans', and the spell that they seemed to be able to put over people.

"And now, Luke, thanks to these documents, we know exactly why this all took place. he was luring people into compromising situations then filming and photographing them, effectively collecting evidence that could be used as blackmail material at a later stage.

"From what I have been able to ascertain he had planned to use his charm to persuade his influential friends to make decisions that would help keep America out of a war against Germany. Should his charm not work, then he then had a lot of compromising material which he could use as leverage."

"So did he ever use any of this material?"

"That is a question that I cannot answer, but we are opening a real Pandora's Box of intrigue and I am sure that answer still lays hidden at the house. I have a list of names of the people they had incriminating evidence on although I am sure there are a lot more that will come to light if you are able to get your paper to follow this through. perhaps we might even be able to identify all the missing people; it would bring closure to a lot of families."

"I believe it could, and I know I can put together a story that will open up everything that has been hidden if Skip lets me run with it and I can't see why he wouldn't. What about those wooden boxes I found?"

"I think we both suspect that we know what they might contain; confirmation would put to rest the mystery of all those disappearances, but that is for the authorities to deal with. Eric Linderman was a sick man. on one hand he was the most charming man you could meet but then he was also a ruthless cold blooded killer who saw no value in your life, if you were Jewish or anyone else despised by Nazi principals. That is why there must be a full investigation, and there are so many things that have to be laid to rest."

"Are we one hundred percent sure that the Lindermans killed themselves when they realised they could not follow through on their original plans? Surely after spending all those resources to get this material they could have still used it to slow down our aid to the Allies or something."

"Yes, we know Eric and Edith did commit suicide. After Pearl Harbor, war with Germany would only be a formality, and when it did happen, the Lindermans, overcome by grief, took the coward's way out and killed themselves. They were bound together and jumped off an adjoining cliff face; their bodies were discovered the next day and identified by Peter Linderman.

"Eric sold himself as a proud American of German descent and as such a man who could not bear the thought of Germans and Americans fighting each other. But we now know he was in fact a Nazi and a long time supporter of Adolf Hitler; many of the documents quoted his doctrines.

"Just like Hitler who took his life when he realised his evil dream for Europe was over, Eric preceded him with the same result after realising his dream of an America that not only would remain neutral, but one day would bow down to a glorified Nazi empire, was over."

"You said after their deaths the house transferred into Peter's name."

"Yes, Luke it did, after the bodies of Eric and Edith were found at the base of the cliff. Peter was evidently heartbroken. He was a man who idolised his brother and he never left the house again right up until the day he died twenty years ago. When asked, he stated that he could not leave the house as he was waiting for Eric to come back, although he had identified the two bodies. He became not only a recluse but delusional, I guess it is what he wanted to believe.

"Since Peter's death, the house has been vacant, its security and other costs paid for out of some sort of financial agreement made with Eric's original lawyer.

"After the Lindermans' deaths, their domestic help, Mr and Mrs Best, continued to turn up at the house each day to cook for Peter and keep the house clean and in a state of good repair When Mrs Best died in the eighties, the Lindermans' lawyers organised a regular supply of meals for Peter out of the extensive estate.

"History does not recognise the real Eric Linderman: rape, sodomy, orgies, beatings, abductions, torture and murder, all machinations for the purpose of blackmail. Who knows how many atrocities this evil man actually was associated with either directly or indirectly? How could one man commit such wickedness? Did he not know we are all sons of Adam?

"You must expose the actions of this vile individual and correct the myth surrounding how good he was. You can do it, Luke, in print, in your paper, think about it, Luke.

"I will get us a glass of my finest port. After all this I believe that we both could do with a drink."

Chapter 29
(April 1941)

Hector Fifefield had been an easy touch; it had not taken much for him to be coaxed into letting his guard down. Now with the right prompting, along with the slowly increasing effect of the drugs that he had been discreetly administered, he was slowly being led into a very dangerous state of mind. How Hector, a giant of American business, a man who thought nothing of crushing his opposition like a fly with a swat, could allow himself to be so easily manipulated defied logic. However, to the Lindermans, Hector was just one more person who would succumb to their charms and manipulation.

Eric knew well that Hector could prove to be a dangerous adversary if this all went wrong, so the recording of what was going to happen had to be incredibly good, even by Eric's standards.

A previous encounter with Hector had spurred a series of conversations revolving around a woman's place in society and how this had changed over the centuries. There was no doubt that Hector saw women as subservient with their main purpose in life being to provide childbearing services, domestic chores and as a source of sexual gratification to men. It was additionally clear that he thought it was quite justified for a man to force himself on a woman for his sexual pleasure, with marriage being nothing more than a legal document to allow this.

Eric had also come to the conclusion that Patricia Fifefield was the actual powerhouse in their marriage; Patricia was not a woman to be messed with. It was her family wealth that got Hector to the position of power that he now had. Seeing the apparent lack of power Hector had in his own household coupled with what he actually believed to be a man's acceptable right, Eric had concluded that Hector was a very frustrated man and he had seen a weakness, one which he was going to use to his advantage.

The woman was tied to a wooden frame that saw her slightly bent forward. Her legs, which were slightly spread, were tied to the frame, likewise her hands, whilst a gag tied firmly around her head muffled any sound that she tried to make. Additionally the back of her dress had been lifted up, exposing the tops of her black stockings and the back of her silvery white underwear.

"What is this? Who is this woman, Eric?"

"She calls herself Josie, but I doubt that is her real name, but we'll call her that. Josie is a lady who enjoys certain activities and is willing to provide a service that not many other women will. I am not a doctor, but she has an acute case of Gaudensper dolorem syndrome. That's quite a mouthful, I know, but it simply means she can only enjoy sexual satisfaction through pain."

"What are you trying to say, Eric?"

"She enjoys rough sex; the more it hurts, the more she enjoys it. That's why she loves to carry out rape fantasies. She's very good at acting the part of a rape victim, but rest assured that she's enjoying it. The more she tries to scream, the more she is acting out her own macabre fetishes. You're totally free to have your way with her, and the more the violence, the more she will be satisfied. Women like Josie are hard to find. There would be many men dreaming of time spent with someone like her."

Hector looked perplexed. What Eric had just said had aroused him on many levels, but really, was Eric serious or was this just a game his host was playing?

"Honestly, Hector, Josie would probably be happy to do this for free, but she has been more than financially compensated, so enjoy your time with her. And you can do whatever you like to her, if you know what I mean."

"And you, Eric, what will you be doing?"

"Hector, I am very open minded and there is very little in this world that would shock me. I am, however, happily married to the woman who knows all my needs and addresses them fully. I will be in the next room enjoying a whisky, happy in the knowledge I am helping a friend. You are a good man, Hector; Josie is my present to you as a sign of our friendship and as friends we need to look after each other."

"Are you sure about everything that you have said?"

"Yes, Hector, totally sure. Please feel free to be rough with her. Don't worry about any blood or anything like that, we can clean it up later. Remember, the more it hurts her the more she is enjoying it, and at the end you can choke her gently but make it seem real and make it feel real, enjoy the moment because she will."

There was still a level of reluctance from his guest, but Eric's words were calming and reassuring.

"Start by slapping her hard across the buttocks and call her a bitch. She told me earlier that it arouses her and is a good way to get started. When you have finished just leave her there. I will untie her and see she gets safely home. If you untie her it would ruin her fantasy."

After a moment's hesitation Hector raised his right hand, bringing it down across the woman's buttocks with such force her whole body reverberated. The woman's flinch and her muffled scream had got the blood excitedly pumping through Hector's whole body as his heart rate noticeably increased. Although his own hand stung, his own pain just increased the intensity of the pleasure he was now feeling.

"Did you like that, bitch?"

Hector's words were swiftly followed by a second slap to her buttocks. His hand was now throbbing, but he was fully aroused and did not even notice Eric quietly leaving.

As Hector pulled the woman's underwear down he was fully overcome by decades of violent lustful fantasies that, for the first time in his life, he could now act on. As the drugs that Eric had secretly administered into his system helped blur the line between fantasy and reality, Hector had reached a place from which there was now no going back. The more the woman resisted the more excited he became.

Hector had not long retired to bed when Eric and Peter re-entered the room. The woman, still restrained was in a lot of pain. Whatever her name actually was, it wasn't Josie, and she didn't suffer from the make-believe syndrome that Eric had invented just to ease the doubts of his guest. However, all of this was irrelevant as she was Jewish and in Eric's eyes that made her fully expendable.

The woman was bleeding from between her legs and still gasping for breath after the choking she had received. She was also in pain from the other violent treatment inflicted on her. Eric showed no emotion as he prepared to put the woman to final use.

"Peter, please get the movie camera."

There was a false section in the wall between the main room and the hidden passageway facing the stage and when opened from the inside it allowed Peter to roll out the sixteen-millimetre camera mounted on its rolling trolley for occasions just like this. As Peter carried out the task that his brother had requested, Eric leaned forward to whisper to the woman.

"You think you are the chosen ones but now where are you? You are nothing, absolutely nothing and our Führer will see that all like you are wiped from the face of the Earth. But I do have to tell you this before I say goodbye, your life has not been wasted, the things that you have done in the last hour will actually help the Führer's cause to convince Americans on what is the right choice, so how ironic is that for you? But now, young lady, it is time to say goodbye."

As he spoke these words, Linderman's heart chilling breath on her neck would be the last thing the woman would remember as she gasped her last breaths. Eric Linderman's hands gripped around her throat with such intensity that he could feel the veins in his head standing out.

Peter returned shortly as Eric slowly released the grip that had taken away that what was keeping the woman alive.

"Are you ready, my brother?"

Peter nodded in return.

"Let's start by filming from a few feet back, then as you get closer focus on the fact she is not breathing."

Eric seemed excited at the scenario he had set up, but now it was time for Peter to work his magic once again. Activating the camera, he trained the lens on the woman's lifeless body, the blood coming from her crotch and the red marks on her neck. Finally, the camera captured her lifeless head, leaving no doubts about her state of life.

This film footage would be spliced to follow directly on from the movie footage that Peter had taken of Hector climaxing, his hands firmly clasped as he choked his helpless victim. Peter may have been shy and possess limited social skills, but he was a natural behind a movie or a photographic camera. What his words could not say, Peter's artistic projection told tenfold.

"Let's get her in the back room. We will dispose of her body the usual way, later in the afternoon after Hector has left. There should be a good wind blowing out to sea, so we will let the Bests go home early just like last time."

Peter nodded as he made his way to open the door of an adjacent room. This was not the first time that a victim had to be disposed of. It was not a pleasant experience, but he and Eric now had the process down to a fine art and he found comfort in knowing, just like his brother had told him, it was in the long-term interest of the Fatherland.

Hector had awoken to blurry images of what had happened the night before, although the remnant effect of the drugs prevented the whole events of the previous evening from becoming clear. Flashbacks of what had occurred sprang into his mind causing moments of disbelief; did things really happen as he suspected they might have?

Although he planned to leave in the early afternoon, Hector decided it was best to leave early and had informed his chauffer accordingly.

Knowing that he would have to face Eric when he left, Hector's blurred thoughts turned to the previous night. As he dressed, he wondered how to approach the subject.

Eric, however, knew exactly how to play the game as he smiled pleasantly, not giving Hector the need to approach the subject himself.

Hector's chauffer got out of the driver's seat holding open the rear right-hand door of the Lincoln.

A handshake helped ease the uncertainty of the situation as Eric leaned forward to whisper in his guest's ear.

"Josie left early this morning and said to say thank you for last night. She admitted that she is a bit sore but stressed that she would not have it any other way and wanted me to personally thank you. Additionally she stated that nothing that happened last night would ever leave her lips."

Eric knew exactly what Hector needed to hear and the look of instant relief was evident. Eric's reassuring words had taken away any worries or concerns. Additionally it had confirmed what his flashback had been telling him, something that once again aroused deep seated evil fantasies. However, now believing his actions of the previous night would not have any consequences, Hector was free to continue his impeccable public life.

Chapter 30
(2019)

Errol soon returned, in his right hand, the neck of the bottle containing his favourite port; in his left was balanced a small silver tray containing two crystal glasses.

"Caribbean Royale, Luke?"

Luke nodded, making the assumption that the liquor in question was of the highest quality and probably only brought out for special occasions.

"You are right, Uncle, we probably have no idea of the extent of his crimes but surely Linderman must have had accomplices at all levels to get away with what he did. Surely he could have not done all that by himself, the kidnapping, the abuse and then disposal of the bodies—it all would have taken a lot of time and effort."

"Of course he would have had help, Luke; that goes without saying. There would have been plenty of sympathisers if you knew where to look. Many Americans are of German heritage and at the time there would be plenty unaware of, or in complete denial of what was actually happening in Europe. However, apart from Edith and Peter, he makes no mention about anyone else in his documents, well not in the documents that I have seen. I do suspect their family lawyer must have known something about what might have been going on, as there are several references to him in one document. Maybe he was a Nazi sympathiser himself, we just don't know."

"There must be more information at the house about his accomplices. When this is all exposed and the police get involved then all the information will come out."

"I presume it will all come out, Luke. Then there are, of course, Mr and Mrs Best, the loyal staff who must have seen things of a questionable nature. I suspect they turned a blind eye to a few things that they might have seen, but I don't believe they were involved in any way.

"Although the house had servants' quarters these were only used during the time Eric's parents were alive. During the renovations Eric had a small house built about a hundred yards away and the Bests moved in there; neither property was visible from the other. Each day the Bests would walk to the house and whilst Mrs Best prepared most of the meals Mr Best looked after the maintenance by either doing the work himself or organising contractors."

"Surely someone must have seen a connection between all those people going missing and the Lindermans. The police are not stupid and the fact that the victims were all Jewish and lived close must have raised alarm bells."

"Yes, Luke you would think so, fourteen people in a two hundred mile radius and all Jewish. I.t was no surprise to hear that Tortoise had his suspicions, but as he said, he was shut down at the highest level."

"Even so, how could fourteen people just go missing?"

"We must remember, Luke, it was a different time and although attitudes today are quite different, the hatred of our race is not new and was quite deeply engrained into some aspects of society. You are so much younger than me and lucky enough not to see some of the things that were deemed acceptable in my time. There are those who hated Jews because their father and grandfather hated Jews, so they continued that hatred without even meeting a person of Jewish descent. If you knew where to look, then for the right money there would be those more than happy to kidnap and supply a person to the Lindermans."

"There must have been others apart from Tortoise who had their suspicions; abduction is abduction regardless of who the victims are, why did the police never investigate?"

"Of course there were suspicions and accusations, Luke, but as time went by Eric gained more credibility as he associated with the rich and powerful; his character became beyond reproach.

"Nothing could ever be proved and even if any evidence was found, with the important contacts that he was acquiring, any evidence would be soon criticised and dismissed."

"The police should still have had a duty to follow up on any claims."

"Yes, Luke, you are totally correct, but it was eighty years ago, who knows what the police did or did not do? The truth became irrelevant for whatever happened, Eric Linderman's reputation was never tarnished. Consequently the more he got away with, the bolder he would have become with his actions."

Chapter 31
(October 1941)

Police Chief Reilly slowly exited the black and white 1936 police sedan, closely followed by two of his junior officers, Patterson and Thomas. The chief hesitated before using the heavy brass knocker attached to the solid oak entrance door. Leighton Best opened the door with a sense of professionalism.

"Good afternoon, Officers can I help you?" Leighton's voice was deep and authoritative.

"We are here to see Mr Eric Linderman, is he in?"

Leighton, however, did not need to answer the question as Eric Linderman walked into view from the adjacent room. His words were as charming and friendly as always.

"Chief Reilly, please come on in. For what do I have the pleasure this evening?" As he spoke he indicated for the two accompanying officers to also come inside.

"I am sorry, Mr Linderman, but I am here on official business I have a search warrant for this property."

"Please call me, Eric it is so much less formal. May I be so bold as to ask why the warrant, Chief?"

"I am sorry, Mr Linderman, I mean Eric, but there have been some ridiculous allegations made about some people who have disappeared, and Judge Samson has issued this warrant. I hope you understand it is a formality that I am obliged to comply with, so if we can carry this out then the sooner we can leave and let you to get back to your afternoon."

"Chief, I fully understand, please feel free to search anywhere in the house. Missing people! Goodness me, you are right that does sound ridiculous, so please do not hesitate to conduct your search. The sooner we get this sorted the better."

The chief indicated for his two officers to start performing their examination as Eric Linderman led him through to the formal lounge.

"Please have a seat, my lovely wife will join us unless you would like to look around yourself."

The chief knew that he really should be assisting his officers but somehow felt obliged to follow Eric's invitation to sit down. The sound of a female voice from the hallway caused the chief to stand up and turn ready to greet Edith Linderman as she walked in.

"Chief Reilly, so nice to see you, it has been a while."

"It's nice to see you too, ma'am, but as I said to your husband this is unfortunately official business as I have a search warrant."

"I did see your officers having a look around. Can I offer you a coffee whilst they are doing their job?"

"No, I am fine thanks, ma'am"

"Well then, Chief, do tell me why you would have a search warrant for our house."

"I was saying to your husband how ridiculous this all is, but there have been several missing people reported over the last few months and as a formality we are required to search your house."

"Well then, Chief, please feel free to look everywhere. I am sure if there were any people hiding in our house Leighton would have found them. But if he hasn't I would prefer if you found them rather than me. Imagine getting dressed and discovering one of these missing people watching me. You wouldn't need a warrant, Chief as it would be I who would be asking you to search this house."

Edith Linderman placed her hand on the chief's shoulder as she laughed in a way that caused her husband and the chief to follow suit. Edith, like her husband, had perfected the art of manipulating people. Whether it was flirting, putting a person at ease or making a person feel uncomfortable, the Lindermans both had the right action for any occasion. Edith and Eric kept the chief occupied for a solid fifteen minutes with Edith turning the subject of conversation around to Gladys, the chief's wife and her community support group, whilst Eric quizzed the chief about local events. Having lost track of time, the chief suddenly looked at his watch.

"I am so sorry we have taken so much of your time and it's getting late now."

The chief called out to Patterson and Thomas who soon made their way downstairs.

"You didn't find anything did you, boys?"

"No, sir, nothing."

"Well there we go, I knew you wouldn't, but we had to comply."

"That's no problem, Chief. I would rather you did you job properly so you can find where those missing people really are."

"Thank you for your understanding, we will be off now."

"Chief, one thing before you go."

Eric was clearly starting to write out a cheque.

"I am sorry, sir I can't accept that."

Eric looked at the chief as if the chief had just made a mistake.

"Now, now, Chief I hope you were not thinking that I was offering you a bribe."

The chief looked very embarrassed,

"This is something I have been meaning to do for a long time and I am ashamed that I have not made the time to do it sooner. I am aware the department has a fund to help those officers injured in the line of duty. Well, I feel honoured to support the brave officers who do their job so we can all sleep safe at night. Please take this little gift and make sure it goes into that fund."

The chief looked in amazement as to the amount the cheque was written out for.

"Thank you very much, this is very generous. I will personally see that it goes into the fund, and once again we are very sorry to have bothered you with this silly misunderstanding."

The chief turned to his men.

"Right, men, let's go. We've used up enough of these fine people's time."

Chapter 32
(November 2019)

As Skip drove to work, his curiosity surrounding the content of the call from Luke the previous evening was such that he found it hard to concentrate. It was a call that had woken him from what should had been an early night's sleep. Skip, however, did not have the opportunity to express any displeasure, as Luke had completely dominated their conversation.

Could this really be the breaking exclusive that would save *The Eye*? Probably not, however, if it really was as big a story that Luke claimed that it was, then at best it might give *The Eye* an adrenalin rush that might coax another six months out of the business.

One good story alone is soon forgotten unless it can be followed up, and in a world that demands access to everything almost straight away, Skip knew that the bold tactic of teasing the audience only worked if you truly had a total exclusive.

Luke had in fact done just that himself as he had not told Skip the full details, only that what he had was a lost piece of history and something that could have changed the outcome of the Second World War, which in turn could had changed the events that prompted the Cold War. Luke had also made it clear to Skip that he was only going to hear the full story face to face and not over the phone, something which almost prompted Skip to invite Luke over right there and then. However, at 10:45 p.m. and with a reassurance that nobody else had access to the information, common sense saw him suggesting a meeting first thing in the morning, something Luke agreed to, insisting that they both turn up early.

As Skip's old yellow Honda burst into life, the intensity of the intrigue increased. Skip was actively trying not to get too excited at the possibility of a real game changer. He had been in the industry a long time and had heard many promises of that once in a lifetime exclusive from eager young journalists; most failed to deliver the wow factor whilst the rest were usually cut down to size by lack of facts or content that was libellous.

Luke was different from most other journalists and Skip's journey to work was a time of reflection as to how much he trusted Luke's potential. However, there would be no excitement until he knew exactly what he was dealing with.

The office lights were on, and it was quite clear to Skip that despite his early arrival Luke was already there. The sound of the door opening drew his excited colleague from a side office where he had laid out a collection of papers and photographs over a large sheet of white card on which he had drawn lines and notes in a variety of colours.

"Skip, I have it all set out for you to see."

"Good morning, Luke."

"Sorry, good morning, Skip."

"Well then, Luke, you are obviously very excited about what you have so I won't draw out your enthusiasm to show me. I am of course very intrigued to know what would make you call me late at night and then be here so early. So here I am, and you have my undivided attention."

"I have it, the story I have promised you. It's something that could have changed American history and I have the exclusive and it starts with a man called Eric Linderman.

"Eric and his wife Edith were committed Nazis and lived about four hours east of here on the Maryland coast. During the late nineteen-thirties and early nineteen-forties, Eric Linderman had secretly recorded many influential people in very compromising situations, both photographically and on movie reels.

"Evidently Eric and his wife were very charming, they held amazing parties and slowly got people into their confidence before setting them up. None of the victims contemplated that the Lindermans were just waiting to get them into a situation where they could be blackmailed. Events such as sex sessions with prostitutes, gay orgies, bizarre S and M activities and even the forced rape and beating of abducted victims were organised and recorded. The surprising thing, however, is that even to this day nobody knows all this ever took place, but now I do, and I have all the proof."

Luke pointed to a few of the pictures obtained from the folders that he had laid across the table. Till this point Skip had not taken much notice of the contents of the tabletop as he was more focussed on what Luke had to say, but know it became clear that the pictures showed people and groups of people indulged in very compromising activities.

"I don't understand, Luke, why would this man Eric Linderman go to all the effort of collecting all this material?"

"Well nobody was aware that he was actually a Nazi sympathiser. Everybody knew he was originally born in Germany, but he sold himself as a genuine loyal American of German descent. Eric Linderman feared that if America ever joined the war on the side of the Allies then Germany, although in a strong situation, would not have the resources to fight the British, the Russians and the Americans all at the same time. He realised that America, for political reasons, could never side with Germany so the best option was to keep us neutral, and he intended to do that by having material that he could use to blackmail influential people into making decisions that would stop America siding with or even helping the Allies."

"OK, I am beginning to get the picture, but why did he never use all this blackmail material for the use that he'd intended it for?"

"When the Japanese attacked Pearl Harbor Eric knew he would never be able to stop what was now destined to happen as America and Germany would soon be at war, and as such, he and his wife were so overcome by grief that they took their own lives.

"I have all the information and I know it was my destiny to write the story of what could have been. I was led to this story by what were my nightmares, but as scary as they were they drew me to the place where all this information was kept. This is far more that a coincidence; by having those dreams I was chosen to tell this episode of history."

"OK, hold it just there for a moment, Luke. You say that you were led to the place that this information was kept at, just exactly where is this place?"

"At Eric Linderman's house. Under the house is a large hidden room along with several other smaller ones. The main room is surrounded by a secret passageway where the cameras and projectors were set up. There were even some devices that appear to be used for torture."

"And you just walked into the house and retrieved information that had been undiscovered for nearly eighty years. I think I am missing something here."

"No, we didn't just walk in."

"We! Are you telling me that you had someone with you?"

"Yes, an urban explorer called Kent Clark. The house has been abandoned for a number of years, but Kent was able to pick the lock."

"So you broke in?"

"You make it sound like a criminal offence. As I said, the house was abandoned."

"Breaking and entering is a criminal offence; I don't believe I have to tell you this but no matter how big the story is, I can't publish anything when the supporting evident was obtained by theft."

"I know, Skip, but this is different, it's something that could have changed American history. I believe people were abducted and taken there to be tortured and killed; we even suspect their remains were possibly burnt and could still be there stored in sealed boxes. The public has a right to know, these were very influential people at the time that we are talking about."

"Have you got any names of these people?"

"Yes, I have a list right here. A couple of these names are from the folders and information that you see here but as I could only collect what I could put in my backpack, the rest of the names are taken from the photographs that I took of other folders and documents."

Skip took the list, his eyes slowly making their way down the names. As he read each name to himself 'bloody hell' and 'holy shit' were the only words to leave his lips. Finally he turned his attention back to Luke.

"Have you any idea who some of these people were?"

"I haven't had time to research them all yet, but I will."

"Luke, for a smart man you are beginning to frighten me. Let me save you a bit of effort, amongst this list are some family names that still hold considerable power in American politics, not just power but major influential power. You are making some serious accusations, publishing this just based on what you have told me will be like poking a hornet's nest whilst you are standing completely naked. Does anybody else know about this?"

"No, nobody else does."

The realisation that he had just told Skip a lie about his Uncle Errol sent a feeling of uneasiness through his body.

"What about this man Kent, what does he know?"

"Nothing about what was in the folders; he has not seen any of the pictures, and I have not discussed any of this with him. He has, however, seen the Nazi memorabilia, the torture devices and the hidden cameras. Maybe he will draw his own conclusions, maybe he will try to go back to retrieve his gear that he left there."

"What! He left his gear there, Luke, this is just getting worse and worse."

Luke had never seen Skip with a look on his face like the one he currently had.

"And what about Rachael, Luke, have you told her? Bits of careless pillow talk maybe."

"No, I haven't, she knows about the house but not exactly what I found there."

At least this time he was telling part of the truth. Rachael knew the story, but Luke had not showed her the list of names.

"Well that's one good thing I guess. Now let me tell you what is going to happen. You are going to your office and do two things. First, you are going to document everything that has happened right up to us having this conversation. Do not leave anything out. Secondly you are going to print off two sets of the photos that you said you took inside the house. I am going to arrange for us to meet with Janice from legal right here at one o'clock, at which time you will bring us four copies of the document that you have typed up plus the printed photos. Until then this door will remain locked, and nothing is to be removed from this room, do you understand?"

Deflated and surprised by Skip's reaction Luke nodded.

This was not supposed to be Skip's reaction; he should be excited and enthusiastic to follow this up and go to print with the story. Yes, the house was broken into, but it was not like anybody was living there, and it was only the documents that were taken, it was not as if they stole jewellery or any other items of monetary value.

"And, Luke, this should go without saying, but you will not mention anything to anybody about this, so get typing and one last thing, just drop everything else that you are working on. Wilson will pick up your other work till I tell you otherwise. Have you any problems with anything I have said?"

A sideways shake of Luke's head told Skip that his employee would be fully compliant with the requests. As they left the office Skip firmly closed and locked the door behind them.

Although it was only twelve forty-five, Luke's arrival at the office containing the documents, saw both Skip and Janice already there and in deep discussion, dialogue that abruptly came to a stop as Luke entered the room.

Janice Gray, also known informally as the bitch from legal, was not a person to be messed with; in a court of law she would be the person that you would pray was defending you rather than prosecuting. Despite a reputation for taking no prisoners she seemed a bit perplexed as to the magnitude of what lay before them. Janice's initial response was to hand Luke a disclaimer that she insisted he sign. The wording stated that Luke's actions with regard to obtaining the information that he had collected were independent from and unknown to Skip or any person associated with *The Eye*.

Although happy to sign the disclaimer, Luke could not help but wonder why there was a sense of urgency to produce this disclaimer.

What exactly was this all leading to?

Taking the four copies of Luke's statement, Janice gave one copy to Skip and returned one back to Luke; the other two were for her own keeping. Line by line, paragraph by paragraph, Janice led the two men through the text, stopping to quiz Luke on various points that were then noted and highlighted on one of her copies. Two-and-a-half hours later, the painful experience finally came to an end. Now satisfied that Luke could offer nothing more of any relevance, Janice placed all the documents and photos from the house into her briefcase along with her two copies of Luke's statement.

"I will have to take all this material to consult with my colleagues. Are you sure that this is everything you have, Luke?"

"Of course, what else could there be?"

"Janice will get back to me, in the meantime, Luke, you need to go home and do not return here until I inform you that you can. You will be paid your normal wages on condition that you are not to tell anybody about what has been said here today, including Rachael, is that clear?"

Luke nodded nervously.

Chapter 33

The warmth of Rachael's body was very comforting. With Skip's warning playing on his mind, combined with the fact he had heard nothing else since, Luke had let his imagination start to get away with him. How he longed to discuss what was troubling him with the person he hoped would be his forever soulmate and companion to share life's problems with. Instead, all he had been able to tell her was that discussions with the paper were ongoing and that she must not tell anybody about anything related to the bus or to the house.

As she lay closely against his body, Luke took note of the rhythm of her heart. Whatever the rate, it was definitely slower than his. An involuntary arm movement roused his girlfriend.

"Is something wrong, hon? Is there anything that you want to talk about?"

It was if Rachael had a sixth sense. Was she subconsciously detecting the raised frequency to his heart's rhythm?

"No, everything's fine. Go back to sleep."

Reassured by Luke's words Rachael soon slipped back into a state of sleep. Luke knew that as much as he wanted to share his burden it was definitely in Rachael's best interest that she knew nothing of the recent events in Luke's life.

There was a sense of something not being just quite right even before Luke actually placed the key into his apartment's door. Hesitating for a moment as he made a quick glance along the hallway behind, noting nothing out of the ordinary reassured him that all was indeed well, a feeling of temporary relief that held true until the now opened door revealed the state of the apartment.

Removed and emptied out drawers, overturned furniture and displaced personal items led to the reality of the situation: Luke had been burgled.

Satisfied that the perpetrator was no longer in the apartment, a quick inspection of the apartment to assess exactly what had been done, revealed that to the best of his knowledge nothing had been taken. His iPod, his camera, even the forty dollars tucked into his underwear drawer were all accounted for, items that would have been the first to be taken. Someone had clearly been looking for something specific.

The phone call to the police led to a very unsatisfactory response; a burglary was clearly very low on their list of priorities, especially when answering 'I don't think so' to the inevitable question of 'Was anything taken?'

A mixture of shock, surprise and disappointment mingled to produce a dry throat and the need for a caffeine pick me up.

Luke had only managed to get one sip of the freshly brewed coffee into his mouth before the ringing of the doorbell drew him out of the kitchen. Initially assuming that a passing patrol car may have made the effort to show up following his phone call, led only to disappointment as he opened the door to a large and unfriendly looking man.

"Yes, can I help you?"

Luke's question seemed obvious enough for a simple reply in return, however, it only evoked a stare in response, something that make Luke feel at little uneasy.

"Are you looking for someone?"

The man finally spoke in a voice that was deep and had an authoritative tone to it.

"Luke Spitz, I presume. We need to have a talk. Can I come in?"

"You obviously know me, but I am afraid I don't recognise you. So who are you and what do you want to talk to me about?"

"My name is Mr Smith, and I would like to talk about an old house that was hiding some secrets. Now may I come in?"

Luke felt the rhythm of his heart speed up; there were a few things wrong with this situation. Firstly the man's name was quite clearly not Mr Smith, so why then did he not use his real name? Secondly, how did this man know about the house and its contents? Luke realised this could either be a very good or a very bad thing; either way he was about to find out. With a heightened sense of awareness he opened the door fully, allowing Mr Smith to come in.

"It's not really a convenient time; my house has just been broken into."

"That's the trouble with the world today. You just never know when somebody is going to think they have the right to enter someone else's residence and take whatever they like. But people like you and me, we would never dream of doing anything like that would we? It's just so very wrong, breaking into someone's house and stealing things that do not belong to them even if they have been there a long time, isn't that right, Luke?"

Luke suddenly had a very uneasy feeling about where the conversation was leading.

"You don't have any recording devices operating, do you?"

"No; of course not."

"Well then you won't mind putting you phone on the table where I can see it."

Luke obliged with the request.

"Four days ago, you gave some items to your employer Mr Skip Newton; he in turn gave them to his legal rep who confided in a colleague who then decided they should pass the details onto some interested parties. Let's say there are certain people who would be very upset if this information was ever made public. Any potential exposure of this material would start a process where it would only end up being declared fake; this in turn would cause both you and Mr Newton's paper to lose all credibility and the ensuing legal action would destroy you both.

"Even although my employer and his family's good character would remain intact, the resulting publicity would still be unwelcomed. My client cannot afford to have any accusations directed at his family, no matter how ridiculous they are. Therefore, I have been asked to clean up this mess, and that is something that I will do. Whether I do it nicely or have to be persuasive in a not so nice way will be totally up to you."

"You can't just come and delete history; the public has a right to know."

"Luke, Luke, Luke. Don't try getting righteous with me. You're a thief who broke into private property and stole things that did not belong to you. In fact, Luke, you could be arrested if this came to light. There are some very nasty penal institutions, and my client is a very powerful person. He would certainly make sure you spent some time in the worst of the worst, the sort of place where you have to be on your guard twenty-four hours a day, especially in the showers.

"Your friend Mr Clark has seen the error of his ways for his part of this unlawful act. I went with a couple of friends and had a little talk with him last night. Mr Clark now wants nothing to do with you, and as far as he is concerned, your visit with him to the house never took place. Mr Clark is, in fact, so upset by his actions that he is going to take down his website and move to another city.

"What about you, Luke? Do you now see the error of your ways?"

Luke knew he had been threatened by someone he could not hold his own against. If this man had scared Kent, then he didn't stand a chance. He had no option but to nod agreeably.

"I certainly hope that you really do mean that, Luke."

At a loss for words, Luke stared back blankly.

"I am sure you noticed how run down the house is and what a bad state of disrepair it was in. I guess there were a lot of things in a house that old that could have started the fire that happened last night. Those poor security guards; if they'd only notified the authorities, they may have been able to save the building. But they obviously tried to fight the fire themselves and perished in the flames as a result, I am sure the authorities have probably discovered their bodies by now.

"The loss of life is such a shame, but every time we do something in life, there are consequences. Sometimes, they are good, and other times, they're not so good. But you realise this, don't you, Luke?"

Luke nodded but felt sick to his stomach. His run in with the security guards may not have been pleasant but they were only doing their job and they were both somebody's son, maybe even a husband or father, and now they were dead, and it was his fault.

"Now for the reason I'm here. Everything that you gave to Mr Newton has, unfortunately, been lost and it is very unlikely they will ever be discovered again. As well as that, any secrets the house still had are of course now gone. A friend of mine just happened to be flying his drone in the area this morning and informed me that there's absolutely nothing left. The building has collapsed onto itself; even the garage and its contents are no more. It's such a shame about that stolen truck that jackknifed and was abandoned on the bridge, stopping the fire trucks from getting to the house in time to save anything. Really, what are the odds of that happening?

"Where does that leave us, then? Well. Mr Clark assured me that he has nothing from his visit in his possession, and due to the circumstances of our visit, I fully believe him.

"So what about you, Luke. Are you hiding anything? Maybe something you copied and gave to somebody else?"

Luke slowly shook his head from side to side, and Mr Smith stared ominously in his direction.

"Maybe that beautiful girlfriend of yours, I believe her name is Rachael. Did you give her anything from the house? Now is not the time for lies, Luke, so look me in the eye and tell me, is there anything else that I need to know about?"

"No, absolutely nothing."

"Good boy, Luke. That is what I wanted to hear. I believe you because I think you know what could possibly happen if anything—and I mean anything—ever came out. So just like Mr Clark recalls the past few weeks, you never went to the house. In fact, you don't even know what I'm talking about, OK?"

"Yes, I understand."

"Well then, I will leave you to finish your coffee, don't bother to get up, I will see myself out. Oh yes, one last thing, Luke, before I leave. The winters here can get so cold have you ever thought about moving somewhere warm? I hear Arizona is nice, you could take Rachael, start a new life there, heck, you might even start a family that would be a good way to forget about here and everything that has happened."

As soon as the sound of the door latching indicated that Mr Smith had left, Luke picked up his phone. It would be too early to get Skip at work, but he might still be at home. Luke quickly dialled the number, and the phone was promptly answered.

"Luke, I am glad you rang. I've been thinking of how to tell you this, but all the items that you gave me the other day have unfortunately been lost, so we won't be able to run the story, and I really think it's in everybody's best interests to forget everything to do with this story."

"So, Mr Smith came to see you as well. Whatever happened to freedom of the press, Skip?"

Skip did not answer Luke's question. Rather, he changed the topic of their conversation.

"I am going to make an announcement at ten today at work, but I will give you a heads up. It really is time for *The Eye* to close up shop. We'll be ceasing all operations immediately after I make the announcement. But I will do everything correctly and everyone will be paid out all that they are owed plus a bonus. Bring a box in so you can clear out your desk and take your things home. I will be locking the doors at five o'clock."

"Skip, wait."

"What is it, Luke? My decision will not change."

"I am surprised at you. So many of our people were murdered around that time. Don't you care that up to fourteen people, all Jewish, could have been killed by this evil man, and now you're preventing the killer being exposed? I thought better of you."

"If you were anyone else, Luke, and I was there now, I would punch your bloody lights out. How dare you lay down the religious angle to try to make me feel guilty? You say you thought better of me. Well, Luke, I thought better of you! I cannot believe you can accuse me of not caring. You have no idea about my family and what happened to them during the war. I may have been born ten years after the conflict's end, but growing up, its legacy still haunted my family. And although it was never talked about, the scars were always there. My grandmother only told me about her family when she knew she was dying. I saw the pain on her face as she told me the full story of how after meeting my grandfather, she moved to America in 1921 to start a new life, leaving her parents and brothers in Austria. After Hitler's occupation of Austria, she would never hear from any of them again despite employing a post-war agency to try to track them down. I saw the pain in her eyes, Luke, so don't you dare tell me that I don't care."

"I am sorry, Skip. I shouldn't have said what I did."

"Too bloody right, you shouldn't have. And another thing, Luke. I am sure you've figured this out already, but let me state the obvious. Whatever happened at that house, despite how despicable it may have been at the time, it happened over eighty years ago. The victims, the witnesses and, most importantly, the perpetrators are all now long since deceased. Do you think the police are going to arrest a dead person? Of course not, but it doesn't mean that the guilty will never be punished. What do you think the outcome was when Eric Linderman approached the gates of eternity? With one path leading to eternal peace and the other leading to eternal hell, where do you think he was directed to go? There are no winners out of pursuing this, Luke. It will only open old wounds and cause distress for people. Just walk away, Luke, while you can."

There was a moment of silence before Skip continued.

"When my ex-wife decided that she would rather spend the rest of her life with a different man than the one that she'd married, I was devastated. I could have climbed up on my moral high horse and made things very difficult for her. But what would I have gained, Luke? Absolutely nothing, that's what! She had made up her mind, and sometimes shit like that happens, because life is not all about fields of sweet-smelling roses.

"I wished her the best with her decision and walked away, never to look back. After tidying up my business commitments, I returned to America, and since coming back, I have met so many interesting people, seen so many amazing things, been out with some beautiful ladies and had some life experiences that I would never have had if I'd still been living in Australia with her. Purchasing *The Eye* was the best decision of my life, even if it's worth nothing now. You can't always put a price on everything in life. Every dollar *The Eye* has cost me was a dollar well spent.

"Kenny Rodgers sings in *The Gambler*, 'you have to know when to hold 'em, know when to fold 'em, know when to walk away, and know when to run'. They are wise words, Luke. So take my advice and walk away while you can, before you have to run."

There was no opportunity to reply as the sound of the receiver hanging up told Luke everything he needed to know.

Chapter 34

As soon as the door opened, Errol could tell his nephew was not in a good state of mind.

"Luke, what's happened? You look like you've been run over by a truck."

"My apartment got broken into."

"What! Are you OK? Did you get hurt?"

"No, I was at Rachael's last night, and I only discovered it when I got back this morning. I haven't told Rachael because I don't want her to worry."

"Did anything get damaged or taken? What about the Linderman documents? Are they still with Skip?"

"Thankfully, they weren't at my place. They're all still with Skip's legal rep. She took them, but that is little consolation as I have a feeling that we'll never see them again anyway."

"Why? What else has happened?"

"I'll get to that shortly. But first, I don't think my apartment was burgled. Nothing was actually taken as far as I can tell. I phoned the police, but they just said to contact my insurance company and that they'll send someone around to take a statement in the next couple of days. I suspect that whoever was in my apartment was looking for something that might have related to what I got from the house."

"Why do you think that?"

"I was just getting my head around what happened when I got a visit from a man who spoke in a pleasant but threatening way. I am going to cancel dinner with Rachael, and I have been driving around all afternoon since collecting my things from work. I was driving nowhere in particular; I just needed to get out of the house. As much as it will hurt, I'll have to break up with Rachael."

"Luke, I am so sorry. What's happened between you? You seemed so happy together."

"I don't want to talk about that at the moment; there are other things we have to talk about first."

"Then tell me about the man who made the threats. Is this something to do with what you got from the house? You have not told me anything except that you passed on the documents to Skip, who gave them to his legal rep."

Following Skip's stern warning to Luke that he should not talk to anybody about the house or its contents, Luke had sent his uncle a text informing him that he'd passed the information on, but couldn't elaborate further on the subject due to its sensitive nature. Then he'd said that he'd be in contact as soon as he could to provide an update. Additionally, he had instructed his uncle not to talk to anybody about the subject. Naturally, Errol was waiting eagerly for any news and was excited at what Luke would hopefully be telling him. But now he wasn't so sure.

"Uncle Errol, I know you're probably desperate to hear how I got on after submitting the information to Skip, so I'm going to be straight with you, and it's not the news that you want to hear. The story is not going to be published by *The Eye*. All the original documents have been confiscated and probably destroyed. Additionally, *The Eye* has stopped publication as of today."

"What?"

"This whole thing has turned into a nightmare; I was so excited when I gave Skip the information, but right from the start, I knew something was wrong. When he realised that I had broken into the house and stolen the documents, alarm bells went off. Then when he saw the list of names involved, he wouldn't even let me tell him the full story until he got his legal rep involved. I was asked to hand over everything for authentication and not to talk to anybody about anything associated with it. That's when I sent you the text. I was also asked who else knows about what had happened. Of course, I had to tell them about Kent, but I didn't mention you. It is very important that you do not tell anybody."

"I haven't told anyone and wasn't planning to, anyway."

"This morning, the man I told you about who visited me really scared me. He works for someone or some people who would be very upset at the release of the story. He obviously had something to do with the burglary. In fact, he or one of his associates scared Kent enough that he has closed down his site and is denying all knowledge of ever meeting me or going to the house. Kent is a tough ex-military man and not someone who gets intimidated easily, so what chance do I have?

"And they got to Skip as well. As far as Skip is concerned, the story is dead in the water and he's closing down *The Eye* permanently. It was made known to me in a nice, but subtly threatening way, that I need to forget about everything that happened concerning the house and move on."

"I had no idea things would come to this. I am so sorry."

"You don't need to be sorry about anything. It was me who chose to go to the house. And I chose to go back the second time once I realised what was there. Unfortunately, that isn't all. I was also informed by the man that last night, the house burnt down completely, destroying everything, including any remaining evidence that could prove the authenticity of the information. The secret passages, the cameras and projectors, worse still, the two security guards will be found dead supposedly trying to fight the fire. That is the sort of people we're dealing with. That's why I will have to break up with Rachael. I can't put her in danger, and I can't tell her I'm breaking up with her to protect her."

"Then, Luke, the story is dead! Eric Linderman's evil legacy continues by taking two more innocent victims, and I will not let it take any more. I should have known that some things should stay in the past and never be resurrected. Listen to me, you will walk away from this. You will move on with your life, and you will not do anything that puts you in danger."

"I felt I was morally right by talking about the freedom of the press. I felt I had a duty to inform the public, but I was so obsessed by first the bus and then the house and its contents that I thought it was OK to just take something that wasn't mine. Skip was right. I did unlawfully steal them, and that makes me no better than a thief."

"Luke, listen to me. You must drop all of this and put it behind you. I should have done the same many years ago. Walk away, and you won't need to break up with Rachael. I will not have you put yourself in danger. There is something I must tell you, and please hear me out. When you first mentioned the name Eric Linderman, I was shocked. Unbeknownst to me, my nephew was ready to take over from where I had stopped by investigating the person who had tormented me since I was a young boy. The truth has now been exposed to us. I only wish that it could be exposed to the history books. Life is not always fair. There are people who go through life with their good deeds never acknowledged, and then there is an evil sadistic killer like Eric Linderman, who is still hailed by some as a hero.

"Luke, I cannot and will not allow your life to be put in danger. You have helped me with my quest as much as you can. I now know for certain what I have suspected for so long. To some, Eric Linderman may still be seen as a man of principle who died for what he believed in. But I now know the truth, so that is enough for me. I believe this world has incorrectly judged Eric Linderman, but God will be his final judge, and neither Eric nor Edith can hide their sins from a God who knows everything. There is a special place reserved for people like him, and he will be there now, suffering along with his idol, Adolf Hitler, both consumed by the flames of eternal torment. So why should I worry about what mankind thinks?"

Luke knew a weight had been lifted from his Uncle Errol's shoulders. It hadn't been totally removed, but it had been eased to a point that his uncle could now accept what had happened. The burden had, however, been transferred a generation as Luke unknowingly allowed himself to pick up the mantle.

"What was once my nightmare has become my destiny. I was led to expose him, but why? Why me? What are you still not telling me, Uncle? I need to know what I am dealing with."

"No, Luke. Promise me you'll walk away. No good can come of this; everyone who was involved is now dead. It's all just history."

"I don't know if I can just walk away."

"You will because you must. We both must. You need to go home and think deeply about what in this world is important to you."

"My nightmares were no coincidence. That bus was real. It might be a burnt wreck now, but it was real and waiting for me in Eric Linderman's garage. Was the bus calling out to me? Could an object actually do that? Because that is what I thought before you told me about your mum. When

I heard the house had burnt down, including the garage and its contents, I knew the bus had been destroyed. I should have felt relief that the object of my nightmares had been destroyed. Instead, it felt like I had lost an old friend. Maybe the bus was not evil and it was just the only way that it could grab my attention. Perhaps the bus was so horrified about the part it had played in what happened that it needed to make amends. I know this might all sound stupid, but I just don't know what to think any more."

"No, Luke. I don't believe an object can have a soul, but I do believe people's souls never die. They live on in a different form, something that we will only be able to understand once we have passed from our world into God's eternity. Maybe, just maybe, my mother knew that only you could have linked the nightmares to Eric Linderman, and that only you could have obtained these documents and shown them to me so that I now know what happened and can be at peace for my remaining years on Earth. The other possibility is that it was time for any remains of the evil that lurked there to be destroyed, and that's exactly what has happened. Maybe now with everything gone, there is nowhere left for it to hide and the area can be cleansed.

"Luke, we live in a world that we don't understand, ghosts, premonitions, strange sightings. I had a friend who was a pilot. One day whilst he was flying, he saw these black lines in the sky and became so obsessed trying to find out what they were that he lost his job and had a breakdown. I felt bad as he'd asked for my help, but I was unable to help him.

"Scholars who have studied the Torah tell us that there are many other dimensions, but we can only comprehend four. When unexplained things happen, I believe there is a point when dimensions cross over, maybe even for only a moment in time. I am an old man and I have no fear of dying. I actually find it comforting to know that when I cross over, I will see my parents again and all these mysteries will be answered.

"But what I do believe is that whatever the reason for what has happened, needed to happen. And yes, you were destined to be a big part of that. Now, however, it is time for you to move on. God has given you a wonderful gift in Rachael."

There was a moment of silence as Luke digested his uncle's words of wisdom.

"I think we have let this evil man consume enough of our lives. I know we must put all our thoughts of him in the past, and that is what I will try to do."

Errol moved forward to embrace his nephew.

"Good man, Luke. Now you must go, you have much to think about."

Luke could only remember one other occasion when he'd ever received a hug from his uncle. Normally, despite being family, a greeting or departure formality was sealed with a handshake.

"Remember, Luke, it's all over. You have your whole life to look forward to. Put all this in past, where it belongs, take Rachael, make an honest woman of her and move on to somewhere far away from here."

Luke nodded; as he turned to walk towards his car, his right hand involuntarily played with the key to the safety deposit box and its attached key ring that were in his right-hand pocket, a pocket that was normally empty.

Chapter 35
(September 2020)

Luke's finger hovered above the red icon ready to cancel the call when the number he was calling was suddenly answered.

"Uncle Errol, I was just about to hang up."

"Well, I'm glad you didn't."

"Yes, me too, as I have some wonderful news. I am going to be a dad! Rachael is pregnant and due next April. Not exactly what we'd planned, but so wonderful for us both, we wouldn't have it any other way. You're only the third person I've told. I have just been talking to Mum and Nina to tell them, but you're the third."

"Well, I am honoured, Luke. Congratulations to you both on your wonderful news. You've just made an old man so happy, and your news could not have come at a better time."

"We've only known for three days now. At first, we were surprised because we were taking precautions. Then I got scared and almost regretted what happened."

"Why is that, Luke?"

"I started to wonder if I wanted to bring a baby into a world that seems to be going mad. Every day, we see minority groups and organisations dictating their narrow-minded agendas to the masses, whilst the government does nothing and sometimes even encourages them. I don't even believe that the government has the best interests of its own people at heart any more, regardless of who is in power. Some of what I have discovered as a result of my investigative journalism career leads me to believe that our leaders allow things like this to happen to take the focus off what they themselves are doing. So I asked myself what the world will be like when my son or daughter is eighteen, and I didn't like the answer. That's when I panicked.

"But then I thought about the events of the last year and the glimpse into history eighty years prior, and I realised things don't really change. There will never be a perfect time to bring up a child; there has always been corruption and leaders ruling by fear, tyranny and lies, so we can't stop having children because it is not the right time. The important thing is that despite what the world tries to tell them, it is up to you as a parent to teach your children right from wrong, and with that, I embraced our impending parenthood."

"Such wise words, Luke. I am glad you were able to make good of your concerns. But on a more positive note, what are you hoping for, a boy or a girl?"

"We don't mind as long as he or she is healthy, and we don't actually want to know the gender. We would like it to be a surprise. We do have our names sorted, though. Philip if it's a boy, and Talia if it is a girl."

"Both lovely names. You're both going to make such wonderful parents. I can't help but think you have had so many changes in your life since you moved out west. Are you happy there?"

"Yes, we both are. If someone had told me two years ago that by now I would be engaged to the world's most beautiful woman with a baby on the way and that we'd be living north of Phoenix, I would have told them they had me confused with someone else. But I wouldn't change anything. I am happy. I'm going to marry the woman of my dreams, and we both have good jobs, new friends here and we're healthy. It seems so funny now, but when I told Rachael I wanted to show my commitment by asking her to marry me so we could start a new life on the other side of the country, I honestly thought she would say no to both requests. Her hesitation was probably thirty seconds, but it could have been thirty months."

"Rachael is a good woman. Don't underestimate how much she loves you, and never think that you are not worthy of her love."

"Yes, I am very lucky. But enough about me. How are you? How are things with your issue?"

"The word is cancer, Luke. We are two adults and we don't have to tiptoe around it. My cancer is not good, but this phone call is about your good news. We can talk about my health another time."

"I would like to know. If you don't tell me, I will only think the worst and worry. Please be honest with me."

"OK, if that is what you want. My cancer has spread further than first thought. I have months, how many I don't know, but it's months, not years."

"Oh shit."

"No, no, no, Luke, it is OK, I am at peace with everything, especially now with your news. When I said it could not have come at a better time what I meant is it's the circle of life, we can't all live forever, so when God takes someone he replaces them with a new life and in our family he is replacing me with your child; it is what life is about. Throughout history billions of people have cried at the loss of a loved one only to weep with joy shortly afterwards at the sight of a new life.

"Luke you are the son that I never had, you have made me happy and proud, and you have no idea how much I value what you did for me with putting closure to that subject, the subject that does not torment me any more.

"You gave me the answer to the question that had troubled me my whole life. Not only did you risk so much to do it, but you ended up having to give so much away, your life here, your job with *The Eye* and your friendship with Skip. The fact the world will never know about the evil of a certain man does not matter any more. I know what happened, and God knows."

"Are you by yourself? Can anybody hear what we are saying?"

"No, Luke, I am by myself."

"Then don't be so sure the world will never know."

"Luke, you know that you can't tell anyone what happened, so what do you mean? Please tell me, I must know as we might never get to finish the conversation."

Luke hesitated before replying.

"OK, you deserve to know and to be honest I need to tell you even although you won't be happy. Before I took the documents to work I copied everything except the movie reels, that includes all the papers and all the photos, and nobody knows. At first it was just a backup in case something got lost, but after the threats it became my insurance policy; if I was ever threatened again I would have told them that in the event of my death, the documents of which there are now multiple copies will be distributed to every news source that I believe would want to break the story. Most probably won't but how many people could they threaten? It only takes one keen editor to run with it. I know the contents will be discredited and the only proof is copied documents and the coincidental fact that the house burnt down. Enclosed with the documents is the full story of how I got to be there and retrieve the items, well most of the story as I have not mentioned you or Rachael at all. I said my family knew nothing about it and it was purely my secret. Additionally I did not mention Kent by name, just that the man who helped me was someone who was fascinated with old buildings. I listed all the names of the people who Linderman had files on, including the man who was behind the visit by Mr Smith. I know who threatened me, it wasn't exactly hard to work out."

"O'Brian."

"So you worked it out as well! David O'Brian, the man widely tipped to take the next presidential nomination and the man who can't afford any rumours about his grandfather taking part in the beating and rape of a young man. O'Brian would have the country's best lawyers onto it and we both know the incident could never be proved, but rumours about both his grandfather's actions and his own attempt to cover it up, including the murder of the security guards, would still make things just too awkward for him to get the nomination and his political career would be over.

"The documents get released anyway in the event of my death, and as you said nobody lives forever, so one day the story will come out, it is just too big a story not to. The consequences could have changed the world as we know it."

"You must be careful, Luke."

"It's OK, nobody knows except you, and you are not going to tell. So now you know what happened and you also know that one day, although it may take fifty or sixty years, but one day the world will find out the truth about an evil man.

"I am aware that you will not be happy with what I have just told you, but you have to understand that this is how I find my closure. I realise Linderman will be punished in the godly realm, but he will still get away with what he has done in the earthly realm unless I did something.

Directly or indirectly there are the missing people from the nineteen-forties, then the dead security guards, the demise of *The Eye*, and Kent's career. So I am sorry but that's the way it is."

Luke braced himself for the expected chastising and lecture about letting go, but the only reply was a gentle and sympathetic, "OK."

"You sound surprisingly calm at what I have just told you."

"Luke, you are a grown man. You need to do, what you need to do in order to find your own closure. I have had a lot of time to think maybe it's the realisation that what was only ever a long way away, could be knocking on my door any time soon. Perhaps it is finally knowing what happened to my mum and now being aware she is now at peace and waiting for me.

"Whatever it is, for the first time in my life I can appreciate every little thing that is around me especially the things that we normally take for granted. Now when I observe something as simple as a butterfly flying around, I don't just see an insect with wings, but rather a miracle of creation made up of millions of interconnected parts.

"Being calm and at peace does not mean that I have forgotten about Eric Linderman and what happened, I just don't let it bother me. To tell the truth, Luke, there are three things about him and the whole scenario that I often wonder about when I am alone in bed."

"Can you share those with me?"

There was a moment of awkward silence as Errol hesitated before continuing.

"OK, I wasn't going to say anything but since you asked. Firstly, what if Linderman and his wife used their extraordinary charm to do good in the world, then to what extent would he have made a positive impact on society at the time?

"And then there is the one question about him that really puzzles me and it's something that we will never get to hear answered to, as everybody who knew what was going on are all now long dead."

"What exactly are you referring to, Uncle Errol?"

"The Lindermans went to a lot of effort and considerable expense to acquire their collection of incriminating evidence. I am sure that the people who were filmed would have paid good money to obtain the original evidence so they could destroy it. Why did Eric Linderman lock it all away with, the material never to be discovered till nearly eighty years later? Even if he was going to take his own life, I would have thought he would have passed the evidence that he had gathered onto his associates so they could use it to their advantage of promoting Nazi Germany."

"Maybe the man was really so overcome by grief that it caused him not to think straight."

"I guess that is the only explanation that makes sense, and I will have to accept that as the answer. However, it does not answer my third question. We have been told, and I have no reason to believe otherwise, that despite his evil ways, Eric was very close to and very protective of his brother Peter, an intelligent but shy, introverted man who idolised Eric. If the two brothers were that close, then why would Eric and Edith leave Peter to be on his own and to spend the rest of his life in the house by himself? Eric had transferred everything he owned into Peter's name, but what good is that to a man who did not even want to leave the house without support from his brother?

"I was told Peter would spend all day staring out the window; in later years a rep from the legal firm that was administrating his affairs became so concerned about his welfare that they arranged a transfer to an aged care facility. Peter, however, would not leave the house; he was somehow convinced that one day Eric and Edith were coming back for him. So he died in that house, sixty years after identifying the dead bodies of his brother and sister-in-law. What sort of man would allow his own flesh and blood to go through that?

"I guess to a man who killed, tortured and humiliated people that would be of little concern, or would it? We will never know what prompted them to end their own lives so tragically and maybe, Luke, it is best that we don't."

Chapter 36
(January 1942)

Peter Linderman rushed down the stairs, his face filled with sadness as he prepared to relay the news to his brother.

"Eric, the boat has radioed in, and they are all systems go for tonight. They will send a small dinghy out to get you once they see the lit lanterns, they should be here at just after two thirty. I guess this is it then."

Eric placed his hand on his younger brother's shoulder in a symbol of comfort and support.

"Our separation is only temporary. I promised our parents I would look after you and I intend to carry out that promise till the day one of us dies. I am sad to be going, and I have so much to lose, but I know where my loyalty stands and in a time like this we must not think about ourselves, we must think about the country we serve. Germany needs our help more than ever, and we can give the Fatherland the help it needs, so it's very important that we do not deviate from our new plan, not one single detail. You do understand how important this is, don't you, Peter?"

"Yes, I do, and I won't let you down. I will do everything just as we talked about. I might not have been born in the Fatherland, but I too am a proud German."

"Good boy, Peter. Now, we must get our guests ready, we still have a lot to do before we can leave."

Both the man and the woman squinted, their pupils still dilated from the darkness of the windowless room they had been kept in. Dirty, scared and with their hands secured, they were soon led out of what had been their home for the last few days.

Eric now trained the gun that he had taken from the entranceway cabinet at the man as he instructed Peter to remove his handcuffs. Peter tried not to breathe as he approached the man who had obviously messed himself at some point; the associated smell was overpowering and as Peter finally found himself having to take a breath of air he gagged, trying hard not to let a reflex action cause him to almost vomit.

"Look at me, Jew."

The man turned his head to eye his captor.

"Remove all your clothes and place them in this bag."

The man reluctantly stripped down to his underwear before once again turning to look at the man who seemed to not only be a danger to his very existence, but someone who now seemed to be taking a sadistic pleasure from his victim's humiliation.

"Did you not hear me? I said all your clothes, which includes the dirty underwear that you have messed in."

The man hesitated and looked at the woman standing beside him. She, however, was staring firmly at the floor.

"Mr Jewman, this is not a time for modesty. If you don't cooperate I am going to cause you a great deal of pain, however, if you do cooperate you will be free. Do you understand?"

The man nodded and proceeded to remove the last of his clothes before placing all the items in the large paper bag that Eric had indicated.

Eric looked in total disgust at the man's body and the remains of his own bodily waste that had stained his upper legs before turning to his brother.

"Peter, look at this excuse for a person, can you now understand why the Führer wants to eliminate the Jew from the face of the Earth? The Jews are indeed the worst, Peter, but we must not forget that there are many other forms of life that need to be eliminated so that mankind can be purified and start again. There are the uncivilised heathens, the homosexuals, the communists, the sexually depraved, coloured people, criminals who are past rehabilitation, the physically deformed, the mentally impaired and the gypsies, just to name a few. When the Führer has cleansed Europe of its impurities then it will be the turn of America.

"A new world awaits us, Peter, and we will be part of the master Aryan race that rules our brave new world. Sometimes I actually struggle to fully comprehend just how privileged we are to be playing such an important part in the Führer's plan for our utopian future."

Eric then turned to the terrified man.

"Look at you covered in your own mess. There was a bucket in the room to toilet in, but you toileted in your pants. Have you no self-respect or dignity? You are a dirty filthy Jew, so tell me what you are."

The man now found a short lived burst of confidence as he replied softly, "I am proud of who I am."

The man's comments visibly enraged Eric.

"I don't think you heard me; do I have to make it any clearer? You are a—"

His sentence, however, was interrupted by his wife, her words having an instantaneous calming effect on her husband.

"Eric, we haven't got time for this nonsense, there is still a lot to do before we leave."

"You are lucky that my wife reminded me of our priorities, so now it is time to wash."

Eric indicated to the bucket of soapy water that Peter had earlier brought in.

"As you will see the water is warm and not cold. This is a sign from me to you that I am actually a nice man and if you cooperate then everything will work out nicely. Now wash your whole body. I want you to be nice and clean without any smells or dirty bits."

The man cooperated without question. Once clean he was directed to sit in a chair that Peter had gone to fetch. Eric then passed the gun to Edith as he collected a small bowl of water, a shaving stick and a cutthroat razor from a box Peter had also brought into the room.

"Now if I was you I would be sitting very still for the next few minutes. I want to give you a nice clean shave but if you move around there is always the possibility of a nasty accident and we wouldn't want that, would we."

The man sat motionless, scared to even swallow as Eric completed a flawless effort of removing the man's facial growth. With the task completed Eric stepped back to admire his handiwork.

"Such a handsome man indeed, you are so lucky to have such beautiful blue eyes. It is a shame you are a Jew as you would have made such a nice looking German. Now it is time to get dressed and look at the nice selection of clothes I have for you, so much nicer than your dirty old ones, my generosity knows no limits, even though you thought I was not going to be nice to you."

Once dressed, the man was again handcuffed and led aside as it became time for the woman to be given some attention.

"OK, my dear lady it's the same story for you. Please remove all your clothes and put them in that bag. I think we both now realise that when I say all, it means your underwear as well."

The woman obliged, stripping naked before placing her old clothes into the same bag as the man had. She did, however, refuse to make eye contact with anybody, instead choosing to blankly stare at the floor.

"Well done, now that wasn't too embarrassing, was it? Everybody knows what a naked body looks like. Now it is your turn to wash. Look, my brother has fresh warm water for you as well; I would not expect you to use the filthy water from our friend here."

Once clean and dry the woman was instructed to sit in the chair whilst Edith Linderman looked her over. Edith was seemingly unsure about a certain aspect of the woman's appearance.

"Not bad but something is still not right. I think I have to make a further alteration to the haircut that I gave you the other day."

Returning with a pair of scissors and some newspaper that she then spread over the floor, she made an attempt to get the woman's hair just how she wanted. After about five minutes she was happy enough to proceed to her second task, that of putting some make up onto the woman's face.

"That's about as good as I am going to get you to look, so now let's get you dressed."

The woman hurriedly dressed in the fresh clean clothes that Edith had provided, keen to cover her modesty and regain some sense of dignity.

Dressed and with the handcuffs again around her wrists, the woman was directed to stand next to the man. Both Eric and Edith nodded approvingly.

"What a fine beautiful couple you make, so handsome and so beautiful. We are nearly there. Remember, if you do everything that I ask of you then you will be soon free. We will be going for a walk but first I have some presents for you both. Here is my gift to you, Mr Jewman."

Eric Linderman had taken off his gold watch before releasing the man's handcuffs so he could place it over his wrist.

"A fine watch indeed, for a fine specimen of a man. Now my wife has some presents for you, my dear lovely lady."

Edith took the woman's hand and then using some of the soapy water she removed the two rings from the distressed but obliging fingers, and then proceeded to force two different rings onto her fingers.

"There we go, you can't complain these rings are worth many times more than the rubbish you were wearing before. Now it is time for our walk. You will both now follow Peter as he leads the way. Remember, full cooperation gains you your freedom and non-cooperation will anger my husband who has the gun and is not afraid to use it."

The procession led up and out of the house to just past the garage where Peter stopped. This was an opportunity for Eric to pass the gun to Edith, allowing him to retrieve a sack that had been placed against a post. Continuing on, Peter led the four others through the garden, out of the gate that was on the north-west side of the property till they were eventually close to the edge of the cliff.

"We are almost done and soon you will both be free. You, Jew man, hold out your left arm and, you Jew woman, your right arm."

Reaching into the sack, Eric retrieved a short length of rope, tying one end securely around the man's wrist and the other around the woman's.

"OK, nearly there. I just need to take a photo then it's all over. I need you both to stand by the edge of the cliff face but be careful not to fall."

The couple reluctantly obliged, standing a few feet shy of the edge whilst Eric retrieved a camera and a pitchfork from the sack. After passing the camera to Edith, he stood back before calling out, "Look at my wife. One, two, three, smile!"

Eric then turned to his wife, laughing as he spoke. "That would have made such a nice photo, what a shame there was no film in the camera."

With that Eric picked up the pitchfork. The man was now well aware of what was in store for them.

"You told us if we cooperated then we will be free, and we have cooperated, so please keep your end of the bargain."

"I am a man of my word and I intend to do exactly what I said I am going to do, that was to set you free... Free from your miserable Jewish lives."

With that Eric lurched forward with the pitchfork. The man stepped back instinctively, his right foot teetering on the edge of the cliff. Another lurch with the pitchfork saw the man lose further ground. The woman tried to propel herself forward, but it was too late as the affixed rope made sure that she followed the man over the edge. Even the sound of the sea gently brushing against the rocks in the distance could not mask the ensuing thud as the two bodies hit the rocks below.

Retrieving the final item, a torch, from the sack, Eric turned on the device, the innocent victims were barely visible from that distance but Eric did not need to see them in any detail to know that they would be dead.

"And that, Peter, was the end of Eric and Edith Linderman and in a way it is a relief. No more will I have to lie and talk about all the things that I do not agree with. No more will I have to rub shoulders with these filthy Americans who have no self-control and allow themselves to be slaves to their own sexual depravity. Today I am free and shortly you will also be, Peter. We just have to implement the remainder of our plans."

Back at the house Eric and Peter collected the cut hair that had fallen onto the newspaper plus the removed jewellery into the bag containing the clothes. This in turn they took to the furnace. Its red-hot interior soon consumed the bag and its contents as the last pieces of evidence were converted to smoke.

The next task was to dispose of the remaining evidence of the incarceration from the storeroom that had served as a temporary prison for it two unwilling cellmates. Any incriminating items in the room were either flushed down the toilet or met a fiery end at the mercy of the furnace.

The two men then used a bucket of detergent to help remove the bacteria that were releasing associated smells that had permeated the room and its contents before rearranging the other items that were stored inside. With the evidence now removed and with a few meagre possessions packed, Eric and Edith both decided to have one last walk around their beloved house. They needed to check everything was correct before shutting down this episode of their lives completely. Hand in hand and starting at the top floor, they walked through each room, knowing they could never see this house as their own again; perhaps it was additionally a symbolic act of closure, allowing the feelings of sadness to be replaced by anticipation as they both focussed on what the future held.

Eric and Edith had died the minute the couple went over the cliff, but very shortly the next chapter of their lives would begin as they were reborn into new identities.

"We must go shortly, or they will be waiting."

Eric looked at his replacement watch before nodding and replying to his wife.

"Can you give me and Peter a few minutes alone?"

Edith obliged, walking through to the adjacent room. Eric could see the tears and the sadness in the eyes of his brother, eyes that knew things would never be the same again. Eric put his arms out and in an act of compassion that very few ever other people ever saw, hugged his brother close.

"These next few months apart are going to be hard, but it will go quickly. We all have to make some sacrifices for the greater good. For so long I had to pretend my loyalty was with America when the true loyalty of my heart lay with the Fatherland. It made me feel sick knowing that whilst the Führer is cleansing Europe from all the undesirable people like homosexuals I allowed and even encouraged this sort of behaviour to take place in my house. It was not because I was happy about the situation but because I knew I had to make sacrifices to achieve what we needed to. And worse, I had to make you view this behaviour whilst you were filming and taking the photos. I am so sorry, Peter, I just hope our parents can forgive me.

"Now, Peter, we have another sacrifice to make, we both know how important it is to get this right so remember everything that we talked about. Once we are gone go to bed and get some sleep. Tomorrow afternoon when you become concerned that we are not around, search the house and find the note that I left on my dresser. Get Leighton to contact the police and when they arrive let the police do their stuff but if they don't spot the bodies, then you must initiate your own search and of course you will discover our bodies down on the rocks. You must have no hesitation in identifying us when they retrieve the bodies, so make sure you are there before anybody looks too closely. Do everything just as we planned so we can be together again in our new lives as proud Germans. You want that don't you, Peter?"

"Yes, of course I want that."

"Good. Hudson will look after all the legal matters. Once we are officially pronounced dead he can start the transfer of everything into your name. Make sure this happens as quickly as possible so when we return you can sell the house and we can move together to our new lives.

"The Bests will keep coming to cook and look after the house, so play the part that you must play well when you talk to them. I promise we will be back in about three months once we have our new identities and lives established. This may not have been our original plan, but we have the files and film safely hidden so we still have a big part to play in determining the outcome of this war. With our help Germany can beat both England and America. You don't realise how important you are in this plan, so be strong and think of our future and the future of the Fatherland."

Although filled with pride that he had such a major part to play in his brother's amended plan, the thought of the responsibility put a nervous smile on Peter's face.

"Now we must go you get the lanterns, and we will meet you downstairs."

As the dinghy and its occupants disappeared into the darkness towards the safety of the waiting boat, Peter started the climb up the rugged pathway, the light from the lantern safely illuminating his footing. Now inside the small tunnel that led to the underground room, he removed the wooden wedge carefully placed to stop the door from closing, allowing the heavy door to firmly latch; access from the outside world was once again denied.

Walking into his brother's bedroom, Peter took the envelope that contained the supposed last words of Eric Linderman. He would, of course, discover it tomorrow as planned but the temptation to read it now was too much as Peter opened the envelope.

My Dearest Brother

I am now of unbelievable grief as I struggle to make sense of the world in which we now find ourselves living in.

I am torn between my loyalty to you and to that which I struggle to accept.

It is known by all how I prayed for peace between the country of my birth and the country that I have grown to love.

The thought of Germans and Americans fighting and killing each other is too much for me to accept, it is a thought so disturbing that Edith and I are choosing the only way that we know how to escape that what I have feared.

I have not forgotten my promise to our parents to look after you, the house and everything we own will transfer to you. I have arranged this with Hudson our lawyer. There are more than enough provisions for your welfare. You must consult with Hudson. He is a good man and will make sure you are looked after.

I have also made provisions for the Bests to continue to cook and look after the house.

I know you will find this hard, and I beg for your forgiveness, and I wish there was another way. Please try to understand that for us, it is for the only thing we can do to find our peace.

You are young and have your whole life ahead. A wife, and maybe a family, who knows what your future holds, so use what I have left for you wisely.

Both Edith and I love you like the great brother that you are not just now in this life but for eternity.

Eric

The letter and its associated details were the words that the police and any officials would see; it was all lies and meant nothing to Peter.

Carefully folding the letter back, he placed it back in the envelope which he then positioned on his brother's dressing table, the place that he would find it later in the morning. Peter made his way back through the empty house to his own bedroom. There was a sense of coldness in the house; with the furnace actively running in the basement the coldness was not related to temperature but rather to the cold chill of emptiness. Peter was alone and despite the fact that the Bests would be here during the day, the evenings of emptiness would continue until the return of his brother and sister-in-law.

Even after Eric and Edith's return nothing would ever be the same as they were now officially dead. The two people who would return would be different, with new looks and identities; they could never be seen in the house again. On their return they would only be around long enough to cleanse the house of any incriminating evidence and to collect Peter and the accumulated files and film reels. With the house in Peter's name, he would then instruct the family lawyer to sell the house, leaving the three of them to put the next part of their plan into action.

Peter had a plethora of mixed emotions. The security of familiarity would no longer exist. This was the only house he could remember living in and it was the only life he had ever known. Peter knew, however, his sacrifice was necessary. He had seen the look of overwhelming joy on the faces of his brother and Edith as they described how wonderful the world would be after the Führer gained full dominance and had cleansed mankind's impurities from Europe. He had seen their bodies almost quivering with excitement as they spoke of being invited to Berlin to be personally thanked. Such a prospect was way beyond what Peter would be comfortable with, but it would not stop the joy of knowing he was part of what they had achieved.

With his bedroom door firmly closed, Peter sat by the table that was adjacent to the window, opening the window just a small amount, causing the curtains to flutter as they lifted up into the air, letting in the distinctive smell of distant salt air and indication of the night's windy conditions.

Opening the single hidden drawer positioned underneath the table, Peter removed the crisp white envelope, placing both it and its contained letter onto the tabletop.

What Eric's shy and sensitive brother found himself reading was the other letter that had been given to him from Eric. A collection of heart filled sentences that must never be seen by anybody else contained the words that confirmed their separation was only temporary and assuring him that Eric, complete with his new identity, would return. This was the note that would bring comfort to Peter until their reunion. Placing the letter back in the envelope, Peter made a promise to himself that he would read the letter every day at the same table until his brother's return, no matter how long that might be.